## MACHINE GUNS SWEPT THEIR FIRE
## IN A TIGHT FIGURE EIGHT

Lyons and Blancanales kept their fire well below waist height so as not to waste the ammunition by putting holes in the tops of the walls.

This was slaughter, pure and simple. But unlike what had happened at the massacre at the Haitian Social Club, this killing would have a positive outcome. If the Algerians were killed they wouldn't visit death on others. It was a harsh equation, but the mathematics of terrorism were stark. When men went beyond the laws of civilized society, they moved into the realm of barbarism, where the rule was that those who lived by the sword died by it.

They were dying by gunfire tonight, but the rule was the same.

DON PENDLETON'S

# STONY

AMERICA'S ULTRA-COVERT INTELLIGENCE AGENCY

# MAN®

## CONDITION
## HOSTILE

A GOLD EAGLE BOOK FROM
# W●RLDWIDE®

TORONTO • NEW YORK • LONDON
AMSTERDAM • PARIS • SYDNEY • HAMBURG
STOCKHOLM • ATHENS • TOKYO • MILAN
MADRID • WARSAW • BUDAPEST • AUCKLAND

First edition April 2002

ISBN 0-373-61942-1

CONDITION HOSTILE

Special thanks and acknowledgment to
Michael Kasner for his contribution to this work.

# CONDITION
# HOSTILE

# CHAPTER ONE

*Bangkok, Thailand*

Some things never changed, and Bangkok, Thailand, was a classic case in point. Mack Bolan was no stranger to Bangkok, but the more it changed, the more it stayed the same. The major streets had been modernized since he had first seen them. They were wider, cleaner, better lit and the cars traveling them were newer and flashier. Towering modern buildings glittering with glass and neon made much of the city look like a mini-Singapore or Hong Kong. The throngs out for the night in the modern part of town were sleek, well fed and dressed in the latest international fashions. They would eat and drink well, and dance the night away when they weren't chatting with their friends on their cell phones.

Bangkok in the twenty-first century was glittering with modernity, but it was all just eye candy. One didn't have to go far from the clean, well-lit boulevards to find the back alleys of real Bangkok.

Bolan knew the underbelly of Bangkok. It was a place that catered to the worst in humanity. Men flew into Thailand from all over the world to indulge themselves in ways that were simply not possible, or legal, in their native countries.

Bangkok's greatest tourist draw had always been the exotic and the forbidden, particularly the sexually forbidden. For decades, the city had an international reputation as the place to go to indulge in any number of exotic sexual fantasies. Child prostitution was very high on that list. Entire Boeing 747 jetliners full of middle-aged men on "sex tours" landed several times a week, and the "tourists" immediately headed for the bordellos stocked with young boys and girls. Others seeking rougher games went to the S and M palaces to whip and be whipped. Every perversion imaginable was available for the right price.

Most of what these men, and women, sought was also not legal under Thai law, but Bangkok was a place that lived by the Golden Rule—the man with the gold ruled. The same thing went for drugs. As much as Bangkok was well famed for its sexual pleasures, it was just as famous for its drugs. Even though Thailand had the same drug laws as most Western nations, every drug known to man was as readily available as rain during the monsoons.

And that was what had brought Bolan to Bangkok again. It was also what was making him a target.

BOLAN WAS THREE BLOCKS away from the upscale clubs and night spots in a rat's warren of garish neon signs, litter-covered streets and drunken men roaming aimlessly with sex on their minds. He wasn't dressed much differently from the other tourists crowding the sidewalks. He was one of the few, though, who didn't have his arm around the slender waist of a Thai girl. Being solo made him a mark for every street hustler shilling for the strip clubs, drug dens and whorehouses that were the reason for this part of Bangkok to exist.

His other problem was that at over six feet tall, he stood out in the crowd. Not quite head and shoulders, but at least by half a head's height. That made it all too easy for his tail to keep him under observation.

He'd picked up the tail almost from the minute he stepped off the JAL Airbus that brought him to Bangkok International Airport. That had been almost eight hours earlier, and he was still being tailed. The tail had changed several times during the day and early evening, but it was still back there. It was coming up on ten o'clock now, and he needed to shake the man off.

Hal Brognola had warned him that there was a possibility that the Bangkok office of the DEA had been compromised, and he had more than enough proof of that now. The men and women of the DEA were dedicated to their work, but even the greatest dedication could falter when faced with the temptations of the East. The mix of undreamed-of sexual adventures, unlimited wealth and any drug known to humankind would sorely tempt a saint. The drug agency kept a close eye on the personnel in their Bangkok office, but no one could see into a person's heart.

Bolan had seen enough, and it was time for him to evaporate. He had business to take care of that didn't require his having company.

The strip club in front of him looked like a good bolt-hole. It was big and its neon signs garishly proclaimed that all the dancers inside were virgins. In Bangkok, that was about as likely as fish riding bicycles through the streets, but it drew in the marks every time.

Bolan stopped to listen to the rap of the shill by the door. "Hey, mister! You wanna come in here? We have very nice girls. Young, you know. They all virgins. We have good drink, no cheap shit. You come in, you like."

Bolan allowed himself to be enticed into the club. As the man at the door had said, the girls on the elevated stage were all young, but in Bangkok that didn't mean that they were virgins. The bordello across the street from the strip club advertised that its girls were all "delicate budding flowers." That was code for the girls being under the age of twelve. If they hadn't been in town too long, they had a chance of being almost virgins. The dancers didn't.

The air in the club was heavy with the stench of cheap beer, stale sweat and Asian tobacco smoke. Underlying that was the acrid reek of lust and pot smoke. In the dim light, he saw that the customers at the tables against the rear wall were being serviced by lap dancers. They were all older than the girls up on the stage, but what the young ones aroused, their older sisters were ready to take care of. It was a winning combination, as the club was packed.

Keeping a sharp eye on the entrance, Bolan quickly made his way through the packed room. He had just taken a seat at an empty chair at a table full of sweating Japanese tourists when he spotted his tail come in. From his features, he knew the man had to be Chinese, and that told him all he needed to know. Bangkok had a large resident Chinese population, so the man could easily be a local instead of a tong gangster.

The Chinese peered through the smoke, trying to find the tall American. When he didn't immediately spot his target, he looked concerned and started into the room. When his back was turned, Bolan got up and made his way toward the darkened tables at the back of the room. He didn't need a lap dance, but he did need the cover of darkness.

By the time the tail turned, Bolan had found another empty chair. Two girls rushed him, seeking to take care of his every need, for a price, of course.

When he saw the tail whip out his cell phone and start an animated conversation, Bolan knew that he had to move on. Two tables down was a hallway that led to the back of the building, and he took it. The corridor was flanked by cubicles every dozen or so feet. The doors to these little rooms were closed tightly, but the sounds of the frantic activity inside made it clear as to what was going on. These were the rooms where those who didn't like lap dancers took their lusts. As with most Bangkok clubs, this was a full-service facility.

Bolan wasn't unarmed, but he wasn't packing his usual hardware. The 9 mm mini-Glock 26 in his belt holster had been airport-security proofed by John "Cowboy" Kissinger, Stony Man Farm's resident armorer, and made a good arrival piece. A big part of Bolan's needing to shake his tail was so he could secure his prestocked hardware cache. The little Glock held only five in the mag and one up the spout, so if he needed more than that, he was in trouble.

The door leading outside wasn't locked on the inside, but Bolan didn't try the door gently. When he was ready, he put a boot to the lock and smashed the door open.

As he had expected, two men were waiting for him. The first one shouted and lunged at Bolan, swinging a pair of nunchakus.

Bolan didn't favor that style of weapon, but he knew that it was blinding fast and could deliver a stunning blow if it connected. Ducking inside the arc of the weapon, he closed with his assailant and delivered a kick to his crotch. The force of the blow almost lifted the smaller man off the ground and forced a wail of agony from his lungs.

Not waiting to watch his first victim fall, Bolan spun to face his second opponent. This man was armed with a riot baton, another dangerous, quiet but nonfatal weapon. Again, Bolan had to step inside the arc of the baton to do what he had to do. There was no finesse to this, just a takedown. This time he used his hands, delivering a blow to the man's throat, crushing his larynx.

The baton fell from the man's hand as he clawed at his crushed throat.

A shout alerted him to another player entering the alley. So far, his assailants hadn't brought guns into play, but that could change at any time. That they hadn't tried that option yet told him that someone wanted to talk to him. And if his information was correct, the man who wanted the conference was a recent Chinese refugee from Macao named Big Gold Liu.

He fully intended to have a private chat with the Red Door tong leader, but this wasn't the time to do it. As with everything he did, Bolan always preferred to pick the time, as well as the place.

The third attacker had upped the ante by flashing a knife. Still hoping to keep this quiet, Bolan closed with him. The man's first slash was intended to be only a crippling attack, and that was a mistake.

Bolan caught the man's wrist and attempted to lever the blade out of his hand. The Chinese didn't have the Executioner's bulk, but he was strong and he knew the moves. When he attempted to back kick Bolan's leg out from under him, the soldier knew it was time to put an end to this kung fu movie farce.

Reaching back with his left hand, Bolan pulled the mini-Glock, jammed it into the man's ribs and fired a single shot. Being a contact shot, the sound of the report was absorbed by the man's chest cavity, and the expanding gas caused even more damage than the slug alone accounted for. With his lungs ripped open and bleeding, the fight was over.

BACK OUT on the street, Bolan moved quickly, as if he were late for a date in one of the area's better cathouses. He wasn't far from his safehouse, and it looked as if his back was clear. Two blocks off the strip, and he was back in a residential area again. He started looking at the enameled street signs for Luan Street.

The ceramic tiles bearing the number 27 looked a bit worn, as did the rest of the wall they were mortared to. The wrought-iron gate and the rows of outward-facing spikes on top of the wall, though, looked solid. The light from the streetlamp at the corner was dim, but he caught a glint of light from a security camera lens at the corner of the wall. The place was well guarded.

The house inside the enclosure was a prewar, two-story concrete villa, the kind commonly built by wealthy merchants. Without making a recon, he knew that there would be a garden in the backyard and maybe a small house for the servants. The current owner probably didn't have much of a personal staff now, and that was just as well.

When he pushed the bell button by the gate, an elderly man came out of the house and walked briskly toward him.

"Good day," Bolan greeted the doorman in Chinese. "Is Dr. Jordan in?"

The man bowed and turned aside as he opened the gate. "Please come in, sir."

Bolan was led into the drawing room, and a Caucasian in his late fifties immediately came in to meet him. The man's cover was that of a medical doctor, which he was, but he was also a longtime CIA agent.

"I'm Richard Jordan," the man said, extending his hand.

Bolan shook it. "Mike Belasko."

"I expected you several hours ago."

"I picked up a tail at the airport," Bolan replied, "and it took awhile to shake him."

"One of Liu's people?"

"Could have been. He looked mainland Chinese."

"Damn." Jordan appeared to be concerned. "I warned the station chief that the DEA was leaking again."

"It looks that way."

"What do you need from me?"

Neither Jordan nor the Bangkok CIA station chief knew who this Belasko guy was. They had just been told on highest authority to offer him every assistance required. Jordan had no doubts in his mind, though, that Belasko was someone's premier Mr. Fix-it. He also had no doubts that the body count was going to start going up in Bangkok, if it hadn't already. He purposely hadn't bothered to ask the man how he had shaken his tong tail because he didn't want to know.

"Right now," Bolan said, "a secure line, and then that package that was delivered here for me."

"No problem."

WHILE BOLAN WAS on the secure phone to Stony Man Farm, Lam Noc, Jordan's Chinese doorman, was also on a phone, a cell phone. He was talking to the man who had offered twenty thousand dollars in gold for the black-haired, blue-eyed long nose who had shown up at the CIA doctor's house. Over the past thirty years, Lam Noc had made a good living as a freelance spy. The CIA considered him one of their most reliable contract men, and he was. He hadn't worked exclusively for them, however.

Like most of the "offshore" Chinese, Lam had an eye for money. Starting in Vietnam, he had become a spy both for the Americans and the North Vietnamese Communists. The long noses paid him well, and working for the Reds kept him from being assassinated by them. When that war ended, he drifted to Taiwan for a while to play his double game before coming to Thailand. Through it all, he remained on the American payroll, but sold information to anyone who would pay for it. He didn't know who this particular American was and really didn't care because it didn't matter. All that mattered was that the Red Door tong wanted him, and twenty thousand in gold was a big enough payday that he could finally get out of this business.

"He is here now," Lam said in the Szechwan dialect. "I will disable the camera in the garden and you can come over the wall back there."

When his call was finished, Lam Noc went to his quarters in the servant's house and locked the door behind him.

# CHAPTER TWO

*Bangkok, Thailand*

When Bolan returned from making his call to the Farm, Dr. Jordan had retrieved the metal shipping crate the Farm had sent ahead. The soldier saw that the diplomatic pouch seals were still intact, so there would be no nasty surprises when he opened it. The first item he retrieved from the shipment was his 9 mm Beretta 93-R and its leather shoulder holster.

There might be newer, flashier pieces available, but he knew the Beretta cold, and it would function perfectly on a diet of whatever kind of 9 mm ammo he happened to come across.

After checking the Beretta's magazines and strapping on the pistol, he took out his .44 Magnum Desert Eagle. It, too, was a well-tried piece and worked better for the one-shot takedown than anything he had seen since he'd quit using his old AutoMag. His well-honed Tanto fighting knife completed his kit, and he was now fully dressed.

That wasn't, however, the last of the hardware in the shipment. Since he was in Southeast Asia, Kissinger had packed an M-16 A-2 for him rigged with a day-night scope mount and a detachable laser sight. The rest of the shipment was the standard gear needed to support him in the jungle for a week, including freeze-dried rations, several two-quart bladder canteens and a medical kit. He'd be packing heavy, but it was a solo recon and he might need it.

"It looks like you're planning to start a war," Jordan said as he watched Bolan assemble his gear.

Bolan's blue eyes locked on his. "That depends entirely on them," he said.

The look made the doctor glad that he and this mystery man were on the same side.

THE TONG HIT TEAM didn't even bother to try to keep out of sight as they came over the back wall of Dr. Jordan's villa. Lam Noc knew better than to betray them. Working both sides was okay with the tong as long as you never forgot who owned your true loyalty.

Lam had reported that there were only the two long noses in the house, so the team's leader didn't expect the hit to take very long. After the debacle in the alley behind the club, Liu had ordered that the mystery American simply be eliminated. To confuse the Thai authorities as to the real target, the doctor would also be killed and the house ransacked.

According to Lam, the patio in the rear of the house

opened into a small study, and he had left the locks open. Even though the team leader had no doubt of the outcome, a silent entry would make this job a little easier. He waved his six shooters forward.

The lead man ran onto the patio on rubber-soled shoes and tried one of the floor-length windows. When he signaled that it was in fact open, the rest of the gunmen followed.

The first two secured the room while the others made their entry. When the leader signaled, they broke up into two three-man teams to find their targets.

BOLAN SUDDENLY looked up from loading his gear. "Where's your man?" he asked Jordan.

"I think he's in his quarters," the doctor answered. "Why?"

Bolan's hand automatically flew for the Desert Eagle and the other snapped the Beretta from his shoulder rig. He spun to face the door, and the Desert Eagle roared as the first of the tong gunmen appeared.

The .44 Mag round lifted the attacker off his feet as it blew a fist-sized hole through his chest.

At the same time, the Beretta in Bolan's other hand ripped off a 3-round burst. The trio of 9 mm slugs drilled through the torso of the second man through the door.

Not to be left out of the festivities, Jordan produced an old M-1911 .45-caliber pistol from a bookshelf and added its firepower to the mix.

In the first exchange, two gunmen had been killed and the third yelled for reinforcement from the hallway.

The small room was a trap, and Bolan needed enough room to maneuver. He triggered the Desert Eagle twice, and the heavy slugs easily punched through the lath and plaster of the wall to silence the man on the other side.

"We need to get out of here!" he told Jordan as he checked the hall outside.

"Follow me."

The two Americans raced down the hall to the living room.

The tong team leader frantically signaled his remaining three men after the Americans. "Don't let them escape, brothers," he shouted.

"No," BOLAN SAID when he saw Jordan heading for the front door. "We'll take them here."

The light coming from the street would be in the eyes of the attackers, and the heavy colonial-style furniture would soak up a lot of fire. Bolan waved Jordan to cover behind a couch and said, "Wait for me to fire."

The Executioner hadn't seen night-vision goggles on the gunmen, so found the darkest corner of the room to make his stand. The pounding of rubber-soled boots running down the hall keyed Bolan's attack. A blaze of submachine-gun fire announced the gunmen, but he waited until all three were in the room.

Out of the dark, the Desert Eagle blazed, once, twice, three times.

Between number two and three, one of the gunmen tried to do the job he was being paid for, but didn't quite make it. A .44 Magnum round made that a certainty.

"Stay there," Bolan snapped at Jordan as he headed out after the last set of footsteps he had heard.

WHEN THE HIT TEAM leader saw the last of his men fall victim to the American's big pistol, he turned and ran out of the house. He had escaped the house of death, but he knew what was waiting for him when he returned to Big Gold Liu with yet another story of defeat. He was a walking dead man, but he wouldn't carry this burden of bad luck alone. Stopping at Lam Noc's quarters, he booted the door open and went in firing.

"No, brother!" Lam managed to get out before the barrage cut him down.

After putting a final bullet in Lam's head, the tong gunman exited the small house and sprinted for the rear wall. He was young and ran well, but not well enough to escape the burst of 9 mm rounds from the patio outside the study.

When Bolan saw the man go down, he stepped back into the study and turned to Jordan. "I need to use your secure phone again," he said.

The doctor was still buzzed on adrenaline and shakily pointed to the back room. He had known that Belasko was bad news, but he had never seen anything like this before.

*Stony Man Farm, Virginia*

THE WOOD-CHIPPING facility in the forty-eight-acre Annex at Stony Man Farm was almost hidden from view by the fast-growing poplar trees that had been planted there. It would still be a few years before the woodlot would start producing chips for the pulp mills. But the chipping plant was more than just an industrial-sized blender designed to chop up trees. Hidden deep beneath the building was the nerve center of the nation's most clandestine organization.

Stony Man Farm was the home of the Sensitive Operations Group, the President's premier dirty-little-jobs crew. SOG's action teams, Phoenix Force and Able Team, took care of the nation's most serious problems out of sight of the press, as well as the other federal agencies.

The man who ran this organization was Hal Brognola, a high-level Justice Department official. In that capacity, he was listed as a special liaison to the President. And while there were several special liaison people who had unlimited access to the Oval Office, none of them had Brognola's responsibilities, nor his power. As the modern idiom had it, he had the Man's ear 24-7. All he had to do was to place a call and be immediately connected to the leader of the most powerful nation on the planet. By the same token, Brognola was also on call 24-7 himself. It wasn't a job for the faint hearted, nor one where a man could kick back and daydream about taking on the back nine at his favorite course.

Stony Man Farm's mission was to watch over the entire world, looking for trouble that needed to be brought to the Man's attention. And while the Farm crew kept watch on everything all the time, Asia was in the tight focus right now. Asian events were always close to the top of the President's daily situation report. From Tokyo's Nikei Index to the latest fistfight in Taiwan's parliament or a Singapore bank takeover, it was all of vital interest to America. Anything, though, that carried a China lead got top priority. China was the five-thousand-pound gorilla of the twenty-first century, and even the sole surviving cold war superpower had to keep a wary eye on the wakening giant lest it get stepped on.

One of the most traumatic recent moves of the emerging Chinese juggernaut had been the takeover of Hong Kong in 1997. Keeping their upper lips properly stiff, the British had handed over the colony to the Communists exactly as per the century-old treaty, lock, stock and the contents of the bank vaults intact. And with that, they had also given the Chinese the key to domination of the Pacific Rim.

One thing that had been lost in the prime-time brouhaha over Hong Kong was the fate of the much smaller colony of Macao. Located a short ferry ride across the bay from its much larger colonial brother, Macao was Hong Kong's sin city. Gambling was a Chinese obsession, but Macao was the Las Vegas of the Orient. It also offered sensual pleasures not completely legal in staid Hong Kong. Another ancient Chinese tradition, smuggling, was the third leg of the tripod that supported Macao. And, anytime you had gambling, prostitution and smuggling in Asia, you also had Chinese gangs. That, too, was a tradition.

When the red flag of the People's Republic of China had gone up over Hong Kong, most of the triads quickly made their accommodations with their new overlords. It was that or face Red Guard firing squads. They would continue their criminal enterprises, but would now pay a cut to Beijing and would take direction from the intelligence branch of the People's Liberation Army. As with all compromises, it had its drawbacks. But it kept them from being exterminated down to the last man, woman and child.

When the Communists took over Macao, they hadn't been inclined to be so lenient with the tongs of Macao, particularly with the Red Door tong run by a crime lord known as Big Gold Liu. The Liu family's Red Door had long been the dominant tong in the colony, and Big Gold headed a long list slated for execution.

The Chinese Communists had a decided puritanical bent when it came to what they called "decadent weaknesses" and what other Chinese called fun and games. But that didn't mean that they didn't indulge in the traditional Chinese passion for gambling and prostitution. It meant only that they took their decadent urges elsewhere. And with Macao so close, it became a popular hangout for the Red Chinese leadership and their offspring.

Unlike in Las Vegas, gambling in China often involved the unlucky losers borrowing heavily from the tongs running the casinos so they could try to recoup their losses. That was convenient for the gamblers and good business for the gangs, as the interest rates were high. Worse than that were the gangs' debt-collection practices. Without the restraint imposed by the British government in Hong Kong, there were more comfortable ways to commit suicide than try to default on a Macao tong gambling debt.

It was a gambling debt that was behind the ChiCom government's hard-core position on the Macao crime families. A dozen years earlier, the youngest son of the Chinese minister of culture had been addicted to gambling. As with many of the offspring of the Communist leadership, this fine example of Maoist teachings had spent the majority of his time wallowing in the sin pits of Macao. Unfortunately, the Goddess of Fortune had not been at his side. His secondary addiction to cocaine might have had something to do with his run of bad luck at the gaming tables. His worst luck, though, was that his debts had been owed to the Red Door tong.

In a series of events not well understood by American intelligence, that young man ended up dead along with four other well-connected young Red Chinese friends. That the men had been killed was bad enough, but they had also been mutilated. When their bodies were discovered, their genitals had been found sewn in their mouths.

That outrage had almost sparked a Red invasion of Macao, but cooler heads prevailed. A large indemnity was paid to the families of the victims, and the incident was glossed over. It wasn't forgotten, however. Nothing was ever forgotten in China.

When the Reds foreclosed on Macao, the Red Door tong fled before they could be captured, and the notorious Big Gold Liu was reported to be setting up business in Thailand. The Thais didn't lack for home-grown criminal gangs, but they didn't have anyone like Big Gold.

MACK BOLAN WASN'T only working the Big Gold situation. A report from a trusted Pakistani source had come in citing the involvement of the Taliban of Afghanistan. This report claimed that the Taliban was moving troops into Southeast Asia, specifically into the mountainous region of northern Thailand, Laos and Myanmar known to the world as the Golden Triangle.

The strangest part of the report was a claim that the Taliban was linking up with the newly relocated Red Door tong. What made that strange was that the Taliban was the most radical of all the Islamic fundamentalists and had never shown any interest in alliances with even other Islamic republics. On the surface, for the radicals to be seeking to hook up with any Chinese group sounded far-fetched. Until, however, you threw the Golden Triangle into the mix. Then it made a certain twisted sense.

Hash and opium coming out of Afghanistan had long been an element in the European drug scene. Even before the disastrous Afghan-Soviet war of the late eighties, they were minor players in that market. The devastation of the war and the disruption following the Russian pullout in 1989 changed that. The cash-strapped Afghans decided that if decadent Westerners were willing to pay good money to kill themselves, they were ready to take it.

So far, the Afghan product had played almost no part in the American drug scene. The limiting factor was that Afghanistan wasn't prime poppy-growing country and Europe used everything they produced. Given access to Asian production, though, and access to established networks to get it to Europe for transshipment, America could soon be awash in heroin. That would kick off a price war with the Mexican product, which would only increase the number of addicts on America's streets.

Even were that to come to pass, though, it wouldn't be the greatest impact Taliban-controlled drug dealing in the United States would have. Unlike with the usual drug-cartel crowd, the Taliban leaders wouldn't use their drug wealth for personal aggrandizement.

Fortified villas, flashy limos and even flashier women didn't fit into their lifestyle. To the Taliban fanatics, money was only useful if it could further their cause by destroying their enemies. When it took over Afghanistan in 1996, the Taliban declared a permanent state of jihad, holy war, on the Western world.

Originally, the State Department believed that the declaration was simply more ravings from the lunatic fringe of the Islamic revolution. Every couple of months, some Islamic radical denounced "the ungodly West" and in particular, of course, the United States. The Taliban declaration was seen as only that. Then the Taliban allowed the notorious terrorist Samir Qattari into its camp, and the nature of the Taliban threat changed radically.

Brognola's gut was telling him that throwing Qattari in the mix along with a link between the Taliban and the Algerian Sword of God faction could only mean trouble. And, in that context, the Taliban joining forces with Big Gold Liu made sense. Even though Qattari had seemingly endless amounts of money, waging war with the West was expensive. There was always the risk that the U.S. would finally convince the Saudi royal family to get past its fears and freeze the terrorist's assets. Should that happen, Qattari would need new financing, and the heroin trade would provide that in spades.

The Taliban's Canadian-based Algerian allies had already been involved in terrorist attacks against the United States, and several of them had been stopped within days of their launching. A couple of their defused operations had made the papers, but not the full extent of what they had planned.

The DEA and other federal agencies could work the heroin import problem, but the mission of stopping a new jihad against American interests funded out of the Golden Triangle was given to Stony Man. No agency in the world had the track record the SOG teams did fighting Islamic holy warriors.

Instead of throwing Phoenix Force and Able Team directly into the fire once again, though, Brognola was trying to start out low key this time. The results of Bolan's recon would give him the information he would need to sit down with the Stony Man staff and plan how to deal with the situation.

# CHAPTER THREE

*Toronto, Canada*

Carl "Ironman" Lyons was angry. He just couldn't understand how Abdul Armani had been set free. The man was a proven terrorist.

"What in the hell is it with you people?" Lyons raged. "This transfer was set up between Ottawa and Washington. It was a done deal. You were supposed to turn the bastard over to us."

"You must understand, Agent Green," the court officer stated, "that Mr. Armani hasn't committed a serious crime here in Canada. He was picked up on a charge of driving with a forged license, and according to our laws, he was released on his own recognizance as any other Canadian citizen would be.

"And this warrant—" he waved the Justice Department paperwork Brognola had provided Able Team in the air as if it had an odor "—I'm afraid that it's simply not valid in this country."

Lyons had worked with both the Royal Canadian

Mounted Police and Canada's intelligence service on many occasions and had found the men and women of those organizations to be consummate professionals. The people who held down jobs in the civilian agencies, however, were another matter entirely.

The Canadians prided themselves on living in a neutral, open country where all were free to come and share their lives and the diversity of their cultures. Each year a multitude of immigrants claiming to be political refugees were granted asylum in the country. The problem was that the Canadians weren't letting in only the huddled masses yearning to be free. In their exuberant spirit of openness, the Canadian government didn't seem to scrutinize too closely those they were admitting onto its soil. Along with those who were honestly fleeing oppression in their homelands, Canada had become the preferred home base for dozens of international terrorist groups.

Every terrorist organization from the Provisional Wing of the IRA to the Sword of God had come to learn that they would be welcomed in Canada. Even better, they knew that no one would keep an eye on them in their new home.

To top it off, the fact that the border with the United States was almost completely unguarded gave them almost instant access to their favorite enemy, the Great Satan of the United States of America. Terrorists could live in their warm little apartments with their rents paid by ''refugee'' organizations, gather their weapons, make their explosives and plan their attacks. When they were ready, all they had to do was drive or walk across the border to sow death and destruction in the United States.

The terrorists were smart enough not to attack Canadian targets, so international terrorism wasn't high on the Canadian government's list of things to be overly concerned about.

Abdul Armani was an Algerian connected with the radical Islamic group that called itself the Sword of God. In fact, if Aaron Kurtzman was right, and the Farm's cyber sleuth usually was, Armani was the Algerian terrorist group's top operations officer. The warrant Lyons had presented charged Armani with conspiracy to commit terrorism, specifically the destruction of the tunnels leading in and out of Manhattan Island during the evening rush hour. Lyons refused to contemplate the carnage had the attack been carried out as planned.

The Justice Department warrant was based on solid evidence, and this sorry excuse for a human being was saying the warrant was invalid. Lyons was ready to go ballistic.

"Ah, Carl?" Rosario Blancanales had noted the warning signs and knew that it was time to try to mellow out his team leader. This was a fiasco already, and the last thing they needed was for Lyons to give the court official a knuckle sandwich. Brognola would blow a fuse, and they would all spend some quality time in a Canadian jail.

"What?" Lyons spun and snapped at him.

Blancanales took it calmly. It was far better for Lyons to bite his head off. "Maybe we should call Hal and have him contact Ottawa on this."

"What in the hell good is that going to do?" Lyons's voice was getting louder and louder. "Armani has already been turned loose."

Blancanales noticed that they were drawing attention in the large, open office and risked grabbing Lyons's upper arm and squeezing hard. "Let's call in anyway," he said, "and let him deal with it."

"Christ on a crutch!" Lyons started ratcheting down. When Blancanales had to restrain him, it was time to chill.

"Is there a phone nearby?" Blancanales asked.

"Certainly. The phones are in the hallway inside the main entrance."

"Come on, Carl," Blancanales said, nudging Lyons. "We're outta here."

They went to look for a phone.

The Canadian court officer drew some satisfaction from the fact that, despite the American's behavior, it was not Canadian Customs through which anyone had to pass to enter the United States.

IN THE AVIS rental car parked outside, Hermann "Gadgets" Schwarz monitored what had taken place in the Canadian court building over an open com link. Blancanales was right to try to rein in Lyons. While the Canadians had been happy to let Armani go, they'd take great pleasure in locking up Lyons for a couple of days to cool off.

"It just so happens," Blancanales said when they were back in the car, "that I got Armani's home of record from the open file on that guy's desk, and I suggest that we give him a visit. If we can put the grab on him, we can try to use our warrant and Justice Department ID to get him back across the border."

Lyons's mood immediately cleared up. Smashing in a door to get his man was infinitely better than having him handed over in handcuffs. He wasn't called the Ironman for nothing.

"Where is it?"

"He's in a suburb of Toronto," Blancanales replied. "And it's not too far from here."

"Hit it, Gadgets," Lyons said.

"Got you covered," Schwarz replied as he reached for the ignition switch.

*Stony Man Farm, Virginia*

"DO YOU HAVE anything from Carl yet?" Barbara Price asked Aaron Kurtzman.

Even though there was no shortage of room in the new Annex computer facility, Kurtzman's new "office" was as cluttered as the old one. Actually, when Price stood and looked at it, since he had more room here, he had added several piles.

Kurtzman wheeled his chair around, adroitly dodging the piles of paper stacked on the floor around his desk without disturbing a single piece. "Not yet," he answered. "And since they're overdue to report in, I'd say that the Canadians are humping the pooch again."

Ever since that Algerian national had been captured at Port Angeles, Washington, right before crossing the border with a trunk full of explosives destined for Seattle, Canadian-based terrorists had been high on the agenda, particularly Algerians. High-level talks between Washington and Ottawa had raised the temperature of diplomatic relations between the two nations, but had produced little else.

She shook her head. "I just don't understand. This should have been a done deal, routine transfer under our extradition treaty with them."

Kurtzman shrugged. "You know how it's been going on up there lately."

"Hal's going to be pissed."

"I think he knew that there was going to be a screwup," Kurtzman pointed out. "That's why he sent the Ironman."

"Let me know as soon as you hear from them."

"Will do."

*Toronto, Canada*

ARMANI'S HOME of record was a second-floor apartment in an older urban area of Toronto. Since it was in an older neighborhood, the population was ethnic for the most part. As in the urban United States, many native-born Canadians had long since fled to the sub-urbs.

"What do you think?" Blancanales asked Lyons.

Lyons took the field glasses from his eyes. "Typical. Up the stairs, kick in the door and grab the bastard."

"Let me make a recon first. I can take off the tie, rumple my hair, put on the accent and nose around a bit."

Lyons glanced down at his watch. "Half an hour, no more."

"Drive around the next block," Blancanales told Schwarz. "I want to do a walk up."

"Remember," Lyons said as Blancanales got out of the car. "Half an hour."

"Got it."

The neighborhood air was redolent with the smells of exotic spices and foreign cuisine. Most of it smelled Middle Eastern to Blancanales, but he detected an undercurrent of Eastern European cabbage. Considering the signs on the small shops he passed, that was to be expected. With a Russian element in the neighborhood, as well as Arabic, everyone would be culturally paranoid. His best bet here would be to put on a heavy accent and pretend to be Turkish and looking for an apartment.

"IT'S YOUR USUAL 1930s construction apartment building," Blancanales reported back to Lyons right as the clock ran down on the half hour. "There's an external fire escape in the back that hooks up to the hallways and only one flight of stairs inside.''

"Does it have a basement?"

"The usual boiler room and storage, but no exit."

"Is he up there?"

Blancanales looked thoughtful. "I couldn't get a confirmation, but I heard what sounded like male voices. I couldn't get the language, though."

"That's good enough for me," Lyons said. "Let's do it."

"In broad daylight?" Schwarz asked. "There's a lot of people on the street right now, Ironman."

"That makes it all the better," Lyons said. "We'll go in as Canadian cops."

FIFTEEN MINUTES LATER, Blancanales drove the sedan up to the entrance of Armani's apartment building. Schwarz had been let off and was around the back keeping an eye on the fire escape. The two men got out of the car and walked purposefully to the apartment's entrance. Inside the door, they drew their weapons and rushed up the stairs to the second floor.

Number 2D was at the end of the hall. Lyons didn't have to put his ear to the door to hear male voices inside arguing in Arabic. If this wasn't the place, it was at least a good place to start. He flashed his fingers out in sequence: one, two, three.

On three, Lyons and Blancanales booted the door, slamming it back against the wall, and rushed in.

As if on cue, the women in the apartment started

to scream. For the life of him, Lyons couldn't figure out why women always had to stand around and scream hysterically when clearing the area would make a hell of a lot more sense.

The three men in the living room were sitting around a coffee table when the door flew open.

The first man was halfway to his feet and reaching for an AK on the floor beside the couch when Lyons's Colt Python bellowed once, putting a .357 Magnum end to his efforts.

The second man also made the mistake of going for a piece. Blancanales double-tapped him with his silenced Glock, sending him toppling back into his chair.

The third halted in midstep and put his hands up. "Don't shoot."

"Are you Abdul Armani?" Lyons asked.

When the man nodded, the Able Team leader punched him to his knees.

A pair of riot cuffs secured the terrorist's wrists behind his back, and a strip of duct tape kept him from crying out as Lyons jerked him to his feet.

"We're coming down the stairs," Blancanales said to Schwarz over his com link.

"I'll meet you out front."

The women were still screaming when the Able Team duo left with their man between them.

Their sedan had been left unlocked, so Lyons opened the curbside rear door, threw his charge into the back seat and slid in beside him. When Armani tried to struggle, the muzzle of Lyon's Colt Python jammed into his ribs, calming him.

AS SOON AS they cleared the edge of the town, Schwarz found a side road and turned onto it. Once they were out of sight of the main road, he stopped.

When Lyons pulled the Algerian out of the back seat, Armani's legs collapsed and he started to talk behind the tape over his mouth. He couldn't bring his hands around to the front, but his eyes showed that he was begging for his life.

Lyons dragged him around to the back of the car and opened the trunk.

"If you so much as move in there," Lyons growled, grabbing Armani's arm in a viselike hold, "I'm going to stop this car and beat you half to death. You understand me?"

The Algerian nodded.

"You'd better because I don't have to take you back alive. Your dead body will do just as well."

Armani climbed into the Buick's trunk and lay down.

"ANYTHING TO DECLARE?" The customs man at the border crossing into New York State leaned down and glanced around inside the car. Even though these guys were in a government vehicle and had flashed Justice Department IDs, he was required to ask the question anyway.

"Just some garbage we didn't want to leave in Canada," Lyons replied.

The customs guy waved them on through with a smile. He liked seeing the new "good neighbor" policy in action.

## CHAPTER FOUR

*Stony Man Farm, Virginia*

When Barbara Price walked into the Annex Computer Room, she found Hal Brognola busy at one of the extra workstations. Now that they had a large enough facility, everyone could play without running over one another. The Annex was so well set up that she had a hard time remembering how they had managed for so many years in their old quarters. The lighting alone was a vast improvement, to say nothing of the extra workstations and the big-screen monitors.

"You have that look again," Brognola said when she approached him. "What's up?"

"It looks like Big Gold Liu really does have a tap into someone who should be keeping his damned mouth shut. Right after Mack got to the Bangkok safehouse, he was visited by a hit team. He took care of business, but said that they had the look of tong gunmen."

"What does he want to do next?" Brognola asked her.

Price's job title was the mission controller for SOG operations, and when Mack Bolan was doing a job for them, it went smoother if he worked with her. Brognola and Bolan went back a long way, but the Executioner always reserved his right to remain independent of the Farm. Part of that independence was being able to work with Price on Stony Man missions, and Brognola had no problem with that.

"Along with getting out of Dodge for a while to cool off," she said, "he wants to go ahead with the recon plan we worked up. He secured his mission pack and is heading for the Golden Triangle right now."

"Remind him to keep us home folks updated on what's going down," Brognola said. "You know he tends to run solo even when he doesn't need to."

"I'll try." Barbara laughed. "Also, Carl called and said he was inbound."

"Good," Brognola said, clearing his screen. "I'll walk back with you. I need to talk to him."

"YOU GUYS sure raised a shit storm up there," Hal Brognola told Carl Lyons when the Able Team leader reported to him in the War Room of the old farmhouse. "The Canadians are upset."

"Screw them," Carl Lyons spit. "How much more of this crap are we going to have to take?"

Brognola had known that the Ironman was going to detonate like that, and it was always best to let him vent. He had to admit, though, that for once, he agreed with Carl one hundred percent. Canada's apparently lax immigration and refugee policy wasn't a new problem for law-enforcement agencies, and not only American. More than one attack on the United States had been plotted in, and staged out of, Canada, in recent years. But now the situation had reached a critical stage.

"The good news," Brognola told Lyons, "is that we put Armani under chemical interrogation. Yes," he continued, "I know that means we can't put him on trial and we're going to have to turn him loose. But we got the information we needed and we're going to give the Sword of God people a transcript of what he told us, both in Arabic and English. One look at that, and they're going to whack him for us."

Lyons face broke into a huge smile. "Outstanding!"

"You guys aren't the only devious bastards in federal service," Brognola told them.

"What did you find out?"

Now Brognola got serious. "The main thing is that the tie between the Taliban and the Sword of God we heard about is a fact. Where it gets weird is that rather than joining forces to attack us like we expected them to do, they're trying to establish a network to distribute heroin. The only military actions they have planned here are against the Haitian, Mexican and South American drug cartels. Their plan is to wipe out their distribution systems and replace them with their own people and move China White."

"That's novel," Lyons said. "I like any operation that eliminates scumbags."

"I usually agree," Brognola said. "The problem is that the police and the citizenry are going to end up in the crossfire," he pointed out. "Their plans for the L.A. area are going to make the Rodney King riots look like the Pasadena Rose Bowl Parade. They're planning to use heavy weaponry and assault troops on several targets. The body count isn't going to be trivial."

"Less work for us," Lyons said.

"Dammit, Carl!" Brognola snapped. "I don't like drug scum any more than you do, but we can't have a war going on in our backyard over it."

"We already do, Hal," Lyons reminded him, "and you know it. Every year hundreds of dealers and gangbangers go down in turf wars."

"And part of that body count are innocent bystanders," Brognola stated.

Lyons shrugged. As far as he was concerned, anyone who hung around the drug scene was as guilty as those who actually got caught. "I can tell that you're leading up to something. What do you want us to do?"

"One of their attacks is planned against the Haiti drug lords in Miami. As you know, they're running neck and neck with the Mexican gangs for total tonnage smuggled in."

"And you want us to go down there and do what the cops can't do?"

"I want you to preempt it," Brognola said simply. "The cops will have to wait for them to make the first move before they can act. And if we do that, it'll be too late. There'll be bodies in the streets."

A smile slowly formed on Lyons's face. "The old 'shoot first and ask questions later' drill."

"That's about it," Brognola admitted. "But we've already asked the questions and know the answers. I can give you three locations the Algerians are supposed to be staying at. I want each of them hit and cleaned out down to the walls. You'll have the standard Get Out of Jail Free kits."

"No reading them their rights?" Lyons had a mock expression of surprise on his face.

"It's way past that," Brognola said. "Armani said that a shipment of AKs and RPGs came in on an Algerian freighter a couple of weeks ago. We didn't have the exact timetable for the strikes, but he thought the attacks would start soon."

Lyons smile faded. "I guess I'd better get down there and start kicking ass and taking names, then."

"Just kick ass," Brognola said. "We'll leave the name taking for the medical examiner and the INS."

"Got it."

*Thailand*

ENTERING THE legendary region of mountainous jungle terrain known to the world as the Golden Triangle wasn't all that difficult. All a person had to do was head north out of Bangkok and keep going until he or she stopped seeing local police or military. That told you that you had entered the "forbidden zone," the Golden Triangle of thriller novels and tabloid media. From that point on, one did have to walk carefully, but the legend was more dangerous than the reality.

Nonetheless, Bolan was taking all of the precautions one should take when in enemy territory. He was skirting a clearing when the snarling sound of approaching vehicle engines sent him into cover. Six machine-gun-toting U.S.-made M-151 jeeps pulled out of the wood line and halted on the trail running through the clearing.

Finding American jeeps in a place like this was no big surprise to him. With over a hundred thousand having been produced, the agile little M-151 was in service with more armies in the world than any other light vehicle, and the Thai army had thousands of them. For Liu's operation to be going on blatantly in the open like this meant that someone in the Thai army was on the tong leader's payroll. That, too, was no great surprise. Official corruption was an established fact of life in Southeast Asia.

The only thing surprising was that several of the vehicles were crewed by men in loose tan uniforms who were wearing the distinctive low, round hats of the Afghan mujahideen. As far as he knew, this was the first time that Islamic muji fighters had been seen in the Golden Triangle. But since everyone from the Chinese nationalists to the French had tried their hand in the poppy-growing business, why not the Afghans?

The fact that they already grew some opium in their arid homelands made them a natural for this, so the question should have been what had taken them so long?

The gun jeeps were wearing hand-painted three-color jungle-camouflage paint, but had no markings that he could see. From the radio antennae mounted on the left rear of each vehicle, they could obviously talk to one another and coordinate their attacks. The biggest threat, though, was that most of them were equipped with U.S.-made M-2 Browning .50-caliber heavy machine guns on pintle mounts behind the front seats.

Old Ma Deuce meant trouble, and that went double when the guns were mounted on a mobile platform. Considering the mujis crewing the vehicles, he would have expected to see them using the Russian 12.7 mm heavy guns, as they were an Afghan favorite. But if the jeeps had come from the Thai army, the Fifties, their mounts and the ammunition would have come with the vehicles.

After a fifteen-minute break for the crews to smoke and eat, the jeeps formed up again and set off down the road. After giving them enough time to clear the area, Bolan continued his recon. If Liu had brought in these vehicles, he wanted to see what else the tong leader had put together to defend his new kingdom.

It was obvious that major capital investments were being made in what had historically been a very low-tech, low-capital operation run mostly by the native mountain tribesmen. If the rest of Liu's plans included updating the processing and delivery systems with modern equipment, the Golden Triangle could once again become the world's largest drug-producing region.

ONCE INSIDE the ring of the gun jeep's patrol area, Bolan started running into roving foot patrols of a dozen men or so. Like the crews of the jeeps, these were mixed-nationality units. It looked as if local tribesmen were acting as scouts and the troops were a mix of what looked like Chinese and Afghan mujis. Apparently, Liu wanted his Taliban allies to get accustomed to working in the jungle.·

With local scouts in the area, Bolan knew that he had to be very careful about not leaving any signs of his passing. The mountain people had lived there for thousands of years and could read a bent leaf and a scuff mark on the jungle floor like Americans read an AAA road map.

He was approaching a stream when he caught movement high in a tree overhanging the opposite bank. He dived for cover as a burst of AK fire cut through the jungle directly over his head, shredding the vegetation. The sniper was overly eager, and that wasn't a good trait in a marksman. In a sniper situation, the man who didn't make a mistake took out his target, and not making a mistake meant having patience. Patience always bagged the target.

Bolan didn't need a scope to take this guy out, but he wanted a closer look at the surrounding jungle to see if he had backup on the ground. Reaching back into the side pocket on his rucksack, he took out his day scope and clicked it into the mount on the M-16's carrying handle.

Before he could start scoping out the far bank, he heard a voice call up to the sniper, and his question was answered. That answer meant that he needed to disappear. Bolan silently pulled back deeper into the jungle until he found a fallen log he could use for cover. Though he couldn't catch the language clearly, it sounded as though the sniper was being berated for wasting ammunition. If that was the case, he could simply pull back, bypass these people and they would never know that he had been here.

The sniper, however, seemed to be defending his shot. Bolan heard the man come down out of his perch and start splashing across the stream. Rather than let him get too close, Bolan parted the foliage in front of him, sighted in and took his shot. The sniper was climbing the near bank when the 5.56 mm round took him high in the chest. His arms flew up from the impact, and he dropped backward into the water.

As Bolan expected, the far side of the bank instantly erupted in a blaze of AK fire. Most of it went wild, but a couple of short bursts had him hugging the dirt.

Shouts cut off the fire, and he heard men start moving through the brush. He also heard the distinctive sound of a voice over a field radio, and that was bad news. A skilled jungle operative would have no trouble getting away from these inept guys, but no one could outrun a radio. He needed to break contact and fade while he still could.

Taking a grenade from his harness, he pulled the pin and lobbed it in the Afghans' direction. The detonation would cover his withdrawal. The explosion was followed by screams as the red-hot shrapnel found homes, and Bolan slipped away.

AN HOUR LATER, Bolan was well clear of the ambush site and felt that he was getting close to whatever the patrols were guarding. The smell of machinery exhaust was in the air, and the jungle animals were mostly silent. Taking his time, though, he moved in closer until he came to another clearing and found the airstrip.

The airstrip was camouflaged to look like a widening of the road that ran through the clearing, but it was unmistakably a packed-earth landing strip with taxi strips at either end leading off into the nearby wood line. Through his field glasses, he saw that the jungle under the trees had been cleared away, leaving the upper canopy to hide the aircraft parked underneath.

The open-air hangar was big enough to hold several fair-sized aircraft, and a refueling dump had been set up on one end, as well. Right then there was only a single civilian chopper with a Thai registry number on the tail boom in residence. If Liu had built himself a hidden airfield, he was probably using the jungle canopy to hide the rest of his operation.

Before, the processing of the Golden Triangle's

raw opium had been farmed out to small huts all over the region. It was a very inefficient system and had resulted in a product of uneven quality. But its advantage was that there was no center of production for anyone to target. The Thai and Myanmar drug busters could show up every so often, burn a few hooches and maybe find a small warehouse, but there was no way that they could locate and destroy them all.

As soon as the troops loaded back in their choppers and flew out, the locals simply put up another hut or two and were back in business.

Bolan figured that Liu, being a modern, Westernized Chinese businessman, would want to get the maximum return for his investment here. That would mean centralizing and modernizing his facilities to some extent. He would be well aware of the need to be able to maximize his transport network to cut his overhead. That would serve his purposes very well, but it would cluster his assets and provide good targets for a strike force.

After making a few notes on his map, Bolan carefully backed out of his hiding place and swung around to the north. The airstrip and the park under the canopy would be heavily guarded, and there was no point in poking a stick in the hornet's nest.

## CHAPTER FIVE

*The Golden Triangle*

Bolan was moving to the north, keeping a sharp eye out for Liu's foot patrols, when he heard a furious firefight in the distance. Sound traveled differently in the jungle than on more open ground, so he knew that the combat was actually not too far away. Rather than going to ground and waiting for it to end, though, he decided to investigate. If someone else was probing the Golden Triangle, he wanted to know who it was.

The jungle in that area was thick, and the gunfire stopped before he could get in position to see what was going on. According to his map, he was approaching a large clearing when he faintly heard men's voices. Not wanting to take on one of the patrols with their blood up, he decided to let the victors get well clear of the area. He did, however, work his way forward until he found a concealed observation point just as a dozen men walked into his field of view.

He wasn't too surprised to see that the patrol was made up of more mujahideen fighters. They didn't have one of the local mountain tribe scouts with them, but their distinctive flat, round hats, beards and khaki uniforms clearly identified them. As soon as they were out of sight, he couldn't resist finding out who they had run across and started following their back trail.

About five hundred yards north, he found where the patrol had taken cover in the tall grass. From the muzzle-blast marks on the ground, he could see which direction they had been firing in. He went about a hundred yards in that direction and came across a man's body, naked from the waist up, lying facedown beside the trail. He'd been shot several times through the head.

Through the blood, he saw that the man was blond, which matched the pale skin of his torso. Taking the roll of parachute cord from his pack, Bolan tied it to one of the corpse's arms so he could roll him over from a safe distance in case the corpse had been booby trapped with a grenade. Since the body wasn't stiff, it wasn't easy, but he soon had him lying face up.

The bullets that had been fired into the man's head had blown much of his face away, but he appeared to be Slavic, probably a Russian. That made the incident worth investigating, and after finding the man's pockets clean, Bolan started canvassing the area. When he saw two piles of empty AK brass a few yards apart, he realized that the dead man hadn't been alone in his last stand. He'd had at least one partner.

Whoever the second man had been, he was good in the jungle and Bolan had to look carefully to find his sign. The first thing he saw was a drop of blood half-covered by a leaf, so the second man had also been hit. How badly he was wounded was yet to be seen, but when Bolan went back into the jungle, the next two blood trails he saw were bigger.

Several times Bolan had to cast about to pick up the man's trail again, but he always found the blood. If the muji patrol had had a local scout with them, they'd have tracked him down, as well.

BIG GOLD LIU WAITED until his helicopter had been towed into the cleared taxi strip under the jungle canopy before he stepped out. The tong leader was as big as his nickname and almost as golden. He was a traditionalist who saw himself as a traditional Chinese businessman running a traditional family business. Not so long ago in Asia, a gangster proclaimed his status and wealth by the amount of gold he wore. Big Gold had abandoned most of the adornment, but he still sported a solid-gold, Rolex Oyster watch. Long before it had been taken over by the CIA as an in-house badge, the gold Rolex had been designed for the Asian criminal underground.

Almost the minute he stepped out of the chopper, he broke out in a sweat and silently cursed. This outdoor steam bath wasn't a place for a civilized man like him to have to do business. Only mountain barbarians could live in this climate, but since it was the key to his future prosperity, he would learn to endure it.

Liu's family had been based in the old Portuguese colony of Macao for centuries. But for the past fifty years, Macao had existed only because her larger sister, Hong Kong, had been there to protect her from the Red Chinese. With the British gone, there was nothing to stop Beijing from crushing him. Every morning when he awoke, he cursed the British, both their past and future generations. If he could have, he'd have gladly pulled the plug on their miserable little island and sunk it into the deepest part of the cold northern seas. What spineless cowards. Their capitulation to Beijing had doomed his city and had cut him adrift from his ancestral home. And all of that because of a gambler.

To Liu's mind a man, but particularly a gambler, was only as good as his word. A favorite son of a Communist official, this particular gambler had been deeply in debt to the Liu family. He had also been infatuated with Big Gold Liu's favorite party girl. The girl, Mai, had been a rare beauty even in a nation known for beautiful women. Her lineage included enough European blood on both sides that she was one of the hybrid beauties that only such matings could produce. Her hair was deep bronze, her eyes golden and, while her body had been Asian slender, her breasts and hips were those of a Victoria's Secret supermodel.

Liu found this rare flower when he had foreclosed on her father's small business because of nonpayment of a loan. Rather than lose his only means of livelihood, the man instead offered his thirteen-year-old daughter to cover his debt. Liu was a connoisseur of female flesh and saw the potential in the child. The price he would get from the first man honored to enter her jade gate would buy him a thousand small shops like her father's.

He took the girl under his wing and taught her the things she would need to know to develop her full potential. These lessons, of course, left the girl's virginity completely intact. Virgins had great value in China, and Liu wasn't about to screw up his investment.

After his ship came in, however, he often visited Mai and considered her his number-one girl. That didn't, however, mean that he had kept her services exclusively to himself; he was always a businessman. Mai was in great demand, and that demand meant great profit. It was only when the Communist gambler tried to take her for his exclusive use that Liu was forced to act.

The young man burst into the house where Mai held court late one night with four of his friends, and they had all been armed. When the madam of the house had tried to stop him, she was gunned down. After kidnapping the girl, the five tried to make it across the border back into mainland China. But again the favorite son's luck hadn't been running with him that night. Liu's men easily captured him and his equally foolish friends before they were able to make the crossing.

When the prisoners had been brought to him, Liu had been faced with a dilemma. All five of the men were sons of Communist officials and therefore they were off-limits to traditional tong justice. No tong leader in his right mind was ready to take on the People's Liberation Army. However, before this incident, the Communists had always treated the tongs and triads with measured respect.

The madam who was killed at the bordello had been one of Liu's favorite aunts. Her death alone would have been enough reason for him to take blood for blood. And with the kidnapping, as well as the unpaid debts on top of that, he'd had no choice but to act. If he had allowed this man to treat him as he had, others would try to do the same. As with the American Mafia, respect was paramount with the tongs; losing face meant losing business sooner or later.

Looking back, Liu could see that he should have simply castrated the five and turned them loose. That would have served to assuage his offended sensibilities in a traditional manner. And, had the ringleader not bragged of his superior sexual skills where Mai was concerned, he might have let him live. But, on top of everything else, the sexual insult was too much.

Big Gold Liu wouldn't have been able to keep control of his own crime family had he not acted.

That was all in the past now, and Liu wasn't one to keep recounting past misfortunes. He had the rest of his life ahead of him and, were the truth to be known, he had grown tired of trying to make good on bad debts. His new enterprise didn't involve him holding his customer's markers until he could be paid. Even with the interest rates he charged, it wasn't a worthy occupation for a man like him. He was creating a cash-and-carry business with repeat customers and he would need a fleet of ships to hold all the money he would soon be making.

The tongs had been involved in the drug trade since the beginning of the opium trade in the eighteenth century. Like gambling and prostitution, it was also a traditional, honorable business for a man of his stature. It was also a springboard to his owning, or at least ruling, much of non-Communist Southeast Asia.

Liu wasn't called Big Gold for nothing. He had big plans, and his golden luck was still running with him. Or at least most of it.

As Liu HAD EXPECTED, Al Hosn, the Taliban representative, was waiting under the trees for him. Liu had never thought that he would ever have to do business with a Muslim fanatic, but the drug trade made for strange bedfellows. Even with their mutual interests, though, the relationship wasn't running as smoothly as Liu would have liked. The Afghan connection was needed so that he could use their established European networks to move his product. The traditional Asian drug networks were full to overflowing, and he didn't want to have to fight endless turf wars with well-established tongs to make room for his shipments.

In addition, the antidrug agencies were all over the Asian shippers like flies on carrion. The loss rates were climbing, and Liu wasn't going to invest a large portion of the Red Door's wealth just to see it pissed away on losses in shipment. The Taliban had offered guaranteed routes into Russia and Eastern Europe for a fair percentage. It was the kind of deal that any Chinese businessman could understand, and above all, Liu was a businessman.

The problem was that the man the Taliban had sent was having difficulty adjusting to living in a land that wasn't ruled by the rigid laws of his harsh desert God. Every time Al Hosn watched a Chinese eating roast pork, the man could hardly restrain himself. The sight of one of the tribal women quietly nursing her child was equally repugnant to him. That didn't, however, keep him from taking the young mountain girls to his bed.

Further, the mujahideen troops Al Hosn commanded were turning out to be less than successful in their new environment. They were battle-hardened desert and mountain warriors who were confident that they could conquer anything God sent their way. But the jungle wasn't something to be fought and overcome. Good jungle fighters were men who had learned to respect the jungle and who moved through it like the tiger. The Afghans saw it as an obstacle and tried to fight it. Even so, there were enough of them to fully secure the area and, if he needed men to die for him, these desert barbarians would come in handy.

"We just had two more attempted intruders," the Afghan said by way of greeting to Liu. "My men killed one of them, a Russian, but the other one escaped in the jungle."

"How close in did they get?"

"Not close," Al Hosn said.

"What would a Russian be doing here?" Liu asked.

"They came here for me," the Afghan boasted proudly. "I am famed as a killer of the Communist infidel dogs, and they have a price on my head."

Liu sincerely doubted that the Russians would have sent a hit team to Asia to settle a ten-year-old debt left over from a failed war. A Chinese would have, but while the Russians were even worse barbarians than the Afghans, they weren't mad. More than likely they, too, had heard rumors about the changes that were going on in the Golden Triangle. Since the streets of Moscow were awash with heroin, they would be concerned enough to investigate.

"How is the work going?" Liu asked.

The tong leader was well informed as to the state of the construction he was financing; Al Hosn was in charge of the work only in name. The engineers supervising the construction were all Chinese, and he received their reports on a daily basis. The Afghan had only to keep them secure from intruders for the job to be finished on time.

Back under the jungle canopy, a factory complex was being raised, the first of several Liu planned to erect. Built into the side of a hill next to a small river, this modern processing plant would process the poppy sap into heroin in a fraction of the time it took using the traditional methods. In other areas under his control, hundreds of acres were being cleared and put into new poppy fields. Within two years, Liu expected to have tripled production and made himself one of the wealthiest men on Earth.

That wealth wouldn't merely serve to provide him comfort. It would be put to work creating a Liu family dynasty that would live for generations after him. His spirit would be worshiped for centuries to come and his name would never die. For a man who had been forced to flee from his ancestral homeland, it wasn't a bad legacy to leave behind.

Liu wasn't unaware that the Taliban intended to use its cut from his enterprise to create havoc in the world. Had Liu been in any other business, such disruption of the trade and commerce would have cost him dearly.

However, for a man in his business, it was never bad for his customers to live in uncertain times. The more they were threatened, the more it drove them to seek drug-induced dreams to calm their fears. Since he would be the world's largest supplier of what they craved, his future was secure.

For an ex-gambler and a pimp, Liu wasn't uninformed of what was going on in the world outside of his narrow field of interest. First and last, he was Chinese and the Han had kept a close eye on the West for a long time now. And, unlike the Taliban, he had a much more realistic view of the West's strengths and its weaknesses.

The Afghans would use their money to attack the West and for a time, they would have it all their way. A weakness of the West was that gold spoke louder than loyalty, and the money would open doors for them that should be tightly guarded. Emboldened by their initial success, and screaming their cries of jihad, the Taliban would eventually go too far. That would awaken the West, and the Afghans would then see the great strength of the Western peoples, particularly the Yankees, brought to bear on them.

Fanatics weren't men of finesse and they never took into consideration that when you teased a tiger, you had best make sure that it was a dead one. Regardless of the ravings of the radical imams, the West wasn't corrupt and teetering on the brink of internal collapse. Regardless of its faults, and they were many as well as public, the West was stronger than ever.

By that time, though, Liu expected to be at the center of a well-diversified personal empire. But he wouldn't invest any of his money in anything that touched upon the Arab world. When the West finally struck back, there would be nothing left there that would be worth having.

Al Hosn and his mujahideen fighters would be gone from the Golden Triangle long before that, though. As soon as everything was up and running, Liu intended to recruit the world's largest mercenary force to guard his kingdom, and the troops would all be Chinese. The Han made good mercenaries, and there were enough experienced fighters among the offshore Chinese that getting the numbers he needed would be no problem, not at the rate of pay he would offer.

"The work goes well," Al Hosn said proudly. "They do not dare be lazy when my men are watching them."

Liu smiled at his temporary business partner. "Show me."

"Come this way."

The processing plant was a concrete-block structure on a concrete slab. Usually, that kind of construction would have been visible to the sensors of a deep-space spy satellite, but Liu had thought of that when he made his plans. The tree canopy above the building was laced with a particular kind of carbon-fiber cable that blocked satellite sensors by diffusing radar beams. A Liu family member in America worked for NASA, and he had come up with that idea.

He knew that sooner or later the Americans would start looking for him. At first, they would try to do it from space because that was easiest, but the cables would guard them from seeing anything. When that failed, they would send in men on foot to try to find out what he was doing. But he had made plans for countering that contingency, as well.

"When are the reinforcements due in?" he asked the Afghan leader.

"Very soon," Al Hosn replied.

"Good," the tong leader said. "I want them in place as soon as possible. And," he warned, "don't let any more Russians in here."

"They will not pass," the Afghan said. "You have my word on it."

# CHAPTER SIX

*The Golden Triangle*

Now that Bolan knew what to look for, the blood trail in the jungle was easy enough for him to follow. Knowing that the man he was tracking was armed, though, made him move carefully. He would be in pain, and that could make him react unpredictably.

Hearing a faint noise ahead of him, Bolan worked his way off to the side and found a place to scan the jungle in front of him. The man was sitting under a tree with his back to the trunk and his legs in front of him. His left leg was bound with a blood-soaked sweat rag. From the man's features, there was no doubt in Bolan's mind that he was also Slav, and again more than likely a Russian.

He had no idea what two Russian operatives were doing in the Golden Triangle. Southeast Asia wasn't a traditional area of concern for Moscow, but Russia was the end market for much of Afghanistan's current heroin production, so they would be concerned about any increase coming from the area. If that was the case, it made them allies again this time, and this ally wasn't going to make it out without help.

"Attention," Bolan said softly in Russian. "I am a friend. Do not fire."

"Your accent is terrible," the man answered in British-accented English. "Who are you?"

"I'm an American," Bolan replied. "And I'm not your enemy. I know you're wounded. I've been following your blood trail, and I have medical supplies to treat you."

"Come out slowly," the Russian replied, "and keep your hands empty."

Bolan slung his M-16 muzzle down over his back. "I'm coming out."

"Slowly."

When Bolan stepped out, he faced an AK in steady hands. "What are you doing here?" the Russian asked.

"I came to find out what's being built here in the Golden Triangle," Bolan admitted. "And you?"

"I came for the Dushmen, the Afghan bandits."

"But they found you and your partner first," Bolan said. "I found his body along the trail."

"We stumbled into them," the Russian replied, "and they took us by surprise. Yuri went down first, and there were just too damned many of the bastards for me to deal with after I got hit."

"Let me look at your leg before you bleed to death." Bolan reached for his first aid pouch.

"I have been in the jungle before," the Russian said to distract himself as Bolan knelt beside him and cut his pant leg open. "But I have never seen anything like this."

"There's worse," Bolan replied as he gently examined the wound.

"What is your name, American?" the Russian asked to keep his mind off of the pain.

"Mike Belasko."

"That sounds like a Russian name."

"It isn't."

"I am Dimitri Polnacek."

"RSV, right?"

"I thought you Americans called it the FSB, for Federal Security Bureau?"

"It depends on who we're talking to." Bolan shrugged. "The bullet's still in there, and I don't want to try to cut it out here. Let's stop the bleeding, then I'll try to get you out of here."

"Why are you doing this?" Polnacek asked.

Bolan looked him straight in the eyes. "Our countries aren't enemies now, and it looks like we have similar interests in this particular region of the world. Believe me, we don't want to see heroin production increased any more than your people do."

"I owe you, Belasko," the Russian said.

"Just call it professional courtesy," the Executioner replied.

After putting a pressure bandage around the wound, Bolan reached into his pouch and came out with a plastic pill bottle. He shook four of the tablets into his hand and held them out for the Russian.

"They're a broad-spectrum antibiotic and should keep the infection down until I can get you to a doctor."

Taking out another bottle, he again shook out four more pills. "The aspirin will keep the swelling down and help with the pain."

Taking the canteen from his belt, Bolan handed that over, as well. "Wash them down good."

The Russian took the pills and followed them with a long drink of warm water. "Thanks," he said as he handed the canteen back.

Bolan stood and held his hand out to the Russian. "Stand up and see if you can walk on that."

The Russian took Bolan's hand, pulled himself erect and took a step. "It hurts, of course," he said, wincing. "But I think I can walk out."

"Good," Bolan replied. "Because if you want to get out of here alive, we have to put several miles between us and their patrol area as soon as we can. We've both stirred them up, and they'll be looking for trouble."

"The Afghans are always looking for trouble."

"I'll take point," Bolan said.

EVEN WITH BOLAN breaking trail, Polnacek's wound made the going much slower than he would have liked, but it couldn't be helped. Rather than fight the terrain, Bolan tried to keep to the valleys. There was simply no way that the Russian could climb the steep hills and ridgelines that characterized this part of the world. As the pointman, Bolan cleared the trail for a hundred yards and then waited for the Russian to catch up before moving out again.

Bolan was waiting again when he caught a flash of movement from the clearing in front of him and smelled wood smoke. The mujis might not have been fully acclimatized to working jungle terrain, but they could identify a checkpoint when they saw one. They had parked themselves right in the middle of a narrow valley where two ridges came down to almost meet. The flat ground was only twenty yards wide between them, and there was no way that he'd be able to sneak the wounded Russian through without alerting the mujis.

If Bolan had been alone, he'd have simply bypassed the Taliban outpost. But the only way around them was over a hill, and Bolan knew the Russian wasn't up for anything that physical. Moving back down the trail, he found Polnacek and motioned him into cover.

"I think there's some kind of checkpoint up ahead," Bolan stated. "With the narrow pass, we can't get around it, not with your bad leg. So I'm going to try to take care of it."

"Is there anything I can do to help?" the Russian asked.

Bolan shook his head. "Thanks, but I just want you to keep out of the way for now."

Taking out his combat cosmetics, Bolan reapplied his war paint over every inch of his exposed skin. This would be no time for a flash of bare Caucasian flesh to catch the eye.

"If I don't make it back in two hours," Bolan told the Russian, "you're on your own. But if you take your time and travel at night, you shouldn't run into too many of the Afghans. I'm leaving my food and water here for you. I won't need it."

Polnacek wasn't a particularly religious man, but he said, "Go with God."

BOLAN HAD CHOSEN a tiger-suit camouflage pattern for this mission, and once again it was living up to its name. Stripped of his excess traveling gear, he moved through the brush like a big jungle cat. The green, brown and black slashes of color blended in perfectly with the late-afternoon shadows in the vegetation. Even so, he took his time working his way around to the side of the shack before moving up to take another look at the situation.

From where he had first observed the checkpoint, he hadn't been able to see the extent of the clearing the mujis had cut. They had created full fields of fire in all directions around the hut, and there was no way for him to make his approach unobserved. The only thing going for him was that it seemed as if everyone was inside the guard shack at the moment. From the smoke, they were probably brewing tea.

Going flat on the ground, he cradled his M-16

across the tops of his hands and started crawling out into the clearing.

EVEN WITH a bullet in the leg, Dimitri Polnacek wasn't content to sit and let another man do his work for him. He had no idea who this mystery American was, but he was certain that he had seen a photo of him before. For a number of reasons, he hadn't mentioned that he had been a young KGB agent when the teetering edifice of communism had finally crumbled into the dustbin of history. Since he was so new to the old Communist spy agency, he was one of the KGB officers who had been selected to be "sheep dipped," as the American CIA put it, into RSV service.

Not all of the old KGB cold war warriors had converted. Too many of them had been "super Communists," and the shock of losing their elite status in Russian society was too much for them to handle. Not a few of the old-timers simply went into their offices, put the muzzles of their Makarovs in their mouths and blew their brains out.

Polnacek was kept on with the new RSV for a number of reasons, not the least of which was that his father was a well-decorated hero of the Afghan war. Yeltsin's crowd was courting the Red Army big time and didn't want to anger anyone. Particularly not someone like General Viktor Polnacek, three times Hero of the Soviet Union and commander of the Guards Parachute Brigade. Also in his favor was the fact that he spoke English like a native of the UK. With the cold war turning into an economic battle, Mother Russia would still need spies.

As a man whose father and grandfather had both been renowned military men, Polnacek couldn't let this Yankee carry all of his water for him. If there was going to be a fight, he was going to be in it as much as he could. Biting back the pain, he crawled until he could see the outpost through the edge of the vegetation.

He parted the elephant grass in front of him with the muzzle of his AKM just enough to have a good line of sight. Reaching into his magazine carrier, he took out his last full magazine of 7.62 mm rounds and laid it beside him. Counting the mag in his assault rifle, that gave him sixty rounds, and a man of his training could do a lot of damage with that much ammunition. One of the Red Army's traditional skills was sniping, and he had been a medal-winning shooter at the KGB academy.

Even though he knew what to be on the watch for, he didn't see the American make his approach. One minute everything was clear, and the next, two Afghans emerged from their little hut and started walking to the left.

Suddenly, the American appeared, a shot rang out and the muji on the left went down. When his partner spun to face the threat, Polnacek carefully squeezed off a shot and was rewarded by seeing his Dushmen go down, as well.

The hut cleared in an instant when four more mujis stormed out, the AKs in their hands wildly blazing fire. With Bolan on one side and Polnacek on their front, they didn't last long. The Russian got another one while Bolan was taking out his partners. As a firefight, it was brief, but Polnacek liked his battles short and one-sided.

"I THOUGHT I told you to keep hidden," Bolan snapped when he returned after clearing the hut. "You could have gotten killed."

"As could have you, my friend," Polnacek replied. "I happen to be a better than average shot and thought you might need some help."

He glanced at the bandage on his leg. "That was the least I could do in return for what you did for me."

Bolan knew that he would have done the same and gave the Russian his due. "Let's see if they left anything there we can use."

There wasn't much in the hut, but the real prize was the muji gun jeep parked behind the guard shack. When Bolan walked over to it, he saw that it had taken a few stray rounds, but looked functional. When he switched it on, he saw that the gas gauge showed three-quarters of a tank. That was more than enough to get them back to what passed for civilization in northern Thailand.

"Do you think you can drive?" he asked the Russian.

"Better than I can walk right now."

"Good. You take the wheel and I'll man the gun in case there's any more of them in the area."

The Russian slid behind the wheel of the M-151 and fired up the engine. "Where to?"

"South," Bolan said as he chambered a round in the pintle-mounted M-60 machine gun. "We'll pick up the national highway about twenty miles from here."

Polnacek shifted into first gear and they were gone.

AFTER TWENTY MILES of jungle road, Bolan and Polnacek started running into signs of habitation. At the first village they came to, Bolan bought gas and refilled their canteens from the village well.

"How do you want to work it from here?" he asked the Russian. "I can leave you here for your own people, or we can try to drive back to Bangkok."

"Isn't this vehicle a bit conspicuous if we hit a police checkpoint?"

Bolan planned to ditch the M-60, but the Russian was right. Even without the gun, a camouflaged gun jeep would draw the wrong kind of attention. "Let me see if I can hire us another ride."

A lengthy transaction with the owner of the sole vehicle in the village got Bolan and Polnacek a ride to Bangkok in a battered old Toyota pickup truck, and all it cost them was the jeep. The deal also included the owner as their driver and a load of firewood in the back to hide their weapons.

*Stony Man Farm, Virginia*

AT STONY MAN FARM, Bolan's confirmation of Afghan mujahideen involvement in the Golden Triangle had the effect of dropping a grenade in an overflowing garbage bin. Everything was in the wind now.

It also meant that for once, the tip Hal Brognola had received proved golden. One of the biggest problems in his line of work was evaluating intelligence information. The data stream was constant, almost a daily flood, but for every gem in the stream, there were a thousand lumps of dog excrement. And the garbage often hid the good bits from sight. Intel evaluation wasn't a science; it was a fine art involving everything from basic detective work to satellite recon. But it always ended up with a gut feeling as the most important factor. No matter how good the intel looked on the surface, if your gut told you that it was bogus, it probably was.

He saw dozens of reports every week about the so-called Taliban government in what was left of Afghanistan. One day a man would be flogged for being caught singing the words of a Western song to himself as he worked. The next, one would report the execution of a man caught flying a kite. As bad as most of these reports were, they had little to do with anything that might affect the U.S. in any way. If the Taliban wanted to brutalize its own people, that was an internal problem. But when the Taliban decided to export that kind of behavior, it was entirely another matter.

Coming as Bolan's report did on the heels of a proved Taliban-Algerian connection, Brognola was now inclined to believe the report that the Afghans had also hooked up with the Red Door tong. But for once, with Striker in place and Phoenix waiting to depart, they might be able to shut it down in time to keep it from affecting America.

Bolan's intervention in saving the wounded Russian was also very fortunate. Brognola wasn't surprised to learn that the Russians were also concerned about Liu's takeover of the Golden Triangle. Post-Soviet Russia had fallen to the same ills that plagued the rest of the free world, including drugs. They were the end market for most of the heroin that Afghanistan already produced, so the last thing they needed was for the Taliban to get a new source for even more.

Working with the new Russian Federation was still dicey, but Stony Man had had good results so far. And, since this was shaping up to be a real job, if the Russians wanted in, he'd welcome them.

## CHAPTER SEVEN

*RSV Headquarters, Bangkok, Thailand*

It was obvious to Bolan that the Russian Federation had fallen on hard times recently. The three-story building housing the RSV headquarters was a dump. It didn't have any broken windows, but that was one of the few indications that it hadn't been abandoned. The old KGB had been pretty stingy with most of its overseas facilities, as well. But it was apparent that Thailand hadn't been very high on the new democratic government's priority list until now. That new interest, however, hadn't yet been translated into improving the RSV's living conditions.

The inside of the building wasn't quite as bad as the exterior, but Bolan didn't need to hear the muted roar of dozens of fans to tell that the air conditioner was out of order. He broke sweat on the stairs leading up to the office of the "section chief" on the second floor.

The RSV "section chief," Anatoly Komarov, had

the look of a Soviet apparatchik of the bad old days. He had that unmistakable fifties-style Marxist seediness and a permanent frown etched on his broad Slavic face. His cheap rayon shirt was sticking to his chest, and what little hair he had left was in an obvious comb over. When he opened his mouth, though, Bolan learned how he had escaped the massive democratic housecleaning that had gone on in Lubyanka.

"I owe you one, as you Americans like to say," Komarov said when the introductions had been made. "For saving young Dimitri Gregorvitch. His father and I are old schoolmates, and the general would have skinned me alive if he had come to harm under my command."

Polnacek laughed. "No, Anatoly," he said in English so Bolan could be in on the joke. "He would have simply shot you in the belly and then smoked his cigars and drank his best whiskey while he watched you die. He lost his skinning knife a long time ago."

"You defame your father, Gregorvitch," Komarv said. "He would have gotten a new knife just to avenge you, and you know that.

"But," Komarov continued as he turned back to Bolan, "since he is safe now, we can talk of more pleasant things."

The Russian paused for a long moment. "I have a feeling that I should know who you are," he said. "It is obvious to me that you are a dangerous man and, under the old regime, we kept files on men like you."

"As we kept files on the dangerous men of the KGB like you, too." Bolan met his eyes with a neutral look. "But today my country and yours work together when it's to our advantage to do so. We've worked together in the Middle East several times, and I think we can help each other in this part of the world, as well."

"What do you have in mind?"

"Well," Bolan said, "since we've confirmed that Afghan Taliban fighters are operating in the Golden Triangle, I expect that you would like to see them go back to their own country. I also expect that Moscow would like to make sure that Russia isn't flooded with the heroin that will be produced in the new factories that are being built there."

"That is a precise summation of my orders," Komarov admitted.

"That's also the goal of my government," Bolan said. "I'm the pointman for a larger mission. We're planning to take out not only the new Golden Triangle operation, but the man behind it, Big Gold Liu of the Red Door tong. I'm sure that I can get my people to sign off on a joint venture if you want to join with us on this."

"How would we do it?" Komarov asked. Working with the Americans was all fine and good, but it had to be done in such a way that the Russian units involved remained completely independent.

"As we've done before," Bolan said. "We'd have a joint but separate effort. Your troops would remain under their own officers, as would my people. That way each side will be able to exercise any concerns they might have about national interests.''

"You understand precisely.'' Komarov smiled. "You should be a diplomat. I will ask the interior minister for a team to join up with you in taking care of this matter.''

"Considering what we're facing here,'' Bolan said, "can I suggest that you request a Spetsnaz unit? Particularly one from the Third Company? I believe that Major Alexi Dobyrn is their commander.''

Komarov parked his elbows on his desktop and looked at Bolan intently. "You are a very interesting man, Mr. Belasko, and you have interesting friends. The good major was exactly the man I had in mind.''

"We've worked together before,'' Bolan said simply.

The Russian stared at Bolan intently. "I think I know who you are. You have been of assistance to us in the past.''

"If we're going to team up,'' Bolan told him, "we should start sharing information, shouldn't we?''

"You are quite right,'' Komarov replied. "I'll clear it with my headquarters, but as far as I am concerned, anything I have is yours. And—'' he reached for his phone "—I will start with that right now.''

When Komarov spoke in rapid Russian, Polnacek translated. "He has just told our operations staff to turn the complete file on this operation over to me so I can brief you on its contents.''

"That is correct," Komarov said when he hung up the phone. "But for security reasons, I would like this briefing to be done in our safehouse. I'm sure you understand."

When Bolan nodded, Komarov continued. "Also, I think that we put on a rather fine table there. I know that we have a first-rate bar. That should make the experience a bit more enjoyable."

Bolan smiled. "I'll take you up on your hospitality. I could use a good meal."

"Never fight on an empty stomach."

*Stony Man Farm, Virginia*

BARBARA PRICE FOUND Hal Brognola working in his office in the farmhouse. Even in the middle of an operation, he had to keep the paperwork at bay.

"What's up?" he greeted her.

"We just got the final report on Mack's recon," she said. "He's hooked up with the local Russians again. He found a wounded RSV agent in the Triangle and got him back to Bangkok. After patching him up, the Russian took him to RSV headquarters to meet the fellow in charge and they struck a deal."

"God." Brognola sighed. "It was so much easier in the old days. We didn't have to cozy up to people like that. Working with them always comes with a caveat."

"Considering what he reported seeing in the Triangle," Price reminded him, "we need the manpower they can bring to the party. He said the Russians are sending in a Spetsnaz wet team to back us up.''

''Which means that we need to get Phoenix moving as soon as possible.''

''That's the next item on the agenda,'' she replied. ''The guys should be here this afternoon to check over their mission packs.''

''Considering the situation in Thailand,'' Brognola said, ''what's their insertion plan?''

As with all too many of American's once staunch allies, the Thais were at odds with the U.S. Washington's penchant for alienating the only friends the U.S. had left in the non-Western world had flared up again, this time focusing on human-rights issues. The Thais highly resented what they saw as American meddling in their internal affairs. The current impasse between the two governments was so severe that only minimal cooperation was possible on any level, and even that was difficult.

Until the State Department figured out that American-style democracy simply wasn't going to fly in places that didn't have a tradition of Western ideals, the Stony Man teams would have to operate as if they were on enemy territory.

''Since an in-country delivery isn't on in Thailand,'' she said, ''Aaron and I worked out an offshore pickup. The mission packs will be flown to an American-flagged ship in international waters off Myanmar, and Phoenix will pick them up there by helicopter.''

"That's a bit Byzantine, isn't it?"

"We don't have much of a choice," Price replied. "The Myanmar government is pissed at us, too, worse than the Thais actually, and that was the best we could come up with on short notice. Since the State Department unleashed its latest human-rights campaign, we don't have a real friend left in that part of the world."

"It was sure a hell of a lot easier to operate during the cold war," Brognola grumbled. "At least we knew who our enemies were."

"Peace does seem to bring muddled thinking out in full force," she agreed. "All the 'peace, love and tie dye' types who've been hiding out since the Gulf War are working for the State Department now."

"Maybe we should target Georgetown University's Department of International Studies."

"That would make our job a hell of lot easier if we took them out," she agreed.

"It would." Brognola sighed. "That it would."

*Thailand*

COMPARED TO Hong Kong, or even Macao, Big Gold Liu found Thailand to be a very disordered place. There was little open opposition when he moved his household to Bangkok. That didn't mean, however, that he was met with open arms. Some of the local underworld figures didn't like the idea of a major Chinese organization staking a claim on what they saw as their home turf. Most of those disputes had been taken care of in the back alleys of the city, and the locals had decided to accommodate him.

More dangerous to him, though, was the opposition from within the Thai government. But neutralizing that was actually less of a problem than establishing himself in Bangkok's underworld hierarchy. The Thais understood the age-old Asian system of the greasing of palms, and Liu had plenty of the right grease. In Thailand, as in most of Asia, gold was the grease of choice and, as his nickname implied, he did not lack for it.

Once those obstacles were cleared from his path, his biggest problem turned out to be getting the supplies and construction material he needed up to the region known as the Golden Triangle. That had taken even more bribes and attracted the unwelcome attention of unfriendly agencies such as the American CIA and DEA. To counter that, he'd had to resort to a specialized kind of bribery.

As with their British cousins, Liu knew that Americans weren't as susceptible to open cash bribery as they were to more subtle approaches. Making sure that a man, or a woman, was introduced to the right person, again either male or female, was a far more effective hook than an honest bribe. Also like the British, Americans of both sexes liked them young, but that was no problem in Bangkok.

Further, this was less of a problem to Liu because when he transferred his household from Macao, he also transferred the contents of his sporting houses and the "farms" that fed them. He simply had his people find out which DEA agent was spending the most time in Bangkok's pleasure houses, learn his preferences and then make his wildest dreams become living, willing flesh. In this case, the bait turned out to be a golden-skinned, long-haired girl who, though she was seventeen, looked much younger.

She was also fully trained in her profession and when she was introduced to this midlevel DEA man Liu's agents had picked for their first target, the American fell securely into the net. Quite simply, the man hadn't even dreamed that sex could be taken to the levels that this girl showed him. After their first long weekend together, he would have killed to keep her for himself.

When Liu paid this man a discreet visit to explain that the girl was a favor from him and asked that the favor be returned, he didn't ask the DEA man to kill anyone. He just mentioned his need for information and said that it would be too bad if he had to send the girl to another man to get what he wanted. The DEA man considered treason a small price to pay for the erotic paradise he had found and immediately became a willing part of Liu's intelligence network.

The investment Liu put into this DEA contact paid off when he warned the tong leader of the special agent the Americans had sent to investigate him. That this agent had managed to defeat two attempts to either capture or kill him came as no real surprise. Liu didn't make the mistake of underestimating the Americans as so many Chinese did. They hadn't become the dominant force in the world by accident; they had earned the right to the golden throne. How long they would be able to keep it was another matter, but that didn't play large in Liu's planning at this time. He had to act locally before he went global.

BIG GOLD LIU HAD the traditional patience his culture was famous for. He was also a tong leader, though, and knew that his control of the Red Door depended, in large part, on his taking care of business as expected. Whoever had probed his territory and wiped out the Afghan outpost on the way out couldn't be ignored. Nor could the Russian agent who had been left behind dead. Coming on top of the abortive attack on an American agent at the doctor's house, he couldn't ignore those two probes. To do so would only cause him more trouble.

He had expected that his operation would draw opposition. He would have been a fool not to have figured that into his plans, and Big Gold Liu was anything but a fool. One didn't work his way to the leadership of a gang like the Red Door by being a fool. It was true that being a son of the tong's founding family had helped. But that hadn't kept his older brother Chin from being eliminated when he had done something stupid. In tong life, the learning curve was sharp. He had expected, though, that the opposition would have taken a little longer to react to his moves.

Nonetheless, he was faced with what was, not what he wanted them to be. But he had always been good at dealing with what the winds of chance blew his way. That was why he was called Big Gold. Gold was the color of the god of luck, and he had plenty of it.

So far, he had left his Macanese troops in Bangkok and had let the Afghans provide the security troops in the Triangle. Even though it wasn't working out as well as he would have liked, for now that division of forces would have to remain. He would, however, reinforce both contingents. He had already called for the Red Door organization in Taiwan to send him two dozen fighters. They would all be experienced at working in large cities and would back up the people he already had in his Bangkok operation.

Al Hosn had also been instructed to request that his Taliban leaders beef up his forces, as well. Liu didn't particularly like the bearded mountain warriors, but until now, they had done well. Having a whole squad of them wiped out, though, had served to point out to their hawk-faced leader that his men weren't quite the invincible warriors he so often boasted they were. They were learning the hard way that the jungle favored the knowledgeable and cared little for reputation.

If he didn't have enough in his rice bowl already, Liu was becoming concerned that his American DEA contact hadn't been able to find out where the mystery Yankee was staying, and that worried him. What worried him even more was that the man could have been the one who had made the second probe into the Golden Triangle. Then he received a report from one of his foot soldiers, and everything snapped into place. A tall, dark-haired American matching the description of the man he was looking for had been seen going into the Russian RSV headquarters.

It wasn't outside the realm of possibility that the Yankee had linked up with his country's old enemies against what they saw as a common enemy. That thought angered the tong leader, and he didn't like being angry. The Russians had no business getting involved in his affairs.

This part of the world wasn't in their legitimate sphere of influence, and the sooner they returned the last of their dogs to Europe, the better it would be for them. The days when the feared KGB had left a trail of blood wherever it went were long past. Russia had had her day, and now she had to be taught that she no longer had the power to influence events in Asia. It was time that he imposed a little Red Door punishment on a dying Russian bear.

He called for the leader of his street enforcement units. They weren't as experienced as the Taiwanese who were coming; Macao had been a quiet place. But he couldn't let the Russians go unpunished. And if the mysterious American agent was with them as had been reported, he might become an unfortunate casualty, as well.

## CHAPTER EIGHT

*Miami, Florida*

The greater Miami area was turning out to be one of the nation's hottest tourist spots of the twenty-first century. No one could say exactly why it had come back in fashion, but hundreds of thousands of sun-starved northerners were flocking to the beaches as they had done in the fifties and sixties. That gave a much needed economic boost to most of the communities that made up what most of America thought of as Miami. Certain ethnic communities, however, weren't seeing the benefit of increased tourism, and Little Haiti was one of them.

Little Haiti could be a scary place for the average sun-seeking out-of-state tourist. While it wasn't as scary as going to Port-au-Prince, it was a lot like stepping into the dirt-poor Caribbean island most of the inhabitants had escaped from. Not even the local fast-food outlets blunted that impression; the signs outside were in French Creole. One look was usually all it took for the average tourist to turn and leave. Which, on balance, probably wasn't a bad idea. Little Haiti wasn't like the other ethnic enclaves in south Florida.

Along with the Haitians who had come to America to keep from starving to death on their home island, there were those who had come specifically to work in the drug trade. Florida's geographical location made it a prime destination for the Latin American drug cartels' products. With hundreds of miles of coastline that no one really cared much about, boats large and small came in every night to off-load their cargos. Delivering the contraband by air worked well in Florida, as well. Low-flying private aircraft would parallel the remote beaches and kick out waterproof bundles to be picked up by waiting small craft.

All told, the DEA estimated that more than seventy million dollars' worth of drugs were smuggled in every year through greater Miami alone. The coastline landings accounted for millions more. Next to tourism, it was Florida's largest industry. Oranges were a distant third.

It was true that the U.S. Coast Guard had the greatest concentration of men and ships working overtime in the region to combat this traffic, but the ocean was big and the blue skies were even bigger. It would have taken a large portion of America's naval and land forces to seal Florida's coastline, and the political will on Capitol Hill wasn't there to take those steps. They were much too afraid that it would scare off the tourists.

Therefore, Florida was the unguarded gateway for the Latin American drug cartels, and the Haitian immigrants made up a large percentage of their soldiers and runners. Those who had made it to the land of opportunity sans documentation found it very helpful to have someone who would hire them no questions asked.

For what the Taliban had in mind, Little Haiti was an attractive target. Eliminating the Latin American connections and establishing their own would give them an immense chunk of the eastern market. But to do that meant visiting a hostile takeover on the foot soldiers of the Latin drug lords, the Haitians. That, too, was seen by the Taliban as being an easy job, since Little Haiti was a perfect place to conduct such an operation. The warrens and mazes of small houses and back alleys were perfect for what they had in mind. They could come in on their targets from all directions, make their hits and then fade back without being seen.

THE MEN OF Able team were going over their attack plans in their Miami motel room with the TV turned on low for background noise. Under chemical interrogation, Armani had divulged three locations in Miami that the Taliban was using as safehouses, and they were prioritizing the targets. Once they kicked off, they would have to move fast and keep moving. Greater Miami's police and antidrug forces were the largest in the nation, and they were used to reacting to turf wars.

Gadgets Schwarz caught the wail of police sirens over the drone of the reporter and glanced over at the TV. "I think we're a bit late for the party, guys," he said after watching the breaking news report for a minute. "Someone just waxed a Haitian social club big time."

Lyons looked over, saw the ambulances crowded in front of the dilapidated building and the body bags being loaded into them. From the damage to the building, it looked as if someone had drilled it with RPGs. From the pools of blood on the sidewalk, the people in the club had been taken down hard, as well. While Miami gangs whacked one another on almost a daily basis, the level of damage pointed to this being a Taliban hit.

"We're not too late." Lyons smiled. "The Algerians just cleaned up some drug scum for us. Now we get to clean them up. Turn it up so I can hear what kind of spin the media's putting on it."

Schwarz thumbed the clicker just as the camera shifted to an obviously shaken, ashen-faced reporter. "This kind of carnage hasn't been seen in Greater Miami since the last drug war, but the authorities aren't saying that another one has broken out. In fact, the scope of this attack has taken the police completely by surprise."

"One thing is clear, though. All of the victims were from this heavily Haitian neighborhood, and the attackers, while not yet identified, are described as being white and Latino. The few eye witnesses are being questioned now, but the police aren't divulging what, if anything, they have learned about who is responsible for this outrage."

The reporter took a deep breath. "Back to you in the studio, Trent."

"It looks like they got a couple of noncombatants, as well," Blancanales commented when he saw a woman's body being zipped into a body bag.

"That's bad form," Lyons said. "We'll have to teach them better manners. And—" he looked up from the map showing the locations of the Algerian hideouts "—there's no time like now to start doing it."

When Blancanales raised an eyebrow, Lyons explained. "They just pulled off a clean attack and got away without leaving any casualties behind. Normally, they'd be a bit on edge waiting for retaliation, but I don't think that's going to be the case this time. Except for us, and we're not telling, no one knows that they're here or what they're doing. They'll be kicked back, smoking their hash, reloading their magazines and planning their next hit."

Lyons grinned broadly. "I think that we ought to show them that they aren't the only ones who know how to blow into town, shoot the place up and fade. In fact, we've been doing that for a lot longer than they have."

"They did fight the French for years," Blancanales reminded him.

"But there aren't any sand dunes for them to hide behind around here," Lyons pointed out. "In Miami they're just another bunch of cheap punks holed up in a small house in a bad neighborhood."

"With AKs, Ironman," Schwarz added. "Don't forget the AKs."

Lyons shrugged. "We'll just wear our body armor."

"Oh Jesus."

SCHWARZ PULLED the van off the road a block from the target. "I'm not so sure that we ought to be leaving our ride here," he said as he looked around the darkened street. "This isn't exactly Middle America here."

The few people on the street were clustered in the alleys and street corners and looked to be buying and selling. What they were selling was easy to determine from the acrid smoke wafting in the air.

"Don't worry," Lyons said. "We'll just leave a Police Official Business sign on the dash when we get out."

"I don't think too many of the locals here can read," Schwarz replied.

"They'll be able to read this." Lyons hefted an M-16 fitted with a grenade launcher under the barrel.

"Good point."

Blancanales made his way around to the side of the

small house to cover the back. "I'm ready," he called over the com link.

"We're go on three," Lyons's voice said into his earphone. "A one and a two and a…"

The night exploded as a pair of 40 mm grenades left the launchers and crashed through the front window of the house.

Lyons and Schwarz quickly reloaded and fired two more HE rounds before selecting full-auto on their M-16 selector switches.

Their magazines were loaded with NATO M-109 heavy ball ammunition, so it wouldn't have too much trouble cutting through the walls of the house. And it didn't.

*Stony Man Farm, Virginia*

HAL BROGNOLA WAS in the Farm Annex watching the retrans from the Miami TV stations. One of the nice things about their new setup was that they had enough TV monitors to watch nearly everything that was being transmitted anywhere in the world. Right now, though, South Florida CNN's raw feed and the local Miami news station was up.

"It's going down," Aaron Kurtzman said as he cut in the audio of a local station's crew on assignment. The scene being transmitted was all too familiar to the late-night TV audience and the fans of reality shows such as *Cops*. The red-and-blue flashing lights, the yellow crime-scene tape, the ambulances and the bodies coming out in bags.

"The neighbors say that they didn't see anything out of the ordinary," the reporter was saying. "When the gunfire broke out, they all say that they ducked for cover in their own houses and didn't try to look out."

"That's one down," Brognola said. "It's too bad that they couldn't have gotten started a day earlier. It would have saved that massacre in town today."

"They needed a recon of the targets, Hal," Barbara Price reminded him. "And since we didn't have a timetable, Carl thought they had a little time."

"I know," he replied. "We can't always short stop these things."

*Miami, Florida*

THE SECOND TARGET was a house situated on a beach well away from its neighbors. With the openness to work with, the attack plan would be modified this time.

Taking out the two 5.56 mm M-249 SAW machine guns, Lyons clipped a two-hundred-round assault magazine box to each. This time they were going for a complete kill as this house was reportedly where the Algerian terrorist leaders were staying. Usually, they would have started with this place, but they wanted to suck the local police into the first location and hopefully tie them up with that investigation.

Lyons and Blancanales remained by the front of the house while Schwarz worked his way around to the beach behind it. He was packing an M-16/M-203 over and under with a hundred-round assault magazine snapped into it. Those who somehow managed to cheat fate and get out of the house would find that they hadn't run far enough.

"I'm in position," he radioed Lyons.

"On three," the Ironman replied. "One…two… three!"

The quiet little neighborhood erupted to the sound of two SAWs firing on full-auto. The 5.56 mm slugs cut through the house's lightweight frame construction like a buzz saw. Fragments of the siding, shards of glass and aluminum from the windows and pieces of decorative pottery flew as the machine guns swept their fire from right to left and back again.

This was slaughter pure and simple. But unlike what had happened at the massacre at the Haitian Social Club, this killing would have a positive outcome. If the Algerians were killed, they wouldn't visit death on others. It was a harsh equation, but the mathematics of terrorism were stark. When men went beyond the laws of civilized society, they moved into the realm of barbarism where the rule was that those who lived by the sword, died by it.

They were dying by gunfire this night, but the rule was the same.

Schwarz had a ringside seat to the slaughter and not much to do but watch. Two Algerians staggered out of the back door, but didn't make it more than a few feet. To discourage any more such foolishness, he sent a couple of 40 mm grenades through the back door.

Sirens were wailing in the distance when the trio got back in their van and drove away.

"DAMN," Lyons said when he saw several figures running out of the third target for the Cadillac convertible parked in front. "We must have left someone alive in the first house."

He turned in his seat to reach for his M-16/M-203 combo. "We can't have that now, can we?"

Blancanales reached for one of the SAWs and made sure that it had a full assault pack clipped in place. "Let's do it to 'em."

Lyons and Blancanales took their places behind the van's sliding side door as Schwarz set up his bootleg turn. He made the approach at thirty-five miles per hour so as not to alarm the Algerians as they stuffed their bags into the Caddy. Twenty yards away, he snapped the steering wheel all the way over to left lock and hit both the gas and the hand brake at the same time. The van wasn't very graceful when it swapped ends, but it did it anyway.

When the van stopped sideways in the road, Blancanales whipped open the side door. As soon as he had a sight picture, Lyons triggered the M-203. The grenade detonated in the middle of the Caddy's grille shredding the radiator. One of the terrorists standing by the front fender went flying.

Before the echo of the explosion died away, Blancanales was snapping out long bursts from the SAW, working the muzzle from one end of the car to the other. Bodies and chunks of the car's bodywork were flying everywhere. Those who moved after they hit the ground got a .357 in the head from Lyon's Colt Python.

Lyons was zeroing in on the man who had been blown clear of the Caddy by the grenade when Schwarz yelled, "Wait! Grab that guy. We need more information."

The Algerian had been stunned by the grenade's blast, but was coming to when Lyons dropped on his back and had his wrists in riot cuffs in record time. Grabbing one arm, he jerked him to his feet and dragged him to the van.

"Move it!" he said.

When Schwarz powered away from the ambush scene, the total elapsed time had been less than a minute and a half. Turning at the next corner, they were out of the neighborhood and en route to the interstate heading north.

*Stony Man Farm, Virginia*

"MIAMI'S GOING bat shit," Aaron Kurtzman said with a grin as he monitored the raw news feed from the city. The anarchist streak in him loved seeing a

full-blown panic over nothing. "The mayor's screaming for the National Guard. Cops are pouring in from
all over the state and even the "roving TV reporters"
are wearing flak vests and Kevlar helmets."

"It'll get calmed down real quick," Hal Brognola
said. "The federal agencies are moving in to take
over the investigation, and they've been tipped that
this was a CT strike by parties unknown. The first
thing they'll do is assure the public that a war hasn't
broken out in their fair city."

"At least not this time," Kurtzman said.

Brognola called up a screen and studied the message. "The best part is that we're going to use this
as an excuse to make a DEA sweep of Little Haiti.
That'll give us a chance to put a bunch of the drug
movers in custody and generally clean up the neighborhood."

He shrugged. "Their public defenders will have
most of them back out on the street in under a week,
but there should be enough to hold some of the worse
offenders."

"How does it feel to be playing cop again, Hal?"
Barbara Price asked him.

"I'm still with Justice. And old habits are hard to
break."

Just then, Carl Lyons's voice came in over the satcom link. "Hal," he said, "we stashed the hardware
and are on the interstate out of town. And we have
another package for you. We're getting pretty good
at picking up garbage from alongside the street."

"Who do you have?" Brognola asked.

"Don't really know, but I didn't want to waste a perfectly good terrorist. I figured you could give him the Armani treatment and ship his ass home with his confession tied around his neck, too."

"Great. Stop off in Atlanta and I'll have him taken off your hands there."

# CHAPTER NINE

*Bangkok, Thailand*

Dimitri Polnacek was a young man and was making a rapid recovery from his gunshot wound. The AK round had been slowed by the brush before it hit him, so it had done minimal damage to his leg. Since he was on his feet, with the permission of his superior, he had attached himself to Bolan as his liaison officer with the RSV. Bolan had also accepted Anatoly Komarov's offer to take up temporary residence in their Bangkok safehouse.

It was a little nicer than the official RSV headquarters, but just barely. It did, though, have a more homely atmosphere as it was home to a number of Russian operatives, both men and women, either coming off or waiting to go on their missions. As was common in CIA safehouses, the place was well protected and everyone was armed. The Russian agents were both culturally and professionally paranoid, so they took their security seriously. Every man and woman wore a holstered Makarov pistol, and every room had a rack of AKMs and ammunition pouches close to the door. Best of all, the food was excellent, and the Russians welcomed Bolan as an old comrade-in-arms.

Bolan was in the common dining room working his way through an excellent beef Stroganoff when a rippling hush fell over the room. He looked over at the door and saw one of the most exotically beautiful women he had ever seen crossing the room. Her long hair was dark bronze, her skin golden with eyes to match. She was petite, Oriental sleek and moved like a cat. She was living proof that the Tartars had left more than the famous recipe for a sauce in Russia. She was dressed in a black jumpsuit, and a Czech Skorpion machine pistol on a shoulder sling rode at her hip within easy reach.

She stopped across the table from him and smiled. "So," she said, "you are the American hero I have to thank for getting young Dimitri Polnacek back to me in one piece. He is a lovely boy."

"Mike Belasko," Bolan said, standing as he introduced himself.

"I am Marita," the woman said as she checked him out. "I think I am going to enjoy thanking you."

There was no doubt in Bolan's mind that this woman could deliver the goods; she had that unmistakable look of a sexual predator. But he was going to have to refuse the invitation this time. Getting involved with his fellow operatives wasn't a good practice. Particularly not with a Russian.

He smiled and shook his head. "You don't owe me anything, Marita. I was just helping a fellow operative."

Marita got an amused expression on her face as she looked up at him. "You disappoint me, Belasko. I was looking forward to seeing what you Americans are made of. But," she said with a shrug, "apparently not this time."

Polnacek and the other Russians in the dining room burst out laughing.

"Yankee, don't turn her down," one of them called out. "She's offering you something beyond price. Our little Marita is famous all over Russia for what she does, but she only does it for you once. The rest of the time you just have to dream about her and do it for yourself."

That got more roars of laughter.

"Maybe after we have wrapped this operation up," he told the woman.

"Maybe," she purred.

Walking past him, she got a plate of food and sat down to dinner.

"She's really very good at what she does," Polnacek said. "Both on and off duty. She's our most capable assassin and is able to get through the defenses of almost any man she goes after."

"I can see how she does that."

BOLAN WAS settling down with an after-dinner glass of vodka when an explosion rocked the building. The Russians dived for the arms racks in the room and rushed out into the corridor.

Polnacek snatched an AKM, a chest pack of magazines and joined the fight. Bolan wasn't about to stay out of the action and rushed after him.

Leaving the AKs for the Russians, he pulled his Beretta 93-R from shoulder leather and flicked the selector switch to 3-round burst mode.

The dining room was off of the main hallway, which connected directly with the building's entrance. Through the smoke and dust, he saw half a dozen black-clad tong gunmen storm the stairwell to the second floor. Another half dozen were working the first-floor rooms, and several more were waiting outside to get through the ruined front door. Since he wasn't going to make it to the stairs, Bolan joined the Russians defending the lower floors.

Taking cover behind a door sill, Bolan and Polnacek started blasting every head that appeared at the entrance. A third Russian exposed himself just long enough to toss a grenade onto the front steps. The screams that followed the explosion told that he had scored.

Marita was in the forefront of the first-floor room-to-room battle, her Tartar battle cry ringing out and her little Skorpion submachine gun spitting flame. The men she led scrambled after her, yelling as they threw grenades to clear the way in front of her. Even though they were blasting their home to bits, they didn't care.

When the last of the tong gunmen had been cornered in the large parlor, Marita took a pair of grenades from one of her men and, in rapid succession, pulled the pins and tossed in the bombs. Almost before the frag from the last grenade had stopped flying, she rushed in, her minisubgun blazing.

Her sudden rush took her comrades by surprise, and they hesitated a moment before they could follow her. In that instant, one of the gunmen rose from behind a piece of heavy furniture, an AK in his hands.

Marita spun to face her attacker, and her submachine gun locked back on an empty magazine. Screaming her anger, she tried to duck for cover before the tong gunman could track and kill her.

From the open door, Bolan saw her plight and snapped off a 3-round burst into the gunman's chest. The gunner's would-be kill shot went wild as he crumpled to the floor.

"I owe you another one, Yankee," Marita called out as she slammed another magazine into the butt of her weapon before putting insurance shots into every tong member she saw.

A final flurry of shots sounded upstairs before a Russian voice called out an all-clear.

THE BATTLE in the RSV safehouse hadn't been all one-sided. One of the Russians on duty at the door had been killed when the RPG rocket came knocking.

Another one had been gunned down as he snatched an AKM from the arms rack. A third had died trying to limit the tong gunmen's penetration of the upper floors. Several more had been wounded, and the Russian medic was tending to their wounds.

"I think someone's been talking too much," Bolan said when Polnacek joined up with him again. "It looks to me like that assault team had your layout in here down cold. They knew exactly what they were doing."

Polnacek was coldly furious, but that truth hadn't escaped him, either. "Someone's been letting their Boris do their thinking for them again," he snarled.

"His little man," the Russian explained when Bolan looked puzzled.

"That what's wrong with us Russians being in this part of the world," the RSV agent said. "The women are entirely too enticing. All Russian women aren't like Marita because she isn't really Russian. And," he added, sighing, "those drunken fools love to brag to their girlfriends."

Marita looked like one of her ancestors as she moved from room to room barking orders, the Skorpion ready like an extension of her hand. When one of the attackers was found alive, the woman took over his interrogation as soon as he was bandaged. Jamming the muzzle of the little subgun into his testicles was all the prompting the man needed to start answering her in Chinese as fast as he could.

When she was finished with her questions, Marita

stood and looked at Bolan. "You are more interesting than I thought, American," she said. "This piece of diseased dog excrement says that his tong leader sent him here to kill you. You must be a very important man."

"I'm not really important," Bolan said, "but I am here to put his boss out of business. Permanently."

"Then get on with it!" she snapped.

Turning back, she pointed her machine pistol at the wounded gangster and ripped off a long burst, walking the rounds up from his crotch to his forehead. Pulling back the smoking weapon, she spit on the corpse before dropping the empty mag out of the butt and snapping a fresh one in its place.

"She's not very fond of the locals," Polnacek explained. "Particularly the Chinese. She lost some of her relatives to them in the Mongolian war of 1969."

In this part of the world, it was hard to find anyone who hadn't lost someone to the wars, revolutions and coups of the last half of the twentieth century. Some, apparently, took it more personally than others.

"Since they're looking for me," Bolan said, "I think I should move to a place that no one knows about and I have that place already. I was keeping it in waiting until the rest of my team showed up, but there's room enough for both of us, as well. Since you're working with me, it might be a good idea if you came, too."

Polnacek looked around the wreckage of the safehouse. "You might have a point, Mr. Belasko. This place is a proper shambles."

THE NEXT MORNING, Anatoly Komarov looked worse than usual. The aftermath of the attack on the safehouse was running him through the wringer. It looked as if he had slept in his shirt, and his comb-over was plastered to his forehead. His eyes were bloodshot and he badly needed a shave, to say nothing of a shower. As busy as he was, though, he had sent word that he wanted to speak to Bolan.

"Belasko," Komarov called out when he looked up and saw Bolan, "come in and close the door behind you."

"I want to thank you for your assistance last night," he told Bolan. "I understand that you saved the life of our little Marita and that was well done. The RSV would not be the same without her unique talents."

"She's a comrade," Bolan replied, "and I was in the right place at the right time."

Komarov smiled. "I also understand that you turned down her offer to thank you earlier. I strongly suggest that you not turn her down this time if she tries to show her appreciation again. You would regret it. You would also make history in our agency, but that is another matter. We already think that you Americans are completely crazy. Turning her down twice would prove it beyond all doubt."

"I'll take that recommendation under advisement," Bolan replied.

"Now," Komarov said, placing both hands on the desktop in front of him and leaning forward, "to business. I have ordered that my people start cleaning up the dog shit in this town, one turd at a time."

He held up a hand. "I know that this is not 'our home turf,' as you would say. But it is not good for us to cower like children and let a gangster like Liu do things like that to us. It is true that I would rather clean the Mafia dog turds out of Moscow, but I am not there, I am here. So, to insure that the reputation of the Russian Federation is not sullied any further, I am going to take a bite out of Liu. Would you like a piece to chew on, as well?"

Komarov was a man after Bolan's own heart. Big Gold Liu needed to be taught that he wasn't yet a sovereign nation unto himself.

"I would enjoy that," he said honestly, "but my mission is to shut down his operation in the Golden Triangle first. Then, if I haven't had a chance to kill him up there, I'll join you. Having your people harassing him here will make my job up north easier as it will split his forces."

"I am going to split his heathen head," the Russian growled. "In the old days, no one would have dared to attack a KGB safehouse. They feared us back then."

He sighed. "This democracy is going to be the death of us all, Belasko. How can we put fear in our enemies when our new government is weaker than yours? The RSV is as timid as your poor CIA is now, and people like Liu do not respond to anything other than the lash in the hand of their master. This only happened because we forgot that simple truth.''

Komarov locked eyes with Bolan. ''I was in Lebanon during the troubles when one of the bandit gangs kidnapped an officer of ours. As the action officer charged with getting him back, I had full authority to act as I saw fit. It was easy to learn which gang had captured Gregor and find out who their so-called leader was. It was easier yet to learn where this man's brother lived and to capture him. Easiest of all was castrating him and sending the eggs to the gang leader with a note that every male in his family would share the same fate if our man was not released to us unharmed. We got Gregor back that same afternoon.''

''I remember that incident well,'' Bolan said. ''I, too, was in Lebanon during that time.''

''It served to show the bastards that we were not to be trifled with,'' Komarov said. ''Unfortunately, your people were not wise enough to know how to handle those barbarians. The torture and death of the American captives in Beirut was shameful.''

Bolan could only agree with that.

''And now,'' the Russian said, smiling, ''it is time that the Red Door tong learn not to tease the Russian bear. He may have lost a tooth or two to this new democracy of ours, but his claws are still intact.''

''When are you going to move on them?''

"We are in the planning stages right now, and it will be soon."

"How are your contacts in the Thai government on this?" Bolan asked. "How are they going to react?"

"They will not interfere. In fact, they have been advised to stay clear until the last body has been counted."

In many ways, the new Russia wasn't all that much different than the old Soviet Union had been. Attacking a Russian always carried a risk.

"Is there anything I can do to help you set it up?" Bolan asked.

"Thank you for asking," Komarov said. "But for now, I think my people need to 'get a little of their own,' as I think you people say. Their pride has been abused."

Bolan smiled. In Russian terms, "getting a little" might end up taking a big chunk out of Liu's operation.

"Any time I can help, just call."

"Thanks. I will keep you in mind."

BIG GOLD LIU WAS satisfied that the attack on the Russian safehouse had served his purpose. It had cost him several of his lower-level men and it was true that no one had reported killing the American. But several Russians had been taken out, and their sense of security had been shaken. They would be more careful of getting in his road now.

To make sure that the Russians left him alone from

now on, Liu had ordered Al Hosn to send him a team of Taliban urban fighters to further reinforce him. Not all of the Afghan barbarians were wild mountain men. Many of them were civilized enough to be able to operate in a big city like Bangkok. He wanted to take advantage of their hatred of the Russians to keep the pressure on the RSV. He didn't see the Russians as being a big threat to him in the long run, but until his poppy operation got off the ground, he didn't want to be distracted by anyone.

With the Afghans keeping the Russians in check, that would leave his men free to deal with the mystery American. Liu's DEA contact hadn't been able to find out anything more about the man, and he wondered if his spy had been compromised. Even if he hadn't, if the man wasn't going to be of any benefit to him, Liu had other uses for the girl who was holding the DEA man in thrall. There were other Americans who would also find her charms irresistible. Also, the girl had complained that the DEA man was completely ignorant when it came to the civilized arts of love.

That also came as no surprise. Liu didn't discount the Yankees, but when all was said and done, they were only clever barbarians.

# CHAPTER TEN

*Stony Man Farm, Virginia*

"That was a damned good op," Hal Brognola told the Able Team trio when they returned to the Farm. The War Room in the farmhouse had been set up with a cold buffet and coffee service for a working lunch as they went through the debriefing.

"The guy you grabbed was the number two of that hit squad," he said as he consulted a paper. "And, like Armani, he was a wealth of information. In fact, if the Algerians want to make their mark in the world of international terrorism, they need to take a few lessons in internal operational security. They don't have the slightest idea what 'need to know' means. It looks like they tell everyone down to the guy in the motor pool what they're going to do next."

He keyed in a command, and a map of a coastline appeared on the big-screen monitor. "And what they have going down next is that they're moving a major shipment of China White to the States by sea."

He looked at Lyons. "It's due in any time now, so I'm afraid that you're going to have to get back on the road to the coast to link up with a customs boat."

"Are we going to have to work with those guys?" Lyons looked surprised.

"No, and the boat isn't really a customs vessel. It's just playing one for the purpose of this operation."

That sat well with the Able Team leader. Most of the time he didn't mind working with the Feds. But going after a boatload of Algerian terrorists, and God only knew who else, could turn out to be a bullet fest, and that would mean a lot of hand wringing and court appearances when it was all over. Since he didn't do court appearances or screw around with Miranda announcements, he usually passed on teaming up with too many Feds.

"Thank God," Lyons said. "What's the plan?"

"Take the boat out," Brognola said, "wait for the ship to enter American waters and then do your usual number on it in the guise of a customs inspection. According to our informant, there should be no more than half a dozen shooters on board, all of them from the Algerian Sword of God movement."

"Do you want more people to talk to?"

"Not this time," Brognola said. "So you won't have to worry about that."

That brought a smile to Lyons's face. He didn't like anything that inhibited his courses of action. "When do you want us to move out?" he asked.

Brognola glanced at his watch. "How about catching the chopper in half an hour?"

"Two hours," Lyons said bluntly. "I need to wash up, eat and change clothes."

"Two hours it is, then."

ABLE TEAM'S fifty-two-foot customs boat was pounding through the Atlantic like a rubber ducky in a hyperactive six-year-old's bathtub. Though the boat had a civilian registry now, it had obviously spent most of its life as some kind of Coast Guard small craft, which made it perfect for a run like this.

In the wheelhouse, Rosario Blancanales was at the helm while Hermann Schwarz was doing the white-knuckle number on the grab rail and trying not to turn an unappetizing shade of green. "Do you have to slam into each and every one of those waves?" he asked. "Can't you try to miss one every now and then?"

Blancanales grinned. "If I do that, we might miss our target. This navigation stuff has to be right on if we want to make contact at the right time."

"My lunch is going to be making contact with your boots if you keep this shit up."

Carl Lyons was in the cabin belowdeck going over the team's hardware. He didn't think that they'd need the RPGs and the grenade launchers, but it was nice to have them on hand. From the satellite photos, the target ship looked as if it had a single-thickness hull and the RPGs would punch through the thin steel like tin foil.

"Ship ahoy, I think they say," Blancanales called down the hatchway.

"On the way," Lyons called back up.

At the wheelhouse navigation station, the radar plot showed a target of the proper size just under the horizon. When the two courses intersected, the cargo ship would be several miles inside U.S. waters and subject to customs inspections.

"It's show time," Lyons announced.

Going out onto the deck, he untied the lines on the side rail and pulled up the magnetic sheets that had covered the U.S. Customs markings painted on the bow. Sailing under false colors was an age-old pirate's trick, and Lyons was into pirates. After both sides of the boat were showing the U.S. Customs ID, he went to the stern and put the American ensign up the staff. To all intents and purposes, they were now official.

Back in the wheelhouse, Lyons put on his customs agent's cap and a long canvas foul-weather coat. The coat was long and bulky enough to hide the arsenal he would be packing on board. Fighting on shipboard where every wall was bulletproof could get dicey.

RIGHT ON SCHEDULE, the cargo ship MV *Darvos* appeared over the horizon. When they got closer, Lyons saw that it was flying a Liberian flag. It wasn't the usual Liberian tramp steamer, though, in that it wasn't a complete rust bucket. The hull and deckhouses had been painted not long ago, and the salt spray hadn't made much of an inroad against the paint yet. Blancanales steered to intercept it.

When they got in close enough, Lyons hailed the ship over the loudspeaker. "Ahoy, MV *Darvos*," he said. "This is U.S. Customs. Stop all engines and prepare to be boarded."

He could see the ship's captain enter the bridge and grab his field glasses to study them. A second man quickly joined him, and an apparent argument broke out. Finally, though, they were hailed back.

"Customs boat," the captain called, "I am stopping my engines."

Even with its engines at stop, the ship took more than a mile to slow to a halt. When she was dead in the water, Blancanales maneuvered his boat up on the leeward side so Lyons and Schwarz could go up the rope ladder without getting hammered by the waves.

Of the two men waiting to meet them when they got up on deck, one was obviously the ship's captain. The gold braid on his cap was a dead giveaway. The other man could only be one of the Algerian gunmen. His barely controlled anger overlaying fear was also a dead giveaway. Lyons decided that he would concentrate on rattling this guy's cage. It shouldn't take too much to get him to lose it big time.

"I am Captain Lozario Carmanos, master of the MV *Darvos*," the captain stated.

Lyons took him for a Filipino. He smiled and extended his hand. "Customs Agent Carl Green," he said. "My assistant is Jim Black."

"How can I help you, Agent Green?" the captain asked.

"Just a routine stop. We do this on a rotating basis. Regulations, you know."

The Algerian just glared, so Lyons tweaked him. "It's no problem, of course, unless we find someone who has something on board that they shouldn't have. You know how it goes."

The captain certainly did, and he, too, started looking a little nervous.

"Okay," Lyons said, turning to Schwarz. "Do you have the manifest and crew list, Jim?"

Schwarz produced the clipboard. "Can we go inside, gentlemen?" he suggested. "I don't want to get the paperwork wet."

The captain led the Able Team duo to the deckhouse and opened the door to the crew's galley, then offered seats around one of the tables.

Lyons remained standing and looked directly at the Algerian. "Who are you?" he asked.

"He's a paying passenger," the captain spoke up. "Not one of my crew."

"Your name, please?" Schwarz asked, his pen poised over the form he was filling out.

"Abdul Mahout," the Algerian answered in heavily accented English.

"Is your visit for business or pleasure?" Lyons asked.

"Pleasure."

"Enjoy your stay in America," Schwarz said with a smile, "but make sure to check in with the INS before you leave the ship.

"And—" he consulted his form before turning to the captain "—it says here that you're carrying a cargo of agricultural products. Is that correct?"

"That is correct," the captain replied.

"What is the exact nature of this agricultural product?" Lyons said.

The captain checked himself after starting to glance at the Algerian. "Spices mostly."

"What kind of spices?" Lyons pressed.

The Algerian couldn't hold it in any longer. "I have to go now," he told the captain.

Carmanos looked like a man caught between a rock and a very hard place.

As soon as the Algerian cleared the door, Lyons's hand dived under his coat and came out with his Colt Python. Holding the captain's face in one hand, he drilled the muzzle of the Colt into his right eye and thumbed the hammer back. "Where are the Algerians sleeping?"

Carmanos collapsed and Schwarz almost felt sorry for the man. He was doing what the ship's owners had ordered him to do, and now it was going to cost him.

BLANCANALES WASN'T picking up all of the conversation over the open com link channel. The mass of steel of the ship's hull and the steep angle from the deckhouse down to the customs boat was garbling the transmissions. What was worse, he caught a glimpse of a man moving along the ship's rail toward the deckhouse.

"Ironman?" he called up on the com link.

When there was no answer, Blancanales chopped his throttle and let the boat drift against the bow rope. Grabbing his M-16 from the clips holding it to the bulkhead next to the nav console, he headed out onto the deck and climbed up on top of the wheelhouse. It was only another eight feet, but it gave him a better angle of fire up to the *Darvos*'s deck.

NOW THAT the captain was gagged and cuffed to a handrail, Lyons whipped off his long foul-weather coat, revealing body armor and the tools of his trade. Along with his .357 Colt Python, he had his Assault 12 shotgun slung over his shoulder. Schwarz shucked his coat, as well, and swung his 5.56 mm CAR-15 into firing position. A Beretta 92 rode on his hip, and he had a bandolier of fragmentation and tear gas grenades.

Carmanos had said that his Algerian passengers were quartered on the A deck up by the bow and had confirmed that there were only six of them.

"Pol," Lyons whispered over the com link, "we're moving out now."

Climbing to the top of the wheelhouse had also improved the com link reception, and the message came in loud and clear. "Roger," Blancanales called back.

MAHOUT HAD his men armed and ready. Having been chosen for inspection was bad luck. But as soon as they eliminated the Yankees and their boat, the captain could make full speed for Norfork and they could still off-load the cargo. Killing the two customs agents and the one they had left in the boat couldn't be that difficult; he hadn't seen them carrying any weapons.

Splitting his men into two teams, he led them up onto the main deck.

FROM HIS PERCH on top of the wheelhouse, Blancanales caught a glimpse of several men moving forward. "I've got three guys coming your way," he radioed Lyons.

"Roger, we're on them."

Lyons had been just about to step out of the deckhouse, but having the Algerians come for them was going to settle this much faster. The open deck of a freighter didn't offer much cover and concealment. Better yet, Lyons and Schwarz had steel bulkheads to shield them, and there were only two hatches leading out onto the deck. Taking cover behind the starboard hatch, Lyons drew his Colt Python and thumbed back the hammer. Schwarz flicked the selector switch on his CAR-15 to rock and roll as he took the other hatch.

Rather than let the Algerians get in too close, Lyons waited until the lead man on his side came into view and tripped the .357. The heavy slug caught the gunman dead center in the chest and punched out his spine.

The shot caused the others to scatter, but there was no place to hide. Lyons's second shot went into a leg sticking out from behind a cargo boom.

When the Algerians scattered, Schwarz stepped out enough to get his weapon into play. A first long burst swept the deck from port to starboard. One of the Algerians had been slow to hit the deck and took two 5.56 mm rounds for being slow. It was now a full-bore firefight, and the terrorists had no place to hide.

A hail of full-auto AK fire swept the deckhouse, but the steel walls were better than Kevlar and the hatches were half-inch-thick armor. Ducking back behind the hatch, Schwarz palmed a frag grenade, pulled the pin and lobbed the bomb out onto the deck. The detonation brought screams, and he followed that up with another magazine on full-auto.

"Ironman!" Blancanales said over the com link. "One of them got around you."

Lyons spun to see what looked like a crewman with an AK in his hands. "Gadgets! Cover me!" he yelled as he stepped out to get a clear line of sight.

The AK was coming up when Lyons's shotgun roared. The load of double-aught buck swept the gunman off his feet, and Lyons ducked back under cover.

Schwarz had done such a good job of covering his partner that there were no terrorists left standing. The two broke cover and swept the deck. When Lyons found the body of Mahout, he kept his Python on target while he put the toe of his boot into the Algerian's side. When the body didn't move, he holstered his weapon.

"We're clear up here," he radioed down to Blancanales.

ABLE TEAM LEFT the *Darvos* dead in the water. A pair of .357 slugs in the main fuel regulator to the diesel engine had made sure that it would stay where it was in American waters. A replacement part would have to be flown in and installed before the ship could leave the area. As soon as the ship was below the horizon, the magnetic signs went back on the side of their boat's hull to cover the customs markings, and the U.S. ensign came down from the staff. Now they were just another civilian pleasure boat out for a cruise.

Down in the radio room, Carl Lyons put in a call to the Farm and Hal Brognola answered.

"You'd better have the Coast Guard come and get this thing under tow," Lyons told him, "before it drifts back out to sea. And you should warn them that there might be weapons on board. We tossed everything we could find over the side, but we might have missed a gun or two."

"What's the body count this time?"

"Seven, including one of the crew," Lyons said. "He kind of got in the way and had his hands on an

AK. We put the bodies over the side, too, so Captain Carmanos is going to have an even harder time explaining his cargo. He's not going to have anyone to blame it on.''

"He's also going to have a hard time explaining this to the ship's owners," Brognola replied, "because the Coast Guard's going to confiscate it. That's our new program to discourage the owners from pretending that they don't know what their hulls are hauling."

"Suits me," Lyons said. "That's almost more fun than sinking the damned thing."

## CHAPTER ELEVEN

*Bangkok, Thailand*

Big Gold Liu's burgeoning Thai empire included more than just the heroin operation he was building in the Golden Triangle. Bangkok was a big city, and there was money to be made in the smaller but more traditional Chinese enterprises of opium dens, gambling and prostitution. When the tong leader relocated, he'd simply moved his Macao urban operations into town and set up again. It took a while for these new businesses to become established, a few short months and a dozen or so bodies of the opposition laid out in the back alleys. But they were running hot and bringing in a steady income now.

Bangkok wasn't Las Vegas, but it was almost a twenty-four-hour-a-day operation as far as the various pleasures the Chinese district went. Like the bordellos, the gambling houses opened early and stayed open until the last man stumbled out, his pockets empty.

EVEN IN THE HEAT of the late afternoon, the two men on the Honda Gold Wing motorcycle were dressed in black biker leathers with matching full-face-shield helmets. Black leathers were currently in high fashion with the youth of the Thai elite, though, so they didn't draw much attention. The man on the back of the bike was carrying a long, thin bag upright between his legs as the bike weaved its way through traffic of the predominantly Chinese district.

Turning off the main route, they went down a crowded side street lined with gambling houses and stopped in the middle of the block in front of a medium-sized, two-story building with a red door. As the driver steadied his mount with one foot on the pavement, the man behind him unzipped his bag and drew out a Russian RPG-7 rocket launcher with an antitank rocket loaded in the muzzle.

At that range he didn't even really need to aim as he leveled the tube and triggered the weapon. The RPG round's main rocket motor barely had a chance to start burning before the 85 mm shaped charge warhead impacted on the brightly colored masonry facade over the door and detonated.

The blast blew half the facade off the front of the building, throwing concrete and ceramic fragments far and wide. The two black-clad bikers hunched their shoulders and let their leathers and helmets deflect the debris.

As soon as the rubble stopped falling, the driver pulled a folding-stock AKM from under his arm and emptied the full 30-round magazine into the cloud of dust in one long burst. When the assault rifle's bolt locked back on an empty magazine, he twisted his throttle, released the clutch and burned rubber down the street.

The Honda was soon lost in the stream of traffic.

IN ANOTHER PART of the Chinese district, a cab pulled up to the curb in front of one of Big Gold Liu's larger gambling palaces. The driver got out, his cap down over his eyes, locked the doors and walked away as if he had an appointment at the corner bordello. When he reached the end of the block, though, instead of going into the Jade Joy Club, he stopped on the sidewalk. Looking back at his car, he pulled what looked like a cell phone out of his pocket, waited until the front of the club was clear of pedestrians and punched in a number.

The cab disappeared as two hundred pounds of RDX detonated. The front of the gambling club disappeared, as well, until it came raining back down in the form of small chunks of brick, wood and concrete. The explosion brought people streaming out of the surrounding buildings screaming and wailing. Some of the onlookers rushed into the shattered building and came out with their hands full of Thai bank notes. Others started bringing out the stunned occupants.

In the confusion, no one noticed the cabdriver walk around the corner and get picked up by a man in black on a Honda Gold Wing. The two made another clean getaway.

WHEN THE REPORT of the first attack came in, Big Gold Liu put his entire organization on full alert. At first, he couldn't tell who had dared to attack him. But when more attacks were reported the picture became clearer.

He knew that he could count out the Americans at first glance; they never did things like this. Plus, with the U.S. and the Thai governments practically on the verge of war, the Yankees didn't have enough manpower in the city to pull off something this widespread. None of the local gang lords would have dared to attack him in this manner, so that only left the Russians.

He now saw that he might have been hasty in ordering the attack on the Russian safehouse. But with the probe they had made in the north, he had felt the need to act. It was too late to second-guess now, but he put out the word for all of his sites to double their guards and to try to keep the front of his buildings clear of parked vehicles.

"HEY, SISTER!" one of the tong guards called out in Cantonese as Marita walked by the Red Door counting house. Big Gold Liu's cash had to be handled somewhere. This "bank" did the initial counting of the daily take before the money was turned over to the tong leader at his main compound to be sent to his offshore banks. "Come over here."

The RSV agent wasn't wearing her usual working clothes this night. The black coveralls she favored for her missions had been ditched for a Suzy Wong dress in green silk that looked as if it had been painted on her. The sides were slit to her hips and promised much each time she moved her long sleek legs. Her glossy black hair was hanging down her back, and the tall spike heels she wore gave her that particular slinky gait that went with a dress like that.

"Why do you talk to me like that, you nasty boy?" she answered in the same language as she stopped with one hip thrown out. That made the slit on that side of the dress open wide enough to show a tantalizing shadow that could not quite be identified from that far away. "I do not know you."

"I want to show you something," the guard said as he stepped away from the gate.

Marita swung her purse around halfway in front of her. "What is that?"

The second guard grinned as his buddy grabbed his crotch and said, "Something you've never seen before."

"Oh, so sorry," she said as her right hand unsnapped the catch on her purse. "Your man stalk has the disease and it has fallen off."

The second guard burst out laughing so hard that he was almost doubled over. It was the last laugh he would ever have.

The silenced Makarov Marita pulled from her purse spit twice, and the crotch-grabbing tong guard dropped to the ground, flat on his face. His laughing partner only had time for his eyes to widen before he took two shots to the head himself.

"Quickly," Marita snapped in Russian as she waved the waiting strike team forward. Two men in night-black coveralls rushed through the gate with silenced machine pistols in their hands while four more dragged the gangsters' bodies inside the compound.

When the sidewalk was clear, Marita took up a position at the side of the gate and casually leaned back against the wall. This time, her purse was held in front of her belly with her right hand inside resting on the butt of her pistol. To passersby, she was just another working girl taking a well-needed break from her busy night.

"Go away, dog," she snapped at one man who stopped to take an admiring look at her merchandise. "I am resting and I don't have time to waste on the likes of you. Go!"

The man walked away muttering about women and their monthly cycles.

A few minutes later, a motorcycle drove up and, when the driver stepped off, Marita slipped her finger through the trigger guard of the Makarov. This guy had tong written all over him.

"Where are the men who are supposed to be here?" the gangster snapped.

"I do not know, Honorable Uncle," the Russian

agent said, pretending to cast down her eyes. "My sister and I were walking by, and the men took a strong liking to her. They went inside, but I do not know where they are. They said they would pay us when they came back out."

"Taiwanese dogs!" he spit as he started through the gate. "I will beat them until they howl."

Marita let him pass in front of her before bringing her hand out of her purse. When his back was to her, she plunged a narrow bladed, razor-sharp stiletto into the hollow at the base of his skull. He went limp without a sound.

Catching him before he fell, she dragged his corpse inside and dropped it.

"Get a move on it," she whispered in Russian over a small radio. "We just had company."

"We're on the way out now," a male voice answered.

Two of the black-clad commandos came out of the gate carrying a foot-locker-sized trunk. One of them spoke into his radio, and a Nissan sedan came around the corner and pulled up to the gate. The trunk was quickly loaded in the back, and the commandos joined Marita in the car before it pulled away from the curb.

At the end of the block, the driver pulled over to the curb again. The man in the passenger seat took out a radio transmitter, flicked it on and pressed a button. A thundering roar erupted from the middle of the block as the counting house disappeared in a blinding flash. Chunks of debris rained to the ground. The Russian driver waited until the worst of it was over before pulling back on the street and speeding away.

JUST AS the counting-house job was going down, three men walked up to the door of a small drinking house known to be frequented by off-duty Red Door gangsters. It was a private club where the men could get drunk, get laid and get a good meal, all at a low price. Big Gold Liu liked to keep his men happy and, while he wasn't going to do it free, he could give them a price break.

Like the RSV team that had hit the counting house, these men were dressed in black combat suits, but they were carrying folding-stock AKMs with the 75-round drum magazines clipped in place. Since the locals knew that this establishment was run by the tong, they gave it a wide berth and the sidewalk in front was clear.

On a silent count of three, the lead man booted the door and stepped aside to let his two partners enter first. And enter they did, their assault rifles blazing on full-auto. The room was occupied by a dozen gangsters and almost that many of their women. The Russians didn't waste time picking specific targets, but simply hosed down everything and everyone that moved with a rain of 7.62 mm rounds.

When the last body had fallen, the third man of the RSV strike team took off his backpack, pulled a fuse igniter and tossed the satchel charge behind the bar. They were half a block away when the RDX detonated.

ANATOLY KOMAROV WAS in his situation room taking the reports of the teams conducting the street sweep against the Red Door establishments. The unaccustomed smile threatened to split his usually dour face.

As much as he was enjoying this operation, Komarov had no illusions that this would frighten Big Gold Liu out of town or even do more than anger him. While the day's take from the Red Door's gambling houses would go a long way to fulfilling the average RSV man's wildest financial dreams, he knew it was but a drop in the bucket compared to Liu's total take. But this action wasn't about trying to bankrupt the tong leader, and the money his commandos had recovered from the counting house would go to refurbishing their shot-up safehouse. Who said that crime didn't pay?

Even so, this effort was aimed at something the Chinese understood well—face. The RSV had lost face when it had been attacked, but Komarov was getting it back now in a way that even a tong leader could understand. Komarov had no doubt that this would turn into a full-blown gang war now, but he was confident of the ultimate outcome. Even the weak sisters in Moscow would have to see that he'd had no choice but to act and they would be forced to back him up.

"What else do we have on the board for tonight?" Komarov asked his operations officer.

"That's about it in China Town," the ops man replied. "But we still have the drive-by of Liu's villa."

"When is that scheduled?"

"Right about now."

Komarov couldn't keep the smile off his face. Hitting his joints were one thing, but hitting his home base was a real slap in the face.

As a Chinese tong leader, Big Gold Liu didn't have to live in a modest house like most American Mafia kingpins were forced to do. He could be as flamboyant as he wanted because he didn't have to fear the IRS. In fact, to rule as he intended to do in Southeast Asia, he had to show everyone that he was wealthy and powerful. In Bangkok, he showed that by living in one of the town's most expensive houses on a hill inside an extensive compound on the outskirts of the city.

This compound was surrounded by ten-foot-tall masonry walls topped with steel spikes pointing outward. The main gate was two cars wide and was topped with a cast ceramic dragon painted in garish colors. On each side of the gate was a minibunker with the barrel of a machine gun sticking out of the firing aperture. Six men guarded the gate, and they were well armed. The rear gate was more modest, but still had the cast ceramic sculpture and minibunkers for its four-man guard and added a chained-shut, wrought-iron gate.

The huge three-story villa in the center of the compound was a well-done mixture of Chinese and Western architecture. The facade was pure Chinese with the steep, gabled, tile-covered roof like a small palace. The back side, however, had more of a Western layout opening onto a large patio leading to a traditional Asian garden. The villa had been built for a once powerful politician who had come out on the wrong side of a coup.

Along with the guards at the gates, more armed gunmen patrolled the grounds and watched the streets from lookout towers. Even more men waited in their barracks to go on guard or to reinforce as needed. Big Gold Liu was as well protected as the king.

Four Toyota pickup trucks drove in a convoy down the main street leading toward the main gate of Liu's compound. Since Toyota vehicles were the most common in Southeast Asia, the tong guards paid them little notice. With the attacks downtown, Liu had put extra men on duty, but none of them really expected trouble. No one in his right mind would attack the Red Door tong leader on his home turf.

Before the pickups reached the gate, they turned off on a side street. As they made the turn, black-clad men in the truck's beds rose with weapons in their hands. Two of them were RPG rocket launchers, and the night went bright with their back blast when they were fired. The two RPG rockets slammed into the firing apertures of the machine-gun bunkers flanking the main gate and cleared out both the guns and their crews.

A storm of AKM fire swept the tong defenders as the RPG men quickly reloaded. Liu's gunmen had the advantage of the massive gate to protect them and countered with a return barrage at the Toyotas in the open.

As the gun battle raged, the RPG gunners raised their launchers again and sent two rockets screaming over the top of the gate. As soon as those two rockets had been fired, the Toyota drivers sped off into the night. Behind them, the RPG rockets slammed into the front of Liu's villa.

"WE HAVE ONE MAN wounded seriously," the RSV ops officer reported to his boss. "And two more with minor wounds."

Anatoly Komarov let the smile drop from his face. Every action carried the risk of casualties, but he always hated to see his people hurt. The Red Door tong would pay, of course, in full measure, but right now he had people who were hurting and bleeding.

"Recall the teams," he ordered, "and have the medical staff stand by."

"It is done, Colonel," the ops officer responded.

Komarov didn't fail to notice the use of his old KGB military rank. He had never been much for using titles and rank to bludgeon his people, but they were in action now and it seemed appropriate.

"Very good," he replied. "I will be in the situation room. When the team leaders come in, tell them to gather there for a debriefing."

"As you command."

# CHAPTER TWELVE

*Bangkok, Thailand*

Big Gold Liu didn't have to be a military-academy graduate to know that he was at war with the Russians, like it or not. Their devastating and well-coordinated attacks on his Bangkok establishments and his villa had left no doubt in his mind about that. This kind of open warfare was a new arena for him, and he realized that he had made a serious mistake in judgment when he had ordered the hit on the Russian safehouse. He had never dreamed that they would respond this way.

The tong turf wars he had conducted in Macao had usually been settled with a minimal body count, most of which resulted from back-alley ambushes. But, as unaccustomed as he was to open warfare on this level, he did know that he was committed. He also knew what he had to do next—attack to protect what was his and keep attacking until the Russians left him alone.

His Taiwanese reinforcements had turned out to be little better than back-alley men. Their failure to properly guard his counting house had been punished. He had left the dead guards in a ditch outside the city for the dogs to eat. He had also threatened that same fate for anyone else who failed him. But he knew that he still needed better men, and that was where the Afghans would come in. Al Hosn was sending him several squads of his bearded mountain warriors, hardened men who knew how to make war against Russians.

When the mujahideen fighters arrived, he would set them against the Russians immediately. His own troops, and the Taiwanese, he had assigned to guard duty at his establishments. His agents were already busy purchasing heavier weapons and stocks of ammunition to defend both his compound and his establishments against anything the Russians could throw at him.

It was going to be a war to the death, and he refused to allow a handful of Russians decide his destiny. Not when he was so close to being the most powerful man in all of Southeast Asia. The completion of the Golden Triangle facilities would have to be put on the back burner until he drove the Russians out of Bangkok and secured his home base.

AL HOSN STEPPED OUT from the trees to meet the Russian-built An-12 turboprop transport when it was towed under the jungle canopy. The An-12 was an assault transport roughly equivalent to the American C-130 Hercules and dated back to the same era as the larger Lockheed machine. It had good short-length takeoff-and-landing characteristics and could carry over twenty tons of military cargo. This day, its cargo hold was full of antiaircraft hardware.

As a veteran of the bitter Russian-Afghan war, Al Hosn knew the value of antiaircraft weapons both large and small. They had made the skies over his homeland so expensive to the Soviets that they had finally retreated. He had argued with Liu about the need for better aerial defenses, but had a difficult time convincing the Chinese of their need. But the ground probes and the attacks in Bangkok finally won the argument for him.

The An-12's load would go a long way to making Al Hosn feel more secure from aerial intruders. His Taliban leaders had been generous and had supplied him with the best weapons available in their warehouses. They hadn't minded parting with their old Russian-made armaments at all. Their take from the Golden Triangle operation would allow them to buy the latest replacement weapons on the world market.

The first things to come off the Antonov's rear ramp were several twin 23 mm auto cannons on wheeled ZU-23 mounts. These fast-firing guns had proved their worth all over the world against low-flying aircraft and helicopters. Even the Yankees had felt their bite in Grenada, as had the Russian pigs in his homeland. For heavier work, he had also ordered several single-barrel 57 mm S-60 guns. Those fast-firing automatic cannons could reach up some twenty thousand feet and bring down even the largest high-flying warplane.

After the guns themselves were off-loaded, the first of the ammunition crates followed. This one plane had been able to carry enough rounds to get the guns emplaced and set up, but it would take several more trips before Al Hosn would feel adequately stocked to defend his territory. In the interim, however, the front of the cargo area was stacked with crates, each holding two Russian SA-7 Grail shoulder-fired, heat-seeking, antiaircraft missiles and their support equipment.

The Grails weren't as good as the Stinger missiles the Americans had so generously supplied to the Afghan mujahideen during their war with Russia. But that was a long time ago, and Stingers weren't as common now. Since he didn't expect to be attacked by the heavily armored Russian Hind gun-ships, the Grails would work well enough against unarmored helicopters.

As each crate of Grails was inspected, he had them issued to his patrol leaders. He was well aware that the intruders who had penetrated into the forbidden zone recently were only scouts. He knew that more, and larger, attacks would come soon, and he wanted to have the missiles in the field and ready for them.

This would be a much different war than the one he had fought against the Soviets in his homeland.

For one thing, he wouldn't be facing the manpower or the firepower of a national army. The Americans might send in their antidrug forces, but they weren't a real army. Even the Russians couldn't mount a real full-scale offensive against him. With the weapons he was being supplied with from Kabul, he could easily defeat anything sent against him.

All of that was in his favor, but the terrain he was being forced to defend made his job very difficult. Afghanistan was a hard country with its open, mountainous terrain, and any war there naturally favored the land's defenders. As far back as the times of Alexander the Great, the terrain of Afghanistan had proved to be more difficult to deal with than the population. This jungle that surrounded him now, though, favored the attacker by offering him a place to hide and strike unseen.

He now understood why the United States, Afghanistan's one-time ally and now the Great Satan of the Islamic world, had had so much trouble fighting the Vietnamese. Nonetheless, his men were learning to work in this green hell, and he was confident that they could do the job. He had a hundred men in the field, both in the gun jeeps and on foot, saturating the buffer zones around the production plants.

If he had been brought into the project earlier, he would have recommended clustering the buildings closer. But Liu had decided to stick to the old system where the natives brought their raw, dried poppy juice to several locations to process it rather than to a central point. They were lazy and it worked for them, but he didn't care if the mountain tribesmen had to carry their product a greater distance. They were infidels, but they, too, were being taught to respect their superiors.

ANATOLY KOMAROV WAS doing a slow burn and loudly cursing all bureaucrats, but particularly the Russian version. The nice thing about working under the old KGB was that operational decisions had been made without having to convene a meeting of parliament. Those worthy members of parliament would argue for days as each one stood up, pitched his ignorant opinion and held out for a fat bribe before deciding what to do. This playhouse democracy in Moscow was hell on operational necessities in the real world.

He was engaged in an all-out war with an opponent who had him outmanned by at least five to one and probably outgunned, as well. If he didn't get the Spetsnaz team he had requested and the extra weaponry, he wasn't sure that he'd be able to hold on against what he knew was coming his way. Even now, every Russian had inborn fears of Asiatic hordes flinging themselves against a thin line of Russian defenders. And it wasn't an idle fear. It had happened too many times in the past and could well happen again.

However, Komarov was an old pro and he refused to be at the mercy of bureaucratic idiots, freely elected or not. Picking up the phone, he placed a call to SOBRE, Moscow's new counterterrorist, tactical police force operating under the auspices of the minister of the interior. In the good old days, that job had been the KGB's and, if extra muscle was called for, Spetsnaz got involved. Back then, though, the authority to strike came directly from KGB headquarters at Lubyanka.

In this new system, the command structure was a little warped, but SOBRE still took direct action when the situation called for it. And, best of all, Yuri Bresilev, their commander, was an old comrade.

"Yuri, it's Anatoly calling from Bangkok," Komarov said.

"Anatoly!" The SOBRE commander sounded genuinely pleased. "It's good to hear from you. How's everything in your tropical paradise? I envy you."

"Save your envy for someone who's worthy of it," Komarov said. "It's a bloody steambath if that's your idea of paradise, and I'm getting my head kicked in down here. I need a big favor of you."

"Anatoly, old comrade—" Bresilev laughed "—or should I say democratic associate. Just ask and it's yours. I haven't forgotten Beirut."

"This place makes the Lebanon look almost sane."

"But that can't be," Bresilev replied seriously. "What's the problem?"

"I have a big-shot Chinese gangster who moved in from Macao recently, and he thinks that he can get away with shooting up my people and my facilities.

And if that's not enough to deal with, I'm supposed to be keeping an eye on the Golden Triangle so that all the heroin in the world doesn't get dumped on the streets of Moscow all at the same time by the Afghans.''

"So the report of the Dushmen moving in was correct?" Bresilev's voice took on a hard note. Like most Russians, he had no love for Islamic radicals of any stripe, and the Taliban was on the top of his list.

"Unfortunately, it was," Komarov said. "Young Polnacek went up there to do a recon to confirm it, and they put a bullet in his leg. Fortunately, though, an American operative was working the area at the same time and rescued him."

"Is the Yankee going to be a problem for you?"

"Not at all. In fact, I'm joining forces with him and his team to take care of the mujis. And I owe him for bringing Polnacek back to me in one piece."

"That was fortunate," Bresilev agreed. "I wouldn't want to have Polnacek's father on my ass."

"Nor I," Komarov admitted. "But a bigger threat than the mujis is that Chinese gangster. He raided our safehouse and shot up a bunch of my people."

"That's not good, Anatoly." The SOBRE commander got real serious. "It gives people the wrong impression about us, and we can't have that. What does Moscow say?"

"They're taking it under advisement." The sneer could be heard in Komarov's voice. "And you know what that means. They'll debate it for a couple weeks and then ask me for another report. And while they're doing that, I'm getting my men killed one by one.''

''For old times' sake,'' the SOBRE commander said, ''why don't I send you a platoon of my best boys on a 'training mission.' I'll break them down into two squads of urban SOBRE to help with your Bangkok problem and two squads of Spetsnaz to give the Yankees a hand. Will that help?''

''If you can do that, my old friend,'' Komarov said, ''I'll be forever grateful. I'll even send our Marita to visit you for two weeks of temporary duty when this is all over.''

Bresilev laughed. ''Thanks, but she got to me some time ago. I'm afraid that I'm old news for her.''

''As am I,'' Komarov said regretfully.

Komarov had a smile on his face when he hung up the phone. Old friends were good to have. Old friends in high places were even better. Now maybe he could get this mess taken care of properly.

Hitting his intercom button, he called his operations officer. ''Valery, get in here!''

''On the way.''

THE SIX MEN who stepped off of the JAL 747 didn't look much different from the other male passengers on the sex tour flight until you got close enough to look into their eyes. They weren't giving every Thai woman they passed the once-over, impatiently undressing her with glittering eyes. These men checked out the crowds in the airport corridor, but it was for an entirely different reason. They were looking for the opposition.

"Over here, David!" Bolan called out when he spotted David McCarter.

"Striker," the Briton said as he walked up and took his hand.

"How was the flight?" Bolan asked as he scanned the horde of deplaning passengers for the rest of the Phoenix Force warriors.

"Bloody drunken schoolboys," McCarter snorted. "Even the Japanese, who should know better, were acting like fools. You'd think they'd never been laid before."

"That's what you get for traveling back in the cattle section."

"But I was in first class with Rafe."

Rafael Encizo joined the pair. "Damn, but I'm glad to get away from those idiots. You wouldn't believe the things they were doing."

Just then, T. J. Hawkins, Calvin James and Gary Manning joined the group.

"Where's Jack?" McCarter asked when he didn't see Jack Grimaldi, their pilot.

"He's exchanging business cards with a couple of the Japanese," Manning explained. "He started entertaining them with his tales of aerial derring-do and they ate it up with a spoon all the way across the South China Sea. To hear him tell it, he taught the Red Baron and Chuck Yeager everything they knew. God, but he can go on!"

"And on and on and on," Hawkins confirmed. "I didn't know there were so many ways to crash a plane and still walk away from it."

"The man does have a fine rap." James grinned. "He can talk the paint right off the wall."

"Well," Manning said when Grimaldi finally appeared, "if it isn't smiling Jack, intrepid hero of the unfriendly skies and all-around ace pilot."

Grimaldi took a small bow. "Gentlemen. Now that I'm here, can we get this show on the road?"

"Don't you have more ticket stubs to autograph for your adoring fans?" Manning asked.

"That's right." Grimaldi grinned and whipped out his ballpoint. "I forgot to sign yours."

"Asshole."

BOLAN HAD LEASED a six-passenger Land Rover, and since the Phoenix Force warriors weren't carrying the tools of their trade, it was a comfortable fit. They all had known Bangkok of old and, along the way, they commented on the changes they saw that had been made since their last visit.

The general aviation airfield was north of town, right next to a Thai air force base. "That's nice and cozy," McCarter said as he scanned the air police gun jeeps on the military flight line. "Nothing like having the locals provide our security whether they know it or not."

"We won't be here long enough to use them,"

Bolan explained. "We're just delivering Jack so he can pick up his ride."

The Bell JetRanger Bolan had contracted wasn't brand-new, but it still had many years of service left in it. Grimaldi piled out of the Land Rover and immediately started checking out his new machine.

"This one's an ex-army OH-58 version," Grimaldi reported. "And that's good because it has the full wiring kit in place if we want to add guns to it. The engine's been updated to a Dash 700, and it has the new broad-cord rotor, so we'll have extra lift capability at high altitude. Considering that you can get into a low-air-density situation even at lower elevations over here, it's—"

"So it's satisfactory?" Bolan cut him off.

"Oh, yeah." Grimaldi blinked. "It's just fine."

"Good, because you need to rendezvous with a freighter in the Bay of Bengal tonight to pick up your gear."

"I thought we were going to do it offshore here?"

"The plan changed," Bolan said. "Hal said the State Department pissed off the Thais again, and we have to be even more careful."

"Wouldn't it be nice to only have to fight the bad guys and not our own government?"

Bolan grinned. "That's a novel idea."

Leaving Grimaldi to go over his machine, Bolan took the Phoenix Force warriors to the safehouse he had arranged through Dr. Jordan's CIA contacts.

# CHAPTER THIRTEEN

*Bangkok, Thailand*

Phoenix Force's new quarters were in a modern two-story concrete-block building with drive-in parking in half of the lower story. The other half of the bottom floor had once been a small shop, but it was empty now and boarded up. The main entrance to the second floor was up a narrow flight of stairs, which made it easy to defend. A second door in the apartment led down into the parking garage. There were beds enough to sleep everyone, and the kitchen shelves and refrigerator were stocked well enough for an extended stay.

"Ah," Rosario Blancanales said when he opened the fridge and saw two dozen cold, half-liter bottles of Tiger beer. "Someone sure knows how to treat his guests right."

He reached in, snagged a bottle of beer and, holding his hand in a practiced grip, twisted the nontwist top off and slugged down a long shot. "Damn, that's good."

"Who are you planning to send after our goodies?" McCarter asked Bolan.

"I thought I'd send you to help with the navigation and T.J. to do the heavy lifting."

"Sounds good to me," the ex-SAS commando said as he grabbed a beer. "I'll limit my intake to a half liter, then."

He looked at the half-full bottle in his hand. "On second thought, maybe two."

JACK GRIMALDI HAD the speeding JetRanger right down on the wave tops over the Bay of Bengal. The whitecaps looked close enough for David McCarter to reach down from the copilot's seat and wash his hands. That Grimaldi was flying that low on a moonless night made it even trickier.

"Whoopie!" Hawkins called up from the rear seat. "Man, I knew I should have brought my surfboard along for this trip. I could just hang on to one of the skids and have one hell of a ride."

"Hey, T.J.," Grimaldi called back on the intercom, "I didn't know that you were a surfer dude."

"I'm not," Hawkins replied. "But if I was, this would be a great time to hang ten."

"Jack's just showing off," McCarter called back. "He hasn't seen enough chopper crashes in his life yet to know that he's flying too bloody low."

"I saw a guy hook a skid on a wave once," Hawkins said. "It was awesome, man. One minute the guy was flying like a bird and the next, he had turned his chopper into floating debris. That part of it that floated, that is. None of the bodies did, so the divers had to go in after them the next day.''

"Okay, guys," Grimaldi said. "I get the hint. But we wouldn't be doing this if the Thai and Myanmar governments didn't have their knickers in a twist, as our copilot would say. I'd much rather fly to some place on dry land and set down like a gentleman. This wasn't my idea of how to get our equipment delivered to us.''

The Myanmar military government was even more angry with the United States than the Thais were. The constant harassment from Washington about human-rights issues when they were fighting an antigovernment movement, as well as a rebel insurrection, had gotten more than a little old. The country's politics were complicated and controversial, but American meddling wasn't making the situation any better.

Grimaldi glanced down at his GPS readout. "We should be coming up on the ship anytime now.''

The words were no sooner out of his mouth than the outline of a ship blocked out a section of the whitecaps. The freighter was showing only normal running lights, but when Grimaldi made radio contact, white mastlights came on. Under their glare, he could see a clear spot on the deck that had been marked with a big *H* in white paint.

From the direction of the waves, the pilot knew where the wind was coming from and circled the ship to face into it before starting his flare out on the helipad. Grimaldi kept the rotor turning as men came into the circle of light with the mission packs on dollies.

Hawkins and McCarter got out to help the crew check the gear off the manifest and stow it on board the JetRanger. They were strapping the last case down when the ship's captain appeared.

"I don't know what kind of spooks you guys are," he said gruffly, "but you've got a hell of a lot of juice. The owners said they'd beach me in Arizona if I didn't play along with you guys on this."

"I'm sorry for the inconvenience, Captain," McCarter said, "and I can assure you that this wasn't our first choice for how to get our equipment."

"I was Brown Water Navy in the Nam for a couple of years," the captain said, relaxing a little, "and I know how these things work. I used to run SEAL teams into godforsaken places in the delta all the time."

"Then you'll accept our apologies?"

"Only if you get the job done," he replied. "Whatever it is you're going to do. This part of the world's so screwed up right now, I can hardly believe it."

"We're going to give it a try," McCarter assured him. "But I can't say that it's going to make much of a change."

"Anything would be an improvement."

The captain glanced at the JetRanger. "That thing's really loaded down to try a takeoff like this."

The weight of the mission packs, the remaining fuel and the three men were stretching the lift limits on the chopper. But McCarter was confident in Grimaldi's skill as a collective-and-cyclic man. If it was at all possible to do, Jack would do it.

"Let me know if you want me to turn my beam into the wind. It'll make half of this candy-ass crew seasick as babies, but it might make it easier for that thing to get off this tub, and I need you guys to disappear ASAP. I have to have the decks clear before a Myanmar patrol boat shows up and wants to know what in the hell I'm doing. Every time I get searched for drugs, it costs the owners a couple thousand dollars in bribes to get the little bastards to go away and leave me alone."

"Get it in gear, David," the pilot called out from his open window. "I want to get out of here."

"Thanks, Captain." McCarter extended his hand.

The captain shook it, then brought his hand up to his cap in a salute. "Go get 'em, tiger."

McCarter was still buckling down when Grimaldi twisted the throttle up and started feeding in collective. The overloaded chopper rocked back and forth on her skids but wouldn't break contact. Grimaldi tried every trick in his book, but it wasn't working. With the wind coming in from one side, the rotors weren't biting properly.

The captain signaled him to throttle down and made motions of turning the ship's side into the wind. Grimaldi nodded and backed off the turbine.

It took some time for the big ship to make the course correction, but when it had completed the turn, the wind was coming from the right direction to add a little lift to the rotors. With the wind blowing over the blades at twelve knots, the chopper felt a little less sluggish this time when Grimaldi hauled up on the collective.

"Hang on, guys," he called out. "We're a go."

With the turbine screaming past the redline, Grimaldi nursed the machine off the deck and away from the ship. If the turbine even burped at this weight, they'd get to go surfing just as Hawkins had wanted, but straight down.

Keeping the nose down, the pilot finessed enough airspeed to be able to feed in a little more collective until they were a full hundred feet off the waves.

"Okay, guys," he said. "You can relax now. As soon as we burn off some fuel, we'll be in much better shape."

"Now he tells me," Hawkins said.

IT WAS STILL DARK when Jack Grimaldi landed his JetRanger in a parking lot beside a small warehouse on the outskirts of town.

"Sorry I'm late, guys," the pilot greeted Bolan and the other Phoenix Force Warriors. "The head winds were a bitch and we're a bit loaded down."

The load Grimaldi had delivered contained the weapons, ammunition and equipment they would have had waiting for them in Bangkok if the political situation had been different than it was. Having the tools of their trade at hand made them feel a little less vulnerable.

The first things they broke out were their individual weapons and the ammunition for them. Only after the magazines were loaded and the first rounds chambered did they feel fully dressed. Then they quickly off-loaded the rest of their equipment into the warehouse.

"This isn't all going to fit in that Land Rover," McCarter commented as he looked at the piles of gear.

"We'll make two trips."

WHEN THE LAST of the mission gear had been delivered to the safehouse, the Phoenix Force commandos went to work securing their new premises. Gary Manning and T. J. Hawkins busied themselves putting up video cameras covering both the front and rear of the building. A third camera covered the parking garage, and all three were wired to a monitor in what would serve as their communications room.

Once their eyes were in place, the radios were set up and Manning let the Farm know that they had secured their gear.

"We have a visitor out front," Manning announced.

Bolan looked out the window and saw Dimitri Polnacek walking up to the front door.

"That's our Russian liaison officer, I guess you'd call him. I've been in contact with the RSV commander here, and we're going to be working with his people on this.''

"The plot thickens," McCarter said.

"We need their help this time," Bolan stated. "Really need them."

Bolan went to the door when the bell rang and called down, "Up here, Dimitri."

The Russian climbed the stairs and shook hands with Bolan at the top. "This is quite a nice little nest you have here,'' he said.

"It's all we need," Bolan replied. "And its main value is that no one knows we're here."

"For now."

Bolan introduced the Phoenix Force commandos to the Russian agent, and McCarter saw to it that he got a cold beer.

The Russian took a drink and delivered his message. "Colonel Komarov wanted me to let you know that he finally got permission for the reinforcements he promised you. He has two squads of urban counterterrorist police and a platoon of commandos coming as soon as they can get here."

"When does he expect them?" Bolan asked.

"That's going to depend on Aeroflot," Polnacek replied honestly. "Our national airline is also having problems working for a living. But it will be as soon as possible. And in the meantime, we're going to keep the pressure on Big Gold to try to keep him focused on his problems here."

"That should help," Bolan said. "We're expecting orders to launch up north anytime now."

Polnacek finished his beer. "If you let the colonel know when you move out, we may be able to cover for you here."

"That would be helpful," Bolan said.

"Did you ask for Spetsnaz?" McCarter asked Bolan.

"It's a big jungle up there and we're going to need help."

*Stony Man Farm, Virginia*

WITH THE successful transfer of Phoenix Force's mission equipment to the team, Stony Man went into the final phase of their end of the mission prep. For the men on the ground to be able to do what they needed to do, the Farm crew had to do its job first. It was axiomatic that no battle plan survived contact with the enemy. That was why he was called the enemy. But going in completely blind without a plan was almost a guarantee of disaster.

Most of the Farm's mission-prep chores were centered around intelligence gathering, and it was their most important function. Knowing what you were going up against gave anyone a better chance of being successful. The Stony Man warriors were good at making things up as they went along; in their line of work, they had to be. But foreknowledge of what they were going up against was the most powerful weapon they could have in their arsenal.

This time, though, the information-gathering process had hit the wall and Hunt Wethers was fit to be tied. He and Akira Tokaido had been fighting a malfunctioning KH-12 satellite for more than a day now, and it steadfastly refused to work as advertised. It wasn't giving them a radar map of the area of the Golden Triangle that Bolan had indicated was hiding the new construction. The Keyhole satellites were fitted with a variety of deep-space sensors ranging from full EM and visual spectra through IR to magnetic anomaly detection. But the most useful for most Stony Man purposes was their radar-mapping capabilities.

The powerful radars on the spy birds could reach down through any amount of vegetation and map the ground and anything that was built on it. In most parts of the world, a radar map was better than a six-inch resolution photo. The cameras could show the headlines of a newspaper well enough to read it, but not if the paper was under a tree. The radar wouldn't show the paper, but it would record the man reading it. This time, through, the radars simply weren't working and Wethers couldn't find out why.

Finally, he gave up and took the situation to Aaron Kurtzman.

"Run a test," Kurtzman suggested. "Aim it someplace else and make a trial sensor run. If it still doesn't give you what you want, we'll blow it up and start all over with a new satellite. That'll mean delaying this for a couple of days while you maneuver the new bird in place. But they need to have the sensor runs.''

''I should have thought of doing that,'' Wethers admitted, ''but we've been so busy trying to trouble-shoot the damned thing, I wasn't thinking.''

Wethers was a good man with an electron. He could make them sit up and sing when he wanted to. But with his background in academia, he sometimes got focused in on the problem instead of casting around to see if there was some way he could break through it. Kurtzman, on the other hand, looked at everything sideways and let his gut lead him where it would.

Kurtzman smiled when his friend walked off mumbling to himself.

WHEN WETHERS RETURNED an hour later, he didn't look any happier. If anything, he looked even more cranked as he handed Kurtzman a handful of hard copy.

''Okay,'' Kurtzman said as he looked over a perfect radar map of a patch of mountainous jungle in a different part of Southeast Asia. ''It looks like we're being stealthed out in the Golden Triangle.''

''But how in the hell are they doing that?'' Wethers asked. It was theoretically possible to stealth objects on the ground against deep-space spying, but no one had figured out how to do it yet beyond hiding underground.

"I haven't the slightest idea," Kurtzman said, shrugging. "But I've been expecting something like this to pop up for years. With damned near everyone in the world having access to spy birds now, it had to happen sooner or later. We haven't gotten involved in that kind of research because everything we have that we don't want anyone to get too close a look at we keep buried."

"How are we going to get the sensor readouts for Striker, then?"

Kurtzman shook his head. "Since you can't overpower whatever it is they're doing down there, I guess we aren't. The guys are just going to have to do it the hard way again this time."

"However," Kurtzman added as he rolled his chair away from his workstation, "we do need to let Hal know about this and see what he wants to do."

"Are you taking bets on what he'll say?"

"Not in this lifetime."

## CHAPTER FOURTEEN

*Stony Man Farm, Virginia*

Barbara Price was waiting in the War Room in the farmhouse when Hunt Wethers entered pushing Aaron Kurtzman's chair in front of him.

"Where's Hal?" Kurtzman asked.

"He's on the horn again," Price replied.

"Sorry I'm late," Brognola said as he rushed in a moment later. "I was talking to the President."

"What did the Man want?" Price asked.

"He just wanted a detailed after-action on the Afghan drug ring Carl fired up in Miami," Brognola replied. "He's ragging on the Canadian prime minister about his terrorist-refugee policies and wanted more ammunition."

"Speaking of Afghans," she said, "when are we going to get a new target for Carl's team? The *Darvos* takedown went like clockwork, and I don't want them to get cold."

Phoenix Force had the bigger mission again this

time, but Able Team's role was supporting it in more than one way. If they could shut down the Taliban's plans to hijack the established American heroin networks, it would slow down the Golden Triangle takeover until Phoenix Force could destroy it.

"I've got something cooking," he said, "but I want to get the Phoenix operation in hand first.

"What's the story on your problem with the satellite?" he asked Kurtzman.

"Well, Murphy was an optimist."

Brognola shook his head. Murphy's Law was a constant that couldn't be ignored. "What is it this time?"

After Kurtzman had filled in Brognola about his theory that the Golden Triangle sites were being stealthed, Kurtzman concluded that they weren't going to be able to provide Phoenix Force with a radar map of their targets as they had planned.

"What can we give them?" Brognola asked.

"Not much." Kurtzman shrugged. "Just the photos and the IR printouts, and you can't see much on them. This one's going to have to be done the hard way. They'll have to make a preliminary ground recon of the targets before we can work up an attack plan. It's going to set back the timetable, but I don't see any way around it."

Brognola turned to his mission controller. "Are you okay with that?"

"I don't see what else we can do," Price said. "Sending them in on an assault without a complete recon of the targets first just isn't in the cards. Particularly since this isn't a direct threat to the nation that has to be eliminated immediately. If it takes them a couple of weeks more or less, it just doesn't really matter this time.''

"I'll argue that point to the President."

"Please do."

All too often, Phoenix Force and Able Team were thrown into the caldron with inadequate premission prep. It was bad enough that no plan ever survived the initial contact with the enemy, but not at least giving the men an even chance was criminal. As mission controller, Price's primary job was to limit the political crimes committed against her action teams as much as she could. After all, they couldn't do their job if they all got whacked the moment they entered enemy territory.

Brognola didn't need to be a mind reader to know what was going on behind Price's blue eyes. This was a discussion they'd had on more than one occasion. And he usually came out on the wrong end of it. There was a good reason that a woman who looked as if she had stepped off the cover of a fashion magazine was running a place like Stony Man Farm. She wasn't a cream puff. The last time she backed down when she thought she was right was back in grade school.

"I promise I'll get him to back off."

"I have the foot-recon plan laid out," Kurtzman broke in. "Striker's solo run earlier gave me enough to work against what little we've been able to get from the satellites. If you want, I'll pass it on to them."

"Please do," Price replied.

"Now," Brognola said, pulling a file from his briefcase, "on to new business. We're still sweating our two Sword of God types on the extent of the Algerian and Taliban penetration here. And after matching it with intelligence from other sources, we're finding a bigger can of worms than we'd thought."

"How's that?"

"We're being invaded and ripped off at the same time."

*Bangkok, Thailand*

THE MAKESHIFT com center in the corner of the Bangkok safehouse had been rigged up with everything the Phoenix Force warriors needed to stay in contact with the Farm and one another. They had the usual satcom link and high-speed fax link to the Farm. For around town and in the field, they had an FM radio that transmitted on the com link frequency.

"Okay, people," Bolan said as he turned away from the fax machine, "this is it. We're a go."

"About bloody time," David McCarter said as he put down his beer and headed for the kitchen table.

The team gathered around as Bolan laid out the material he had just received for the mission briefing.

The table was quickly littered with newly faxed satellite photos and scans, and Katzenelenbogen's plan for a recon in force.

"As you can see," Bolan said, "they weren't able to get us much from the satellite runs so we're going to have to do most of this the hard way."

"What's wrong with the satellites this time?" Rafael Encizo asked. "Every time we really need the damned things, they're off-line."

"Aaron's not sure," Bolan explained. "And that's part of what we'll be looking for. But he thinks that someone has found a way to stealth the sites."

"That's not supposed to be possible," Gary Manning said.

"For every offense that someone thinks up," McCarter reminded him, "some bright lad always comes up with a defense sooner or later."

"At least they could have waited a couple of years on this one," Calvin James said as he studied the topographical maps of the region. "This's going to be a real hump."

"I'll be able to fly you guys in to most of your launch points," Jack Grimaldi said, "and do the extractions."

"Just like it says in the manual on recon operations." T. J. Hawkins shook his head. "Man, I'd like to have a dime for every time I've been left behind and had to boot it out of an LZ when the bird couldn't make it in."

The ex-Ranger turned to Grimaldi. "Nothing

against you, Jack. You're a hell of a pilot and you do things that I've never seen anyone else do with a chopper. But we don't have an aerial fire team backing you up and we don't know what the opposition has tucked away up there. If I remember correctly, the Afghans played hell with the Russian choppers. And since this is a big-bucks operation we're going up against this time, I wouldn't be surprised if they had some kind of anti-air defense. Radar, fifty-ones and Stingers at least.''

"No offense taken,'' Grimaldi replied. "And you're right. The thing I'm counting on is being able to get down in the valleys and use the ridgelines to shield me from radar and missiles.''

"If we're done with that topic,'' McCarter said, looking up from the mission plan Bolan had handed him, "Striker's taking T.J. and Rafe, and I'm going with you other two lads. We're going to do it in an Eagle Flight insertion. Drop off the first team, make sure they're secure and then fly on to the second LZ. After everyone's on the ground, Jack will find a place to park himself and wait for our recovery calls. If one team gets in trouble, the other team will recover and go in to pull the first one out.''

"What's with the Russians?'' Rafael Encizo asked Bolan. "I thought your man said that they were sending a Spetsnaz unit down here to give us a hand?''

"That's still in the wind,'' Bolan replied. "The head of the RSV has the people standing by, but the Russians are dragging their feet transporting them.

Hal wants us to do this preliminary recon ourselves and save them for the assault.''

"That's typical." Encizo shook his head. "Their new government hasn't improved them any. They're still Russians.''

"Anyway," Bolan said, handing him a map and several sheets of paper, "let's go over this recon plan the Bear sent. It looks workable to me.''

ONCE AGAIN Jack Grimaldi was doing his ace-pilot number. The JetRanger hadn't been more than a few feet off the ground for the past several miles. That would have been fine had he been flying over Kansas, but they were in the Golden Triangle. Hawkins had been looking up at treetops all the way into his landing zone. The pilot was keeping his airspeed relatively low to optimize his reaction time if anything suddenly appeared in his flight path. So far, though, all he'd had to dodge were errant branches.

"LZ coming up on zero-one," he called back to the men in the back of the bird.

Bolan, Hawkins and Encizo had their rappelling harnesses hooked to the ropes and were standing in the open doors of the JetRanger. Bolan hooked him a thumbs-up, and the pilot rolled back on his throttle to flare out for his final approach. The clearing he was aiming for wasn't big enough to set down the bird, but the rope drop meant that he wouldn't have to.

To make it work, he had to basically land his chopper on thin air sixty feet off the ground. Then he had to keep it stationary in what was called a ground hover by playing with the pitch of the rotor blades until the commandos made their rappel to the ground. It sounded simple, but it was one of the most dangerous things a man could try to do with a helicopter. If the turbines even burped, the machine would fall out of the sky onto the men hanging under it.

When he had killed his forward speed, Grimaldi saw that he was a little off center of the small clearing and nudged forward on the cyclic as he kept the collective centered. As soon as he had clear ground under him, he called back. "Go! Go! Go!"

On command, the three men kicked the ropes down and stepped out backward onto them. This was a fast recon rappel and they dropped the sixty feet to the jungle floor almost as quickly as if they hadn't been on the ropes. At the last possible microsecond, they braked and their feet touched lightly on the ground. Hitting their quick disconnects, they were free of the ropes and sprinted out from under the machine to take cover in the surrounding jungle.

"We're clear," Bolan sent over the com link.

"Roger, I'm outta here," Grimaldi sent back.

Rolling his throttle back to one hundred percent, the pilot nudged forward on the cyclic to tilt the rotor mast and pick up some forward momentum and increased his pitch. In seconds, he was flying again. He didn't, though, gain more than another twenty feet of altitude. The whole flight had to be made under the treetops or it wouldn't work.

IN THE JUNGLE, the three Phoenix Force warriors of the first recon team went to ground to wait to see if anyone had heard their insertion. It was unlikely, but on the off chance, it was better to wait than to stumble into them. After twenty minutes had passed, Bolan signalled the move out. If the recon went as planned, none of them would say a word until they were back in the chopper and on the return flight to Bangkok.

The LZ was in a valley between two ridges, so their first move was to get up on the high ground. Not only would that give them the tactical advantage of height, but it would also get them away from any foot patrols that might be roaming the area. With just the three of them, they kept a close formation as they made their way up the ridge. Rather than breaking bush, they moved through the natural breaks in the vegetation so as to leave as little sign behind as possible. It was slower going that way, but safer.

THE SECOND INSERTION went as smoothly as the first. And as soon as McCarter, Manning and James were securely on the ground, Grimaldi nudged forward on his cyclic and flew on down the valley. He kept his airspeed low so as to have enough time to get out of the way should something jump out to bite him. Also, his lower air speed cut the sounds of his rotors. If the opposition couldn't see him or hear him, he should be okay.

THE TALIBAN LEADER, Al Hosn, was inspecting the progress of the construction at the third of the poppy-processing plants and he wasn't happy at what he saw. As always, though, the infidels Liu had put in charge pretended not to understand his English when he questioned them. He had given orders that the concrete for the defensive bunkers was to be poured before the foundation for the workers' mess hall was laid. Instead, the mess hall was completed and the excavation hadn't even been started on the machine-gun positions.

Had the engineers been his own men, he would have skinned them alive for failing to follow their orders. As it was, he could only register his displeasure with that fat, smiling Chinese gang lord who would pretend that somehow his engineers had misunderstood what they had been told, so sorry. If he heard another Chinese tell him "so sorry" one more time, he was going to kill someone.

"Commander," Al Hosn's jeep driver said as he approached him, "you are wanted on the radio. They said it was urgent."

"What is it?"

"They did not tell me."

Al Hosn walked to the jeep and picked up the radio mike. "What is it?" he barked into it in Arabic.

"Commander, two of our patrols have reported hearing a low-flying helicopter in their areas."

This was more like it, something he could deal with without having to battle a smiling Chinese. The Afghan took a folded map out of his jacket pocket. "Where?"

He pinpointed the coordinates and saw that they were in the vicinity of the main compound and the number-two processing plant.

"Alert the antiaircraft gun crews immediately."

"That has been done," the radio operator replied.

"Are the patrols carrying the missiles as I ordered them to?"

The radio was silent for a long moment before the operator answered, "Only one patrol is carrying them."

The Afghan's face hardened. "Tell that unit to be ready to fire at the aircraft as soon as they can target them. Tell the leader of the other patrol to return to the compound immediately and report to me."

Al Hosn turned to his driver. "Take me back to my headquarters."

"At once, Commander."

DAVID MCCARTER WAS on point with his team when he spotted the pointman of a muji patrol. As expected for a newbie in the jungle, he was looking in all the wrong places instead of paying proper attention to his surroundings. The Briton signaled for the other two Phoenix Force warriors to go to ground.

By the time Manning worked his way up, the ten-man patrol was almost past McCarter's observation point. But he caught a glimpse of the next-to-last man carrying a long olive-green tube on his shoulder. Toward the front of the tube was the pistol grip and optical sighting unit for an SA-7 Grail antiaircraft missile.

Catching McCarter's eye, Manning tapped the scope on his H&K assault rifle and nodded toward the Afghan with the missile. McCarter shook his head and hooked a thumb to the rear.

As the drag man, Calvin James now became point as the three members of Phoenix Force worked back the way they had come. A couple of hundred yards later, they hooked to the right and bypassed the route the mujis had taken. Another hundred yards farther on, they went to ground and Bolan signaled Manning to bring up the team's radio.

"Flyboy, this is Ground Two," McCarter sent.

"Flyboy, go," Grimaldi answered.

"This is Two. Be advised that there are Grail missiles with the enemy ground units. Over."

"This is Flyboy," Grimaldi answered. "Roger Grails. Any more good news for me today? Over."

"Two, negative. Out."

Grimaldi had been running the valleys looking for a parking place fairly close to where he had dropped off the teams. He wanted to be able to pull them out quickly if they got in trouble. But if the opposition was packing missiles, he had to rethink his options.

Pulling up into clear airspace, he opened his map and looked for a nearby mountaintop.

# CHAPTER FIFTEEN

*In the Golden Triangle*

It wasn't the best time for Jack Grimaldi to be distracted, but he flew with one hand as he frantically searched his map for a place to lay up out of the line of fire. Finding that the opposition had their hands on Grail antiaircraft missiles had just made his life more challenging.

The Russian-made SA-7 Grail was a poor cousin to the American Stinger, but it wasn't without its dangers. It was relatively slow, short ranged and its heat-seeking guidance was more equivalent to the obsolete American Redeye. But just because it wasn't the latest in antiaircraft technology didn't mean that it was harmless. He'd be just as dead if one of them got a hard lock on his tailpipe.

And that was the biggest problem with the bird he was flying. The JetRanger was ex-military, but it didn't have the heat-diffusing, IR-suppression exhausts of the military machines fitted to it. He just had two old-fashioned stainless-steel tailpipes pumping eighteen-hundred-degree hot air into his slipstream. If a Grail's heat-seeking warhead got a glimpse of them, it would lock on in a heartbeat.

The good news was that if he spotted the missile's launch flare, he could turn into it, break the lock and maneuver out of its flight path. It was the "if he saw the launch flare" part that bothered him. He was alone in the ship and, even though he was an ace pilot, he hadn't figured out how to attach eyes to the back of his head yet.

The map indicated that there might be a suitable mountaintop ten miles away on the edge of the forbidden zone. If it was clear enough on top to land without breaking a skid, it would be a perfect parking place. Banking to the left, he headed up the valley toward it. Hopefully, he would be able to keep out of sight until he was clear of the danger zone.

As AL HOSN HAD expected, when he got back to his headquarters, he found that the patrol leader who had failed to carry the missiles as he had been ordered was one of the younger men. He knew the type well—all full of fire, ready to die for God and no common sense. Had he asked, he knew that he would have found that the man was a graduate of one of the schools where the Taliban imams had taught him to honor God. A stint in the Kabul military academy might have been of better use to him. There he would have at least learned to obey the orders of his military commander without question.

"I am curious," he said to the young patrol leader. "You were instructed to carry one of the Grail missiles with you and you disobeyed me. Why?"

The young Afghan stood stock-still. *"Allah Akhbar,"* he said defiantly.

"God is great," Al Hosn automatically replied. "And, in His great, merciful wisdom, He has placed me in authority over this operation. You have disobeyed me and that is the same as disobeying Him."

Al Hosn was an old fighter. He had been killing Russians when this young pup hadn't yet grown his man hair. Worse than the man's youth, though, was that he was arrogant as only a man who had never seen another man's guts on the blade of his knife could be. Unfortunately, the Taliban was mainly made up of such as this one—the young, the arrogant and the inexperienced. They saw the older men who stiffened the ranks with their experienced leadership as being somehow less than pure in the eyes of God. The young hot bloods like him all thought that they had invented dedication to the word of God and jihad against the unbelievers on their own.

Though he needed all the men he could get, he would gladly expend this one in hopes that it would improve the behavior of his young comrades. Locking eyes with the patrol leader, Al Hosn passed sentence on him.

"You are to be executed," he said. "As a lesson

to your comrades that God's will is expressed through your appointed leaders.''

The young mujahideen didn't even change expression. *''Allah Akhbar,''* he shouted.

Al Hosn pulled the captured Russian Makarov pistol from his holster and had it aimed at the mujahideen's head with one smooth move. Only then did the young man's eyes show fear. Even so, he started to open his mouth defiantly, and only the 9 mm round drilling between his dark eyes stopped him from declaring God's greatness yet again.

Al Hosn's eyes swept the small crowd that had gathered to watch the execution, and he was pleased to see flickers of raw fear on many faces. He didn't care how he got their complete and unquestioning obedience, but he would have it.

''Get this disobedient dog out of here,'' he said, pointing to the two mujahideens closest to him. ''And hang his body in a tree until it rots. The next man who fails to do as I tell him to will join him there.''

As the men jumped to obey, the Afghan leader again scanned each face in front of him. ''Any questions?'' he asked.

As he expected, there were none.

He turned and walked back to his radio room. The infidels were probing his territory again, and he intended to have their blood this time.

THE FIRST TIME Bolan had reconned the forbidden zone, the patrols had been frequent, but nothing like they were now. Dozens of gun jeeps were roving in conjunction with the foot patrols, and they were saturating the area. His team had spent much of the day lying doggo while muji patrols passed by. These Afghans weren't any better at moving through the dense jungle than the others he had seen, but there were more of them. And, the closer the Phoenix Force commandos tried to get to their objective, the more of them there were.

For the third time in the past hour, the team was forced to go to ground to let a muji patrol pass in front of them. They weren't having any trouble spotting the patrols in time to fade into the jungle, but it was slowing them.

"We may not be able to do this, Striker," Rafael Encizo whispered to Bolan over the com link after the last of the Afghans had passed. "At least not on schedule."

Encizo had that right and Bolan took out his map. Their schedule was flexible to a certain degree and they could bend it to keep this from becoming a suicide run. This was supposed to be a recon, and there was no point in making a firefight out of it unless they had to.

Bolan stabbed his finger on the map. "What do you think about swinging around to the north and trying it from the other side?" he asked Encizo.

"Suits me."

NORTH OF Bolan's team, David McCarter's group was having similar difficulties. There was simply no way that they were going to get through the defensive patrols without running a real risk of being discovered. Since it was just a recon, there was no point in taking the chance if there was another way to get the information.

McCarter was walking point when a gun jeep carrying an M-60 crossed in front of them a few hundred yards distant and gave him an idea. "If we can persuade those lads to give up one of their gun jeeps," he whispered to his teammates over the com link, "we should be able to drive almost all the way in without drawing too much attention to ourselves."

"Let's do it," Calvin James sent back. "We're stumbling over the bastards every fifteen minutes this way, and we're going to get caught sooner or later."

"Want me to use the rifle?" Gary Manning asked.

"That's what I was thinking," McCarter replied. "You do the driver, and we'll take care of the crew."

The three took up an ambush position along a trail that was well marked with tire tracks. Since the jeeps were road bound in this terrain, it was a likely spot to find what they were looking for. They waited until just the right vehicle crossed their path. For what McCarter had in mind, only an M-151 with a .50-caliber gun mounted on the back would do. If he was going to play this game, he wanted the biggest gun in town.

THEY HAD BEEN in place over an hour when they heard the sound of an engine going through the gears as it approached. Peering from his hiding place, McCarter saw the heavy machinegun mounted on the back of the jeep.

"I have the gunner." McCarter tracked the man with his sights. "Calvin, take the shotgun. Gary, you do the driver. On three."

On the mark, all three men opened fire. Through his scope, Manning drilled his man through the head and he slumped over the wheel. McCarter had to use two shots to get his, as did James, but they got them.

With a dead man at the wheel, the jeep veered off the road and came to a stop against a tree, its engine still running. Manning ran up and switched it off before the rear tires dug themselves too deeply into the dirt.

"Is the radiator damaged?" McCarter asked.

"It looks okay to me," Manning replied as he pulled the dead driver from behind the wheel and slid into his place. Starting the engine again, he worked his way into the brush until the vehicle was hidden from the trail.

The first thing they did was to strip the uniforms from the dead mujis. For this deception to work, they would have to look like any other jeep crew, and that meant hiding their tiger-stripe cammies. They had tried for head shots so as not to stain the mujis' khaki jackets, but not all of the first shots had been on target. Two of the jackets they stripped from the corpses bore bullet holes and bloodstains.

The remedy for that was to use water from the Afghans' canteens to wash off the blood as best they could before mixing up mud to cover what was left. The bullet holes were too small to see from a distance, so they didn't even try to repair them. All three jackets were for smaller men, but they were able to slip them over their cammies even if they couldn't button them up. The flat-topped Afghan hats completed the disguise.

Once they were in their new jackets, the Phoenix Force commandos took the black sticks from their combat cosmetics kits and took turns painting beards on one another. The mujis were all bearded, so a smooth face would be a dead giveaway from even a distance. Up close, the face paint would be seen for what it was, but they had no intention of getting that close. The .50-caliber gun would see to that.

When the Phoenix Force commandos had finished their makeover, they boarded their new ride. With Manning at the wheel, McCarter took his place behind the gun and James slid into the passenger seat. There weren't any black mujahideen, but some of them were rather dark skinned, and it was hoped that he would pass from a distance.

WITH THEIR GUN JEEP, the Phoenix Force warriors had no problem getting close enough to their target to check it out. Anyone seeing them from afar automatically assumed that they were one of the regular patrol vehicles. Following a dirt trail, they had been able to drive up onto a ridge overlooking the site. The angle allowed them to see under the jungle canopy, and they were stunned by the extent of the construction.

"That's quite a little facility they're building back in there," Manning said as he studied it through his field glasses. "I'm really surprised that the Farm couldn't find some way for the satellite to pick that up."

"That question is going to have to wait to be answered, though," McCarter stated. "We're not going to risk going in there tonight to see what they've done to block the spy birds."

"That's for damned sure," James agreed. "I've counted a dozen guards so far, and that's just the ones I can see in the defensive positions."

"That's another reason we're going to play it safe," McCarter said. "They have twin-barrel ack-ack mounts dug in on the north and south, probably 23s, and they work just as well on snoopy bastards like us trying to sneak in."

"I should be able to get a GPS shot from here, though," Manning said, "and then use the range finder to get the distance and azimuth to the center of mass of the big building. That's got to be where they're processing the raw opium."

Manning got the GPS reading on their location to within three yards and, using his laser range finder, pinpointed the center of mass on the largest building.

"I've got the first one," he reported. "Give me a minute and I'll try for the rest."

"Make it quick," McCarter warned. "We've attracted attention."

"Hang on a second," Manning said as he scribbled the coordinates on his map. "Done."

With the recon completed, the three Phoenix Force warriors got back in their jeep and drove away.

"Now what?" James asked.

"As soon as we find cover," McCarter said, "we'll check in with Striker and see how he's doing."

LATE AFTERNOON found Bolan and his team on a ridge well to the east of their target area. He stopped and took a GPS locator reading through a break in the jungle canopy above them.

"We made a little better time than I thought," he said when he translated the reading to his map. "We're about eighteen hundred yards from the edge of their parking strip, and most of it's downhill from here. Call it three hours with the NVG, maybe four. The recon of the target site should take an hour or so. We'll exfiltrate to the south and should be in the clear by daybreak or a little after."

"That's going to be quite a hump in the dark," Hawkins said. "If they're running saturation patrols on this side, as well as the other, we might have to lay up so they don't stumble onto us."

"If that happens," Bolan said, "we'll just wait till morning and try it again."

"Suits me," Encizo said.

Taking advantage of the halt, the commandos ate,

drank and checked over their gear again. For a night raid, everything had to be tied down securely. A single metallic noise in the night would carry in the cool night air.

Night fell swiftly in the tropics, and the jungle grew dark even faster. As soon as the sounds changed to those of the night animals, it was dark enough for them to move out.

MOVING THROUGH the jungle at night took time and, in terrain that thick, they had to move in a single file. Bolan was on point again when he heard noises ahead of him. Peering through his night-vision goggles didn't show him anything except jungle, so he pressed on. A few yards farther, though, he caught the clink of metal on metal and signaled a halt. Even at night, the jungle could be a noisy place, but metallic sounds were made only by man.

Since they were only three, Encizo and Hawkins silently moved forward to join Bolan. The Afghans were worse at night movement than they were during the day. Had they been planning a night ambush, it would have been a slaughter. When the patrol passed, Bolan took another GPS reading and found that they were only a few hundred yards from the edge of their objective. Signaling to the other two men, he got to his feet and moved out again.

LIGHT DISCIPLINE in Al Hosn's camp was good. It came natural to his mujahideen warriors, and he had threatened to skin alive any of the Chinese who dared show an electric light after dark. The work that had gone into stretching the cables in the jungle canopy to shield the site from satellite sensors would be for naught if it didn't stay dark at night.

Al Hosn wasn't technically oriented, but he knew enough to have great respect for the works of the clever infidels. During the Russian war he had seen the photographs that had been taken from deep space with his own eyes. On more than one occasion, the CIA had supplied his headquarters with them so they could plan attacks on the Soviets.

He had been impressed with the detail the photos had shown back then, but he knew that the technology had only been in its infancy then. The infidels were godless, but they could do wonders with their machines.

Along with the total blackout, Al Hosn increased the perimeter guards at night. What shielded his camp could also shield his enemies.

## CHAPTER SIXTEEN

*Tacoma, Washington*

Through his binoculars, Carl Lyons watched the cargo containers being off-loaded from the Indian-flagged merchantman MV *Kali* tied up to the dock in the Tacoma harbor. The cargo, manifested as cedar lumber, had come down from Vancouver, B.C., and a return cargo of used electronic equipment was waiting dockside to refill the coastal freighter's hold. This was all routine business for the Tacoma port, except for the fact that heroin was being off-loaded with the lumber and military contraband was included in the electronics due to be loaded.

Hal Brognola didn't know who had been paid off to look the other way while this transaction took place. But it was going on right in front of the eyes of both customs and the DEA.

Able Team had two missions this time. The first was to follow the containers loaded with lumber to their destination and find out who would remove the heroin from them. The second was to insure that the return cargo of electronic gear didn't reach its ultimate destination.

The U.S. Trade Commission beat the drum hard to encourage the sale of American high-tech products to overseas markets. Supposedly, though, they were to make sure that items of military value to a potential enemy weren't included in that trade. Sadly enough, as with all too much of the federal bureaucracy, they simply weren't doing the job they were paid to do. A number of things were behind this inability to protect the country, but mainly it was a matter of whose ox was being gored. Too many members of the Trade Commission had personal holdings in companies that wanted to make money no matter whom they sold their goods to.

In WWII their actions would have been considered treason and would have resulted in their being hanged. Now it was just called doing business. And because the companies involved were major political contributors, no one in Congress was in a big hurry to shut down this illegal trade. But since Stony Man wasn't in the habit of consulting with Congress, there was something they could do about it.

THE WATER of the harbor at Tacoma was filthy as only a timber-shipping port's water could be. On the surface, it was midafternoon on a sunny day. But a few feet under that chilled, scummy water, Gadgets Schwarz could hardly see a foot in front of him. Fortunately, though, he didn't need to see any more than the SEAL navigation board strapped to his left wrist. Designed to help the Navy's underwater commandos navigate at night, it was leading him straight for the *Kali* tied up to the dock.

In the pleasure boat a quarter of a mile away, Rosario Blancanales lounged on the aft deck with a beer can in his hand while Lyons did the wheelhouse watch by the radio. Along with the nav board, Schwarz had a radio that trailed a floating antenna on the surface behind him, so he could call for help if it was needed. The float of the antenna looked like a small piece of driftwood, so it wouldn't attract too much attention until he got right next to the ship. Then, he'd reel it in.

Along with everything else, Schwarz was towing a net bag full of limpet mines. They were small, barely ten pounds each, had neutral buoyancy and were powerful. RDX was perfect for cutting through steel plate, and the mines would open the hull of the *Kali* like an explosive can opener. The mines were fitted with the magnets needed to hold them to the hull plates and were equipped with both radio and time detonators. Aaron Kurtzman had been able to secure plans for the ship, so Schwarz knew exactly where to place the mines to get the best results.

First, though, he had to find the damned ship in the thin soup of the harbor water. He glanced down at his nav board again and almost ran into a semisubmerged log floating a few inches under the surface.

Dodging around it, he took another reading and continued on his way.

Schwarz was only a few yards from the *Kali* when he finally saw the shape of her hull looming in the murk. He stopped swimming for one last radio transmission before he reeled in his floating antenna and made his attack.

"Floater," he said into his face mask, "this is Sinker, over."

"Floater, go," Lyons replied instantly. "Where the hell are you?"

"Hold your water, Ironman. I'm a few yards from the ship and need to reel in the antenna. I wanted to let you know that I'll be out of communication for a while."

"Are you sure you have the right ship?"

"Damned if I know," Schwarz admitted. "It's a twin screw and the nav screen says that this is it. If it's the wrong one, we can always say we're sorry, right?"

"Get back to me as soon as you're done."

"Roger."

On the boat, Lyons came out of the wheelhouse with his field glasses in his hand and focused on the *Kali*.

"Where's Gadgets?" Blancanales asked.

"He's right next to the ship."

"I'd better get my gear on, then." Blancanales rose and headed belowdeck.

SCHWARZ SWAM FORWARD until he was right next to the ship. Kurtzman had said that the *Kali* was a single-hull design, and that was going to make the hit a lot easier. Once the plates were breached, she would go down like a rock. But to make sure, Schwarz had come up with a plan to insure that she went to the bottom with her contraband cargo. He wasn't going to just blow holes in the bottom; he was going to open her bow like a tin can so the ship's forward momentum would drive her under bow first like a gutted fish.

Swimming up to the bow, he placed his first charge twelve feet below the waterline. The powerful magnets made the bomb stick to the steel as if it had been welded there. Moving back along the side a dozen feet, the next two charges were placed on each side at the same depth as the bow mine. The final two were put a dozen feet to the rear of the first pair. The detonators had been preset back at the boat, so all he had to do was flip the waterproof switches to arm them.

Eight hours from now, when the *Kali* was in open seas on her way back to Vancouver, the bow charge would detonate, followed by the first pair of mines and then the second. The effect would be to open the bow and turn it into a giant water scoop. There was no way that she'd be able to keep from sinking.

His work done, Schwarz consulted his nav board for the course back to Able Team's boat and started swimming again. As soon as he was well clear of the ship, he released his floating antenna again to let Ironman know that he was coming.

BACK ON THE BOAT, Blancanales was suited up in his Scuba gear in case Schwarz needed a rescue. Lyons was at the wheel, bringing the boat in to only five hundred yards from the *Kali* to save Gadgets the long swim back. He was so busy keeping an eye out for his partner that he wasn't paying much attention to the other pleasure-boat traffic.

"Ironman!" Blancanales called out from the rear deck. "We got trouble."

Lyons looked back and saw a pleasure yacht three times the size of his boat bearing down on them at thirty knots or so. They had to see him, but they weren't making way. Snatching up his field glasses, he could see that the two men on the foredeck looked like Middle Easterners. More of their Algerian playmates, he thought.

The bigger boat might be faster than he was, but it would be slower to turn. Lyons racked his throttle back all the way, and the big V-8 in the engine room thundered as the bow of his boat lifted out of the water.

It was going to be a dicey maneuver in broad daylight in a crowded harbor. Everyone from the longshoremen on the docks to the picnicking families at Point Defiance park would have a ringside seat to the takedown. But if they were going to save their own butts, as well as get Gadgets back in one piece, they had no choice.

SCHWARZ MIGHT NOT have been able to see much in the murky harbor, but he could hear the beat of the speeding props and they sounded as if they were coming toward him. Glancing at the depth gauge on his right wrist, he decided to put a few more feet of water between him and whatever was going on up there. The radio antenna wasn't long enough to reach the surface from where he was going, but getting flayed by a boat prop wasn't on his agenda.

With another dozen feet of water over his head, Schwarz felt safe and he went dead in the water. With the murkiness of the water, he couldn't see the hull bottoms above him, but the pounding of the props sounded even louder.

A SCUBA WETSUIT and swim fins weren't the best combat clothing in the world, but this was a run-what-you-brung type situation. Blancanales grabbed the M-16/M-203 over-and-under from the deck stowage and jacked the barrel forward to load a 40 mm HE grenade.

At the wheel, Lyons glanced back at Blancanales and shouted, "Hang on!"

Gauging it until the last possible second, Lyons spun the wheel to his left, almost setting his speeding boat up on her side rail as it avoided the collision.

The yacht's pilot was taken by surprise and tried

to match the vessel's turn, but his big boat needed more time to come about. It did, however, pass within a few yards of the smaller craft.

When the hull of the yacht shielded him from shore-side observation, Blancanales braced himself, raised his M-16/M-203 and laid down on the trigger. The first long burst of 5.56 mm tumblers slammed into the bridge, shattering glass and punching through the fiberglass bulkheads. He caught a fleeting glimpse of the wheelman diving for cover.

Just as the yacht was almost past, he tripped the grenade launcher, and the 40 mm HE grenade detonated on the transom, blowing a three-foot hole in the fiberglass hull.

''Yahoo!'' Lyons yelled as he racked the boat around behind the yacht to give Blancanales another shot at it.

The Algerians had expected to collide with the smaller boat and were hanging on to the railings instead of firing their weapons. Now that they were being attacked, they scrambled for their iron, but the opportunity had been lost. Blancanales had another grenade in the launcher, and he took the time to aim carefully before he fired.

The 40 mm HE sailed through the hole he had punched in the transom earlier and detonated inside the hull. A split second later, one of the yacht's fuel tanks detonated. The explosion broke the keel of the vessel, tossing the gunmen on the deck into the water.

When the second fuel tank cut loose, the boat quickly disappeared beneath the waves.

A couple of heads showed in the water, but Lyons was in no mood to play the Good Samaritan with people who had just tried to kill him. He gave the crash scene a wide berth and once he was back in position to recover Schwarz, chopped his throttle.

"JESUS!" Schwarz sputtered as Blancanales hauled him up over the side of their boat. "What in the hell was going on up here?"

Lyons smiled. "Just a boat full of Algerians who didn't like us watching their cargo being unloaded. They tried to ram us, and Pol dissuaded them."

Several flaming remnants of the explosion on the yacht were drawing attention like a freeway smashup. Even fishermen in rowboats were paddling to the scene. The harbor patrol was a little slow responding, but soon their twenty-four footer was also speeding to the rescue.

"Do you think anyone will miss us if we get the hell out of here?" Schwarz asked.

"Ditch the Scuba gear over the side, both sets," Lyons said. "And stash the hardware while I try to finesse our way out of here. We don't want to be seen running from the scene of the crime."

"This was supposed to have been a piece of cake," Schwarz grumbled.

"Tell that to the Algerians."

While Schwarz and Blancanales changed back into

their street clothes and cleared the boat of suspicious items, Lyons circled around to the west. He cruised slowly, keeping well clear of the gaggle of boats responding to the sinking as if he were trying not to get in the way of the rescue efforts. Working his way over to the south shore of the harbor, he made for the first marina he saw. Pulling up to the refueling point, he killed the engine while Blancanales tied them up.

"Did you see what's going on out there?" a man fishing from the dock asked him.

"Nah," Blancanales said, shrugging. "We just heard an explosion and decided to come in when all the boats showed up."

"Makes sense," the fisherman said. "They scare the fish."

WITH THEIR HARDWARE in nylon bags, the Able Team trio left the boat and walked to their rented Blazer SUV parked nearby. After stowing their gear, Blancanales pulled out of the lot and drove to a scenic turnoff close to the *Kali*.

Unlike much of the cargo that had been off-loaded on the Tacoma dock, the containers from the *Kali* weren't going to be left sitting in the rain for long. Already, semitractors were backing into position to have the containers loaded onto their flatbed trailers.

"Someone's in a big hurry to get at the goodies," Schwarz said as he lowered his field glasses and made another notation on the clipboard in his lap. "That's the fourth truck that loaded up."

"You'd be in a hurry, too, if you were waiting to get your hands on five hundred pounds of the finest grade China White," Lyons said.

"How many of them are we going to count?" Blancanales asked.

"I think we've seen enough," Lyons told him. "It's time we found out where they're taking that stuff."

"Suits me," Schwarz said.

Blancanales started their Chevy Blazer SUV and pulled away from their spot in the park overlooking the docks, heading downhill to link up with the main road leading away from the docks.

With Schwarz doing the map navigation, though, they ran a few stoplights and set a land-speed record for exiting Tacoma proper and taking the first I-5 exit. The tangle of freeways around Tacoma was world renowned. I-5 was eight lanes wide as it funneled traffic to and from Seattle, and the feeder highways created a maze if you wanted to go anywhere other than north or south. This time, though, the crush of traffic worked to their advantage.

Blancanales caught up with one of the semis they were tracking right as it hooked up with I-5 north. "That's one of them," Schwarz said as he checked the number on the trailer against the list from the dock.

While the Tacoma traffic itself was world class, when I-5 got closer to Seattle, it really became a problem. But a slow problem. Afternoon rush hour in northwestern Washington ran from 3:00 p.m. to 7:00 p.m., and at peak hour it made the traffic flow on the L.A. Freeways look like the Indianapolis Speedway.

"Suck in behind him," Lyons said. "We don't want to lose him in this."

Using the Blazer's size as a battering ram, Blancanales sliced into the stream of traffic in the right lane and took the second slot back from the truck. His maneuver was answered by an angry blare of horns, but he didn't bother to reply with the one-finger salute.

Greater Seattle was flanked on the west by the Pacific Ocean and on the east by bedroom and industrial communities that ran for miles inland. Most of the area supported the aviation industry, as well as the Silicon Forest, and was growing almost daily.

"Here we go," Lyons said when he saw the truck's turn signals come on for a right-hand exit to I-405. The traffic on that six-lane highway heading north around the eastern side of Lake Washington was also crowded, but it was moving faster. Blancanales pulled out into the middle lane and allowed another car to get between him and the semi.

The truck continued for several more miles before flashing its turn signals again. "That should be the U.S. 90 east exit," Schwarz said, looking up from the map he had been studying.

# CHAPTER SEVENTEEN

*In the Golden Triangle*

As the pointman, it was Bolan's job to penetrate the camp's inner defenses. Leaving Gary Manning and Rafael Encizo in a supporting position, he worked his way forward an inch at a time on his belly. His night-vision goggles turned the near-total darkness under the jungle canopy into a fantasy of glowing shades of green. Hotter objects were a lighter green than cold ones, so humans would stand out as if they had lights shining on them.

There was no proper perimeter around the camp, no dirt berm line or interlocking bunkers. Instead, a series of fighting positions had been dug roughly ten yards apart. Checking each one, though, he saw no signs of troops on guard. Apparently, the Afghan commander was counting on his roving patrols to protect him. But what worked in the barren mountains of Afghanistan didn't translate well into jungle warfare. Now that they were inside the patrol screen, the camp was open.

Bolan continued for several more yards to make sure the way was clear before click coding Encizo and Manning to move up. As soon as they joined up again, they moved out together. They were too few to break down any further, and this way one man could map the facilities while the other two took care of security.

Though Bolan had seen much of the setup under the trees from the ridge on the other side, he was surprised at the extent of the construction he now saw. The place was like a large village. The heroin-processing buildings were concrete block construction and would require heavy weaponry to take out. There were also several more traditional bamboo structures, some of them quite large, that were probably the barracks and mess facilities for the workers.

From the number of buildings, Bolan figured that the camp's population was at least three hundred. To support all that, there was the usual generator plant, water facilities, fuel dumps and supply points. The financial investment it had taken to create this wasn't small, and that was to say nothing of what it had cost to get the materials into this remote location. Big Gold Liu wasn't a man who thought small.

Before reentering the canopy, Bolan had taken a GPS shot to get a closer hard reference point and it had registered. Now that he was deep inside the camp itself, something was preventing the signal from getting through to the Navstar satellites and he wasn't able to pinpoint the processing plant. That had to be a side effect from the stealthing that Kurtzman had mentioned was blocking the satellite mapping radars.

Putting away the GPS unit, he took out his night glasses and used their built-in laser range finder to map the dimensions of the buildings themselves. He was ranging the last building when he heard a double click in his earphone. Freezing in place, he slowly turned his head to the right to see a pair of figures walking in their direction.

The three Stony Man warriors lay flat, but Hawkins slowly reached down to slide the fighting knife from his boot sheath. Encizo wanted to reach back for the silenced .22-caliber Ruger pistol in his rucksack, but didn't dare make the movement.

Almost on command, the two late-night walkers turned and went into one of the larger bamboo buildings. Bolan figured them to be the early mess hall workers who would prepare the morning meal for the camp.

As soon as they were clear, Bolan took one more reading and signaled the others to move out.

ONCE CLEAR of the camp, the three Stony Man commandos turned to the north to close the gap between them and McCarter's team. With the Grails in the area, he didn't want to expose Grimaldi any longer than was absolutely necessary. They would continue until they were outside the patrol area before finding a place to lay over the few hours left until dawn.

JACK GRIMALDI HADN'T spent a restful night on his remote mountaintop. The mujis hadn't come calling with their curved knives in the dark, but he'd sat dozing in the pilot's seat with his helmet on so he could monitor the com link traffic. Come the false dawn, he stepped out, still wearing his helmet, and relieved himself. Climbing back into the cockpit, he ran a preflight check to insure that he would be ready to go when the teams called for extraction.

The sun had just risen when he got the first call. "Flyboy, this is Ground One. Over."

"This is Flyboy, send it."

THE EXTRACTION of Bolan and Encizo and Hawkins went as per the recon manual Hawkins had talked about. The three men were waiting on the edge of a clearing just large enough for the JetRanger to drop down into. When he was a few miles out, Grimaldi clicked in his radio to let them know that he was coming. "Ground One, this is Flyboy. Papa Zulu in zero-two, over."

"Ground One," Bolan replied. "Roger zero-two, the Papa Zulu is clear."

The team could hear the chopper before they could spot it through the canopy. But an instant later, Grimaldi dropped down through the hole in the jungle. "Go! Go! Go!" he radioed as his skids touched down.

The Stony Man commandos came out of the bush and raced for the bird. Hawkins reached it first and, once he had scrambled aboard, turned to cover the other two. Looking over his shoulder to make sure that his passengers were secure, Grimaldi twisted his throttle past the stop and hauled up on the collective.

The JetRanger almost bounced back into the sky as the rotor blades clawed the cool morning air under the full power of the howling turbine. As soon as the chopper cleared the treetops, the pilot eased off the pitch to flatten the blades and kill the climb. This was no time to expose himself more than was absolutely necessary.

McCarter's LZ was ten minutes away, and the valley he was flying through ran straight to it.

MCCARTER HAD the gun jeep in the middle of his team's clearing and was on the gun when he heard the whoosh of the Grail missile leaving its launch tube. A microsecond later, a plume of dirty white smoke shot up out of the jungle a hundred yards away.

"Jack!" he yelled over the com link. "Launch! Launch!"

Swinging the barrel of the .50-caliber gun to key on the base of the plume, he laid down on the butterfly trigger and the fifty begin to speak. Ma Deuce wasn't the fastest firing machine gun in the world, but that didn't matter. Her half-inch slugs carried two miles and would cut a tree down faster than a chain saw. He didn't have the missile-firing mujis in plain sight, so he started hosing down the jungle in their direction. Even cutting through the thick vegetation, his fire should carry far enough to distract the gunner.

WHEN GRIMALDI HEARD McCarter's frantic call, he reacted automatically. When you had a heat-seeking missile coming up your tailpipe, you didn't have too much time to look around and scratch your butt while you decided what to do. You either did it or you died.

An instant glance to the left showed him the launch smoke plume. He slammed the cyclic to that side and stomped down on the left tail rotor pedal to turn into it. The Grail was like a dim-witted uncle that wasn't too fast on his feet. If he could get the eighteen-hundred-degree tailpipes turned away from the missile, the heat-seeking warhead should loose the lock and go into ballistic free flight.

If he could do that, all he would have to do next was to keep from running into the damned thing with some part of his rotor or airframe and he'd be in the clear.

The men in the back of the bird had also caught McCarter's call and braced themselves for what they knew was coming. Anytime that they were in an aircraft, their lives depended on the skill of the man in the pilot's seat. Flying Jack had never failed them before, but as with ground combat, flying in hostile territory was a risky business. The skill had to have luck riding with it every time.

ON THE GROUND, McCarter was pouring a steady stream of .50-caliber rounds into the jungle. The barrel of the heavy gun was smoking, but he didn't let go of the butterfly trigger to give it time to cool off. Soon the barrel would start glowing a dull red as the rifling burned out, but he would shoot as long as he had ammunition.

The heavy slugs fell like a steel rain, chewing the foliage like a buzz saw. Over the heavy chunking of the fifty, he could hear the sharp chatter of AK return fire and heard the bullets blazing past him, but ignored them. The Stony Man pilot should be able to evade the first missile, but if they launched a second one, they'd have him in the bag. The only way any of them were going home was if he suppressed those damned Grails.

GRIMALDI GOT the chopper turned around just in time to see that the missile was headed straight for him on a ballistic path. The Grail didn't have the guidance lock anymore, but it was still flying.

Reflexively, the pilot dropped his nose and dumped his collective at the same time. Flattening the rotor blades killed his lift, and the chopper dropped from the sky like a brick. The only thing that kept him in control of the JetRanger was that he had put the chopper's nose down a microsecond before he had bottomed the collective.

The effect had been to put the ship into a steep dive and not a second too soon. The Grail seemed to fill Grimaldi's windscreen as it passed right over the JetRanger missing the spinning rotors by mere inches.

In the back of the chopper, Bolan looked over Grimaldi's shoulder as the missile flew past. They had dodged that one, but the next one might not miss.

"Go into a hot rappel!" he shouted up to the pilot. "We've got to get on the ground!"

Grimaldi had regained complete control of his ship and saw a path between the trees leading to a small clearing short of McCarter's LZ. The break in the trees was just wide enough for his rotor blades to clear on the sides.

"Going in now!" he yelled back. Hawkins was already in the door, his rope hooked to his harness and his weapon cradled tightly across his chest. A hot rappel was a hard way to ride to work, but Bolan had made the right call. Fifty-caliber or not, McCarter's guys couldn't stand alone very much longer.

As soon as Grimaldi leveled out on a straight course, Hawkins stepped out of the bird on the rope. He fast rappelled almost all the way to the ground before braking. With his boots a few feet off the ground, he punched off of the rope and went into a rolling PLF. Since the chopper was still moving at fifty miles per hour, it was quite a ride. He ended up crashing into a thicket, but except for scratches and the odd bruise, he was intact.

A second later, Bolan dropped into the center of the clearing with Encizo right behind him.

"David," Bolan sent over the com link, "we're on

the ground fifty yards behind you and we're coming up on your right rear.''

When McCarter cut in, Bolan could hear the heavy chunking of the fifty over his earphone. ''Welcome to the party, lads. Do keep an eye on my right flank, will you? I'm afraid it's inhabited.''

''Roger.''

The three commandos took off running through the brush.

THE BARREL of McCarter's fifty was glowing a dull red. He was just about out of ammunition, but should be able to finish off the last of the can in the gun before it seized up and stopped firing. Then it would be a race to see if Bolan could reach him fast enough.

He heard the whoosh of an RPG rocket leaving the launcher and started swinging the fifty in that direction. Seeing the smoke plume headed directly for him, he barely had time to throw himself off the jeep before the rocket hit the receiver of the gun. The detonation of the shaped-charge warhead sent razor-sharp frag from the steel nose cap flying.

McCarter was stunned when he hit the ground. Fortunately, he was close enough to the jeep that most of the frag sang over his head. A heavier piece blown off of the gun breech, though, punched down through the vehicle's thin unibody and slammed into his left shoulder.

Grunting with the impact, he wiggled under the jeep for cover and brought his H&K into position.

WHEN HAWKINS CAME across the body of a muji RPG gunner on his side of the clearing, he paused. Part of their problem was that with the fifty gone, they had no heavy firepower. But this guy's chest-pack rocket carrier was almost full and the launcher didn't look to be damaged. He knelt to strip the loaded ammo carrier from the body and sling it over one shoulder by the straps.

Snatching the weapon, he took out one of the 85 mm rockets and stuffed it in the front of the launcher. That was the nice thing about an RPG; it was idiot proof. With the rocket locked in place, he thumbed back the hammer on the trigger grip and went looking for a target. Hearing the clatter of at least a pair of AKs on his left, he moved in that direction.

Through a break in the foliage, he spotted a small group of Afghans fifty yards away with their backs turned to him. Hawkins smiled grimly. No one promised that life would be fair, and he was honored to have the opportunity to teach these guys to watch their six at all times.

Throwing the launcher up to his shoulder, he sighted in on the middle of the group. Although designed as an anti-armor weapon, the RPG's shaped-charge warhead had a good frag pattern and worked well on troops. When he pulled the trigger, the rocket's prop charge drove it out of the launcher with a whoosh. A few yards farther on, the main motor kicked in to speed it on to its target.

An unguided rocket was never a pinpoint weapon, and the RPG round drifted as it flew through some low-hanging leaves. One of the mujis heard the whoosh of the launch and spun just in time to catch the rocket in the chest as it skimmed past the man Hawkins had aimed at.

The exploding warhead shredded the upper torso of the muji, sending the hard parts flying as even more frag. In the stunned instant immediately following, Hawkins shed the launcher and came up with his H&K. Short bursts finished what the RPG had begun.

Retrieving the RPG, Hawkins loaded another rocket and went looking for another target.

WHEN BOLAN and his team broke into the clearing, McCarter waved them to cover from his position under the jeep. "T.J. and Calvin are on my flanks about fifty yards out," he called over the com link.

"We'll keep an eye out," Bolan send back.

The fresh trio rushed past the jeep and charged the jungle. McCarter's fifty had done a good job of clearing a fire lane for them, and they started coming upon muji bodies torn apart by the heavy fire.

"T.J., Calvin," Bolan radioed. "We're coming up the middle."

"Striker, I could use a little help over on the left," James called back. "I've got at least a dozen of them cornered here."

"On the way."

"My side's pretty clear," Hawkins radioed Bolan. "I'll link up with you."

Hawkins had just about linked up when he heard a firefight break out fifty yards ahead. "Keep your heads down," he radioed. "I've got an RPG and can fire for you."

"As soon as you get your target, fire," Bolan called back.

Another ten yards brought Hawkins in view of several Afghans firing off to his left. He didn't have the best shot in the world, but took it anyway. The rocket lanced out and fell right in the middle of the enemy. When the smoke cleared, he saw the survivors fleeing into the jungle.

"FLYBOY, this is Ground One," Bolan radioed to Grimaldi. "We're secure down here for the time being. But make it quick—I don't know how long it'll take them to get reorganized."

"Flyboy roger," Grimaldi sent back. "I have your Echo Tango Alpha in zero-five."

## CHAPTER EIGHTEEN

*Greater Seattle*

Rosario Blancanales followed the semitruck as it turned off of U.S. 90 on the state route exit. A half a mile farther, it turned again into an industrial area. The newly built industrial park was typical for this part of the northwest, an enclave off the main road with several streets full of boxlike structures painted in neutral shades and emblazoned with colorful company logos.

Blancanales got caught in the oncoming traffic, and by the time he could make the turn the truck had disappeared behind a row of buildings. "Dammit," he muttered when he finally got a chance to turn in, "we lost him."

"There he is." Gadgets Schwarz pointed to the end of a semi flatbed disappearing around a far corner. "He's pulling in behind that building."

The sign in front of the building read Built Rite Custom Cedar Furniture. The truck backed into the loading dock next to another semi with shipping containers tied down to its flatbed trailer.

"That's another one of them I spotted at the dock," Schwarz stated as he consulted the notes he had taken in Tacoma. "We've found the right place."

"Take it around the next corner," Carl Lyons told Blancanales.

Once the Blazer rounded the corner, Blancanales pulled into the parking lot of a FedEx drop-off point and stopped.

"How do you want to handle this?" Schwarz asked Lyons. "You want to do a recon first?"

"That might work real well here."

Lyons turned to Blancanales. "Pol, you want to do the honors?"

Blancanales smiled. "I guess I could always go in and see if I could order a cedar hope chest."

Schwarz snickered. "Hopeless, don't you mean?"

Looking around, Blancanales saw a Hertz rental depot one street over on the other side of the street. "Why don't I go see if I can rent a car and drive up in it instead of using this thing. There's a chance the truck driver noticed us tucked in behind him on the highway."

"Good point."

THERE WERE no other cars in the parking spots in front of the Built Rite Custom Cedar Furniture office when Blancanales drove up in his newly rented Buick sedan. Of itself, that wasn't too unusual. Industrial parks tended to be wholesale or manufacturing facilities, not retail stores. Nonetheless, there should have been something parked in one of the eight spaces.

Pulling right up to the door, Blancanales killed the engine. "I'm in the parking lot," he said over the open com link, "and I'm getting out now."

"Roger."

When he walked in, the combination showroom and outer office didn't look like much, and it was almost empty. Only two pieces of cedar furniture were on display off to the side, and they weren't all that impressive. To top it off, the man behind the desk didn't look like a typical office manager in Washington State, either. He would, though, have fit right into any Middle Eastern bazaar. The men of the northwest were known for beards, but the man's skinny, short stature, dark skin, hair and eyes could only be foreign.

"I hope you can help me," Blancanales said when the man stood and looked at him.

The man didn't reply, but just stared as if he had never seen an American before. Strike two.

"Do you speak English?" Blancanales prompted him.

Without saying a word, the man turned and walked through the door leading back into the shop area. He was back in a few seconds with a partner.

"We no sell here." The second man pointed. "You read the sign."

On the wall was a hand-lettered sign reading No retail sales.

"I'm very sorry. I didn't see your sign."

"You go now," the second man said, glowering.

Blancanales turned to the two pieces of furniture on display. "Do you mind if I take a couple minutes and have a look around?"

When he reached to take a brochure in a stand in front of him, the first man produced a Makarov pistol from behind his belt and held it in two shaking hands.

Blancanales dropped the pamphlet and had his hands up in a flash. It was much too far for him to try to make it to the door.

The second man spun on the first, yelling at him in what sounded like Arabic. Apparently, pulling guns on civilians wasn't on their program. Regardless of what was being said to him, though, the first man didn't take the pistol off his target, Blancanales's head. It was time for him to do some of that politician stuff he was famous for.

"Careful," Blancanales said softly, "there's no need for a gun. I'm leaving."

"You stay," the second man snapped.

Now wasn't a good time to check to make sure that his com link was open. But if it wasn't, he was in deep trouble. With a scared terrorist turned drug dealer he couldn't talk to on the other end of the gun, there was no way to tell how this was going to go down.

"Don't shoot, please," he said a little louder. "I'm not going anywhere."

"You come with me," the second man commanded.

Under the muzzle of the Makarov, Blancanales was careful not to make any sudden moves as he walked to the door leading to the back. The second man opened the door while his partner kept the pistol on target.

The shop area was large and the doors on the far wall leading out to the loading dock were closed. But two of the shipping containers had already been brought inside. They were open, and a gang of men dragged the cut lumber out and tossed it aside. On a table off to the side of the room lay a stack of plastic-wrapped square packages where two more men were going over them.

Bingo! He'd found the proof they needed.

The two men at the table looked up in surprise when they walked in, and an animated conversation immediately broke out with his two captors. Since the Algerians kept looking over at him, he didn't have to speak Arabic to know that he was the center of the discussion. And he also knew that the specific topic was where to hide his body.

If the com link wasn't hot, he wouldn't be leaving this room alive.

BLANCANALES'S COM LINK *was* hot, and the instant he went under the gun, Lyons and Schwarz sprang into action. "He doesn't have a piece this time, does he?" Schwarz asked.

Lyons shook his had in anger. Since there was no way to know what they were going up against, he decided to go large. The Blazer they had rented was a full four-wheel-drive rig instead of being the all-show, no-guts soccer-mom editions that were so popular. It had the heavy brush-guard bumper and a winch mounted on the front, big mud-grip tires and a manual transmission. With the big V-8 under the hood, the vehicle would make a good battering ram. Particularly going up against flimsy modern construction.

"We'll do a vehicle entry," Lyons said.

"Let me drive," Schwarz volunteered.

"Not on your life," Lyons snapped.

Schwarz immediately backed down and went to get their weapons from the rear of the Blazer. There were certain things that the Ironman did well, and one of them was to drive trucks through the walls of buildings. At least this one wasn't brick or concrete block.

Schwarz had barely secured their hardware when Lyons dropped the clutch and powered away. Schwarz wasn't wearing his seat belt when Lyons started his banzai run. It would take too long to get out of it when they arrived on the scene. But he braced himself for the crash he knew was coming. Lyons rounded the corner onto the street fronting the Built Rite Custom Cedar Furniture office and accelerated.

The road between their target building and the buildings on the other side wasn't wide enough to give him a head-on shot. But by pulling wide to the left before he turned in, he'd hit the front of the office at a pretty square angle. Whipping the wheel to the left, he got as much room as he could before cranking it back to the right and stomped all the way down on the gas pedal.

The big V-8 under the hood roared and the tires squealed as the Blazer slammed into the turn. It was moving at least forty miles per hour when Lyons drove it through the glass of the showroom. The sheet glass and metal framing were no barrier to the truck, and neither was the partition wall that closed the showroom off from the main floor.

THE ALGERIANS WOULD have had to be deaf not to hear the crash as the truck took out the front of their building. But not realizing what was coming next, they froze.

Blancanales knew this gambit well; it was one of the Ironman's favorite entrance scenarios. Waiting until the truck actually appeared through the wall, he spun on the man who had the Makarov aimed at him and kicked him in the crotch at the same time that he slapped his gun hand out of line.

The man wailed and dropped the pistol.

Going flat, Blancanales grabbed the gun from the concrete floor and put the first round in its ex-owner. Coming up from ground level, the relatively low pow-ered 9 mm short round tore a long path through his gut before lodging in his spine.

Rolling over, Blancanales brought his Makarov into action against the two men who had been seated at the table measuring the bundles. One of them had produced a folding-stock AK and was bringing it up to fire on the Blazer.

Blancanales opened fire first and dumped half a mag of Makarov rounds into the man. The Algerian fell across the table, knocking it and the heroin bundles to the floor.

The other man at the table was unarmed, but he was frantically looking for a weapon. To make sure that he didn't succeed, Blancanales emptied the rest of the pistol's magazine into him.

WHILE BLANCANALES HAD BEEN taking care of business, Lyons and Schwarz had been taking care of theirs. Even with ABS, the Blazer's speed was taking it all the way to the rear wall. Tires smoking, Lyons wrenched the wheel to send the truck into a sideways slide to kill the forward momentum.

It had barely stopped sliding when he and Schwarz bailed out, weapons blazing. Blancanales had already cut the odds by three, but that still left lots of targets for them.

The Algerians were surprised to see a truck coming through the wall at them, but they recovered quickly. Every man seemed to have an AK within reach, and the bullets were flying before Lyons and Schwarz got their doors open.

The Ironman's big Colt Python was roaring, spitting .357 Magnum slugs as fast as he could pull the trigger.

One Algerian firing from inside one of the containers thought he was safe until a .357 round punched through the thin steel as if it were a paper bag.

Schwarz had his CAR-15 switched over to full-auto and was spraying 5.56 mm rounds. When one Algerian made a break for the loading-dock doors, he walked into the hailstorm of lead and was almost cut in two.

With his borrowed Makarov empty, Blancanales crawled across the floor to the overturned table after the AK one of his victims had gone for. Snatching it from a dead hand, he cracked the bolt to make sure that a round was in the chamber and added its firepower to the battle.

As suddenly as it had started, the firefight ended.

"WHAT DO YOU WANT to do about this?" Blancanales asked as he surveyed the bodies and wreckage. Once more Able Team had managed to completely destroy a perfectly good building. Drug dealers should be cautioned to conduct their business in places that no one would miss. If they set up in run-down areas, taking them out could be combined with urban renewal. This place, though, had been newly built.

"Do we have any incendiary grenades?" Lyons asked Schwarz.

"I've got a couple of the minimites."

"Get 'em."

When Schwarz handed over the small thermite grenades from his bag, Lyons opened the door to one of the containers on the flatbed parked at the loading dock. Thumbing the fuse, he tossed the bomb on top of the stacked lumber inside. Five seconds later, it burst into flame. The second grenade was tossed into the pile of heroin bundles by the overturned table.

While Lyons was doing his firebug number, Blancanales swept up the papers that had fallen from the table before the flames could get them. On this mission so far, they hadn't had the opportunity to do much intelligence gathering, so maybe this would prove useful.

"Ironman," Schwarz said, cocking an ear, "we need to get out of here. Like right now."

Lyons stopped and heard the wail of emergency vehicles' sirens. "Drive," he said.

Turning the Blazer around, Schwarz drove back out of the front of the building the way Lyons had come in. Thankfully, the Blazer was wearing thick off-road tires, so the glass shards weren't a problem. A crowd had gathered from the nearby offices and stared as he simply turned left and headed for the exit of the park as if they weren't fleeing the scene of a crime. They were turning right onto the main road when the first fire-and-rescue truck appeared from the left and swept past them into the park.

Schwarz didn't even dare look in his rearview mirror as he powered away in the other direction.

Once they were safely back on U.S. 90 headed west for Seattle again, Schwarz slowed to the legal speed limit and pulled over into the right-hand lane. No sooner had he done that than a cop car raced past in the other direction, its gum ball flashing red and blue. It was followed by a pair of ambulances and a fire truck.

"Jesus!" Schwarz said.

"I don't know what you're worried about, Gadgets," Lyons said. "We've got our Get Out Of Jail Free cards."

"I have a hard time getting it out of my wallet when my hands are cuffed behind my back."

"Needless to say," Hal Brognola informed Carl Lyons, "you three are the subject of a four-state manhunt. Unfortunately for the authorities, though, they're looking for three guys who look a lot like the ones you took out at the furniture place. They've been encouraged to think that there's a foreign drug-gang war going on in the northwest. Oh yes, the Canadians are also looking for you guys in Vancouver, B.C. I figured that we might as well rattle their cage, as well."

"So we can afford to show our faces and not have to stare at the walls of this motel for a week till we cool off?" Lyons asked.

After ditching their Blazer in downtown Seattle, the Able Team trio had hopped a cab to SeaTac and got on the first flight to LAX. After another round of rental cars, they were holing up in Riverside waiting for a resupply to replace the weapons they had to leave behind.

"You may be there for a while," Brognola said. "But you don't have to hide."

"When does the *Kali* go down?" Schwarz asked.

There was a pause while Brognola consulted Aaron Kurtzman. "The Bear says another fifteen, twenty minutes. He's got a satellite on it, and we can send you a fax.

"And Rosario," Brognola said, "the stuff from the furniture company you faxed us may turn out to be useful. I've got the guys running phone records, and it seems that your wood workers called a certain airfield in eastern California a lot. Since there's a general aviation airfield not far from that Washington warehouse you trashed, I'm thinking that there's a connection."

"When will you have it?" Lyons asked.

"We're hot on it and will get back to you as soon as we have a picture of what was going down."

"Why don't we move out now and check it out?" Lyons suggested.

Brognola knew that the Ironman hated waiting and released him. "The hardware is arriving this afternoon," he said. "So as soon as you link up with it, I'll have your target information and you can run an initial recon. But don't take them down until we can establish probable cause."

"No sweat," Lyons said. He had his own ways of

finding a good reason to take down a problem area. "We don't mind waiting at all."

Brognola was so distracted by the Phoenix Force report Barbara Price handed him that he let that go.

# CHAPTER NINETEEN

*Bangkok, Thailand*

Since Anatoly Komarov's Spetsnaz reinforcements were on "official" business in Thailand, they didn't have to sneak in on one of the notorious sex-tour planes. They came on a Russian Aeroflot Tu-62 airliner in the guise of a cultural trade delegation. But the hard eyes, the short haircuts and the buff muscles left no doubt that they were professional hardmen.

On the way through the city, the bus was flanked by a small swarm of powerful Honda motorcycles, each carrying two men wearing full-face-shield helmets and black leathers. The man on the back of each bike carried a large nylon bag and had one hand inside of it, and each bike pilot had a nylon bag strapped around his waist. The commandos on the bus also had their weapons bags in the seats beside them.

If Big Gold Liu wanted to try them on today, they were ready for it.

THE SAFEHOUSE still looked a little worse for wear after the tong attack. The spall from the RPG round that had taken the front door down still showed on the concrete, and the windows on the lower floor were decorated with bullet holes. But the building was being repaired and readied for round two.

What had been curbside parking in front of the building was now the home to concrete barriers designed to prevent car bombers from getting too close. A pair of concrete machine-gun bunkers now flanked the entrance, dozens of individual firing ports had been jackhammered into the wall of the second story and RPG screen had been placed over all of the windows. To further cover all of his bases, Komarov had also ordered a pair of guards armed with Grail antiaircraft missiles to watch from the rooftop.

If another attack came, the tong gunmen wouldn't make it inside the building again. Short of their using a tank, the safehouse was now safe.

"This looks more like Afghanistan than Thailand," one of the Russian commandos commented when the bus rounded the corner and the safehouse came in view.

"This is a war," Komarov said dryly. "But we're not going to lose this time. Not to some drug-dealing, whore-mongering bastard."

"Speaking of whores," one of the commandos said, grinning, "I understand—"

Komarov spun on him, his eyes hard. "You'd better understand that I will personally castrate the first one of you bastards I catch with your pants down before this operation is completed."

"I'm sorry, Colonel," the commando said, instantly backing off. "I meant no disrespect."

Komarov cooled down a little, too. "Listen, boys," he said. "I'll personally pay for all of you to let Little Boris go swimming as soon as this thing is over. I'll call it your official mission-completion bonus. But if you try that now, all you'll get is your throats slit for your efforts. These tong bastards are worse than the damned Dushmen, and they run most of the whorehouses."

"How about this American team we're supposed to be working with?" the Spetsnaz commander, Major Alexi Lobov, asked.

"Their leader calls himself Mike Belasko, but that isn't his real name," Komarov replied. "I've seen him somewhere before, and he knows Major Dobyrn of Third Company."

"I know who he is." Lobov grinned. "He's worked with us before and he's good."

"Whoever he is, he stood with us when the tong hit the safehouse and he saved little Marita's life."

"Marita's here in Bangkok?" The major's eyes lit up like a pinball machine.

"She's busy right now," Komarov snapped.

Trying to keep the troops' minds on their mission was starting to get old. Damn this place anyway. Why couldn't this be going down in someplace where all the women looked like the cows they milked? But he had to admit that having the Tartar temptress in Bangkok would keep the boys on their toes and trying to do their best in hopes that she would notice them.

"Of course," the major replied. But the smile didn't leave his face.

"I said forget about it," Komarov snapped.

BIG GOLD LIU WASN'T unaware that Russian reinforcements had arrived in Bangkok, but he knew better than to try to take them out on the way to their safehouse. He now had twenty of Al Hosn's best urban fighters in town, and they had advised him that after their experiences in Afghanistan, the Russians took their convoy-security duties very seriously.

In fact, after seeing the improvements they were making at both their headquarters and their safehouse, he wasn't going to try to attack them there, either. Even with the Afghan warriors on hand, it wouldn't be profitable. His plan was to draw the Russians out of their fortresses where his men could get at them on the streets. That was the kind of fighting he knew best, and he had always had success with it.

Liu didn't claim to be a military man, but every Chinese knew the military wisdom of Sun Tzu, the honorable master of war. His writings had many things to say about the foolishness of fighting another man's war. He would fight the Russians, all right, but he would do it in the way that had brought him victory before.

He had no doubt of the final outcome of the battle

for control of Bangkok, but Al Hosn's last report of intruders in the forbidden zone of the Golden Triangle did concern him. Since he hadn't had any agent reports of the Russians moving north, the intruders this time had to be the Americans. Somehow, they had managed to get reinforcements into the country without his agents spotting them.

The fact that his DEA informant hadn't warned him of that meant two things. One was that the DEA man was about to become yet another victim to Bangkok's back alleys. The other was that he would have to increase the money he was offering for information on the Yankees.

AS WAS THE CUSTOM in the American Special Forces units, the Russian Spetsnaz officers led their troops in person. Major Alexi Lobov had a team of four men with him, and five more commandos were waiting as backup if they were needed. Until he got a better feeling for this new environment, he wanted to make sure that he didn't go in too light and get several of his men killed.

Lobov had been a young lieutenant in a Soviet motorized infantry regiment during the later stages of the Afghan war, and he didn't discount the abilities of the mujahideen. In fact, as the only unwounded survivor of an ambush, he respected them as fighters even though he thoroughly loathed them as humans. The image of what they had left of his platoon sergeant's body had never left his mind. The man had been captured, skinned alive and left to die in the sun.

Lobov got payback for that atrocity many times before he left Afghanistan, and if this went as planned this night, he'd get even more.

He turned back to his men and motioned them forward. The four commandos were dressed in night-camouflage suits with black body armor, black sweat rags on their heads and their faces blacked with combat cosmetics. For this job, they were armed with AK-74 5.45 mm carbines fitted with sound suppressors. These submachine-type weapons fired special counterterrorist, steel-core, hollowpoint ammunition from 40-round magazines at 650 rounds per minute. These bullets meant that one hit was usually all that was required to take a man out of action.

The Afghans hadn't made much of an effort to make themselves popular with the locals. The arrogance of men who believed that they had some kind of special connection with the one true God didn't set well with the religiously tolerant residents of Bangkok. Both Thai and Chinese saw no reason to protect these men. In fact, once the word got out that the Russians were paying good money for information on the bearded intruders, informants lined up outside the RSV headquarters to tell what they knew.

As a result of this flood of "walk-in" intelligence, Komarov had developed information indicating that there were at least twenty of the mujahideen in town and that they were staying in two different locations.

The ones who had been spotted on the streets were always seen in pairs, and the locals gave them a wide berth. He figured that Liu had brought them in because of their reputation when it came to fighting against his countrymen.

But that had been a long time ago and under a much different set of circumstances. If the tong leader thought that what had worked so well in the barren mountains of Afghanistan was going to work in Bangkok, he had a big surprise coming, and the first installment on that bloody lesson was about to commence.

Lobov click coded for his two-man point team to move up closer to the small house he had surrounded. He was going to play this one by the numbers and not risk rushing into an ambush or booby traps.

When the point team signaled the all-clear, the major signaled the rest of his team to move in.

THE TWO LEAD Russian commandos flattened themselves on each side of the door and readied flash-bang grenades. The major pressed his ear to the door and heard muted male voices. He couldn't tell what language they were speaking, but that was good enough for him. On signal, Lobov himself booted the door and it crashed open. The muzzle of his AK-74 was poised and he laid down on the trigger as the two grenadiers tossed their flash-bangs, following them up with long bursts from their subguns.

After the grenades detonated, all three commandos

rushed the room spraying 5.45 mm hollowpoints like water from a high-pressure hose. None of the four men in the first room even had time to get their hands on their weapons.

The remainder of the Spetsnaz hit team rushed in, but all of the targets were down with multiple hits. Weapons ready, they fanned out to clear the rest of the small house.

"Damn," Lobov spit when the commandos reported that there were only the four mujis who had been in the main room and the rest of the house was empty. From the intelligence Komarov had secured, he had expected that there would be at least ten men here. But four dead enemies were a good start. They'd get the rest later.

"Take their weapons," the major ordered. "All their paperwork and anything else you think might be useful to our intelligence people."

On the way out, the Spetsnaz commandos rigged booby-trap hand grenades under two of the corpses and one on the front door in hopes of bagging some more of the Afghans when they returned from wherever they were. As had been the case in Afghanistan, this was a no-holds-barred fight, and anything that added to the enemy's body count was in order. When Russians went after Afghans, everything was on the table.

As silently as they had come, the Russian commandos faded back into the night again. First blood in this round had gone to the Spetsnaz. And if Lobov had anything to do with it, the rest of the battle would go that way, as well.

Now THAT the RSV had opened a new round in the battle for Bangkok, Anatoly Komarov knew that it wouldn't be long before the Afghans retaliated. He had done what he could in the line of physical improvements to harden his sites. But along with the concrete barriers in front of both the headquarters building and the safehouse, the RPG rocket screen on the windows and the machine-gun bunkers in front, Komarov had decided to go the extra mile. He wanted to place snipers on the rooftops of his buildings, as well.

The Taliban mujahideen were God-crazed madmen, but some of them made good snipers. Since both of his buildings were in close proximity to taller surrounding structures, sniping was a real possibility. But the Russians could shoot, as well. In fact, some of the greatest sniper actions in history had been pulled off by the Red Army in WWII, and the best countersniper weapon was always another sniper lying behind his scoped rifle.

When Komarov asked for shooters, he wasn't surprised when young Dimitri Polnacek stepped up to volunteer for the dangerous duty.

"Again your father would be proud of you, Dimitri," he told the young officer.

"He did teach me to shoot," Polnacek replied

modestly. "Plus I haven't had a chance to use one of the Dragunovs in a real situation yet."

Named after its designer, the Dragunov SVD sniper rifle was considered one of the best semiautomatic sniper rifles in the world. It was loosely based on the well-proved AK action, but had a longer barrel and fired the full-power 7.62 mm rimmed cartridge of the old Mosin-Nagant bolt-action rifles. Fitted with the PSO-1 day-and-night range-finding scope and a 10-round magazine, it was good for constant first-round hits out to a thousand meters.

"This is a 'real' situation," Komarov said dryly. "If you've studied the after-action reports, the Dushmen also know how to shoot."

"But," Polnacek said, grinning, "they were not taught to shoot by my father."

Komarov had to give him that. The general was a master with a long rifle, and there was no reason to think that his son wouldn't be as good.

"I'll give you half of the night shift," Komarov said. "But I still want you for regular duty half a day. And as soon as the Yankees return, I'll need you to keep me updated on what they're doing however long that takes."

Komarov turned serious. "I trust that Belasko, but I have to have close liaison with him and that bunch of hardmen he imported. He's working with us very well so far, but as we both know, that can change with a phone call from Washington. Their politicians are worse than ours when it comes to meddling in things that are not their concern.''

"Now that we have Major Lobov's troops," Polnacek said, "we have the balance of power on our side."

"That's what it might look like," Komarov said. "They are good men, the best we call upon. But I would not like to have to send them up against Belasko and his people. I think he would eat them alive."

Polnacek was a bit surprised to hear the colonel say that about Mother Russia's finest. But he knew better than to question the wily old fox's judgment. He hadn't survived as long as he had by making too many wrong calls.

As PART OF his promise to share information, as soon as Phoenix Force returned to Bangkok, Bolan went to the RSV headquarters to brief Komarov on the results of the recon. Komarov was stunned when he saw what they had discovered hidden in the jungle.

"That is much more extensive than I understood it to be," the Russian said, shaking his head. "We are going to need more men than we both have on hand if we hope to succeed at destroying that operation."

"And heavier weapons," Bolan pointed out. "We went in with small arms and almost didn't make it out. Someone has been selling the Afghans your Grail missiles."

"As your people gave the Dushmen Stingers," Komarov said dryly. "But, I have to admit, the Russians who are selling our arms aren't motivated by any ideals as were your CIA. They don't care who is killed with them as long as they get their money."

He looked at Bolan. "Or in this case, I imagine they were paid for with heroin."

Bolan could only nod.

Komarov glanced back down at the report Bolan had brought. "Do you mind if I let my operations people have a look at this?" he asked.

"Not at all," Bolan replied. "When I said we'd share information on this, everything's on the table. We don't have conflicting national interests this time."

"You know, Belasko?" Komarov grinned and shook his head. "After all this time, it takes me a while to realize how much things have changed."

"While my people in the States are going over this," Bolan said, "is there anything my men and I can do to aid your current efforts here in Bangkok? We need to stand down for a day to rest and refit, but we'll be ready after that."

"We're doing okay right now," the Russian said. "But if I need help, I'll send young Polnacek. That way the opposition won't see you coming and going too often."

# CHAPTER TWENTY

*In the Forbidden Zone*

The more Al Hosn walked the battlefield where the stolen gun jeep had been found, the more angry he became. Once more, the infidels had come and gone like Jinn in the night leaving death in their wake. And once more, his fighters had not been able to stop or even hinder them for very long. Even the missile they had fired hadn't killed their chopper. He could blame the missile for its malfunction; it was Russian made. But he had to credit the intruders for their fighting skills. Even so, he was unsure what the infiltrators thought they had accomplished with their raid. According to the reports of the survivors, the chopper had been coming to pick up a recon team at the completion of their mission, rather than letting them off.

That could only mean that they had been on the ground long enough to do whatever it was they had come for. From all signs, they had been conducting another recon, but he didn't understand why they had done it. Except for killing the jeep crew to capture their vehicle, they hadn't attacked his fighters in any way until they were surprised while trying to leave.

Then, there was the matter of how many of them there had been. After sifting through the patrol survivors' reports, he came to the conclusion that there were two groups. It was the size of those groups that was in question. Since his fighters had been so decimated, they claimed that each group comprised at least a dozen men. But since only one helicopter was seen, and a rather small one at that, he felt that the numbers were greatly inflated. From what he knew of Western special forces operations, the groups would have been small, four or five men at the most. That they had been able to inflict so much damage to his men spoke of their warrior skills.

The tong leader wasn't going to be happy when this was reported to him. But the hawk-faced Afghan didn't care. Al Hosn was the one who had lost a dozen and a half men and didn't have anything to show for their sacrifice. In fighting off the earlier intrusion, he had at least been able to count one dead on the enemy side. This time, though, there were no indications that his men had done any damage at all, and he felt a building frustration.

He wasn't a man who was accustomed to being on the losing end of a battle, but he was honest enough with himself to know that he had been overmatched yet again. Since the intruders hadn't attacked this time, he knew they would be back and he had to be prepared for it. The biggest problem was the jungle. His men were still having a difficult time dealing with it. The only answer he could think of was to increase the size of his patrols, particularly at night. The reinforcements he had coming and pulling the guards from inside the perimeters would give him the manpower he needed.

*Stony Man Farm, Virginia*

THE REPORT Bolan forwarded to Hal Brognola and Yakov Katzenelenbogen was extensive. But the more they went over it, the more the numbers didn't add up to success. There were simply too many buildings to be knocked out, and more importantly, too many Afghans guarding them.

Katz shook his head. "There's just no way that we can ask Striker and Phoenix to take on all that," the gruff Israeli tactical adviser said. "Even with the Russians backing them up, they'd only have the element of surprise going for them on the first strike and then it'd get real sticky. Plus, the Grails make multiple aerial insertions real dicey. They'll probably only get one LZ drop before the mujis are alerted that there's a chopper working their territory."

"What do we do about it?" Brognola asked.

"It's actually quite simple." Katz looked up from the map. "We need a cruise-missile attack to take that place out completely."

Brognola shook his head. "There's no way the

Man's going to sign off on that," he stated flatly. "He's having enough trouble making the Thais believe that we're not involved in this thing as it is. The street war in Bangkok has shut down large parts of the city, and even though the Russians are responsible, since Liu's Red Door operation is the target, they think we're behind it. All it would take would be for a chunk of cruise-missile debris marked Made in the U.S. of A. to make it in front of a CNN camera and the President would be impeached."

Katz grinned wickedly. "What if that chunk of missile said Made In What Used To Be The Soviet Union?"

Brognola thought for a long moment. Once more the wily old Israeli fox had come through with a workable solution. The Russians also had air-launched cruise missiles in their arsenal. And being Russians, they really didn't care what anyone thought about what they did. For all the flak they'd taken in the international media about their bloody war in Chechnya, it hadn't slowed them down one bit. The Afghans in the Triangle posed a serious threat to their domestic stability, and they'd probably be delighted to have a chance to hammer a few more Dushmen in the process of eliminating that threat.

"They have this one little item in their arsenal that we call the AS-15 Kent," Katz explained. "It's not as versatile as our own Tomahawks, of course. But it's got a hell of a conventional warhead, and we understand that they've been retrofitting them with laser tracking guidance systems. It can be carried by most of their bomber force, even the old Bears and Bisons, as well as the Blinders and Backfires.''

Katz smiled. ''Maybe the Man could drop their president a not too subtle hint. You know, make him an offer he can't refuse, put some economic-development money on the table or something like that if he'll fire a couple of missiles for us. Hell, we can even pay for them.''

''That's not a bad idea,'' Brognola said thoughtfully. ''Let me talk to the Man about it.''

''I'll get with Kurtzman's crew and start working up the targeting data so we're ready to pass it on to Moscow as soon as they sign off on it.''

Brognola thought for a moment. ''Does Phoenix have a laser designator with them this time?''

Katz nodded. On a past mission, the lack of a laser target designator had put the team in peril. That mistake wasn't going to happen again. ''Damned straight. They can light up half of Southeast Asia if they want.''

Brognola smiled. ''They just need to light up the Golden Triangle this time. How soon can you have the proposal ready for me to take to the Man?''

Katz slid a folder across the table. ''How about now? Can you get this to him right away?''

''I'll see what I can do.''

''I called the chopper,'' Barbara Price announced as she stuck her head around the door, ''and it's on the way.''

"While I'm talking to the Man," Brognola said as he stuffed the proposal into his briefcase, "you might want to call Striker and tell him that he can relax and stop trying to figure out how he and McCarter can take on a mujahideen army and live through it."

"I'm sure he'll be glad to hear that."

As soon as Brognola cleared the room, Katz buzzed Aaron Kurtzman in the Annex. "It's a go on the targeting workup," he said.

"We're almost done."

*Thailand*

WHEN DIMITRI POLNACEK led Bolan into the RSV's operations room, the place was buzzing. The sense of lethargy he had seen before had vanished. Now that the Russians had something useful to do, they were hard at it, and while not everyone had a smile on his face, the optimism was obvious.

When Anatoly Komarov looked up and saw the American, he shook his head in wonder. "I don't know what your President's up to," he said, "but I just got a message saying that, on his request, Moscow has approved a cruise-missile strike to take out Liu's facilities in the Golden Triangle."

"That suggestion actually originated with my people," Bolan said. "Even with Major Lobov's troops assisting us, we just don't have enough power on the ground to take them down without a missile strike to clear the way for us."

Komarov turned to Lobov. "Major, are you in agreement on this?"

Lobov nodded. "It is a good plan, sir. Mr. Belasko knows how to read a situation. We are too few to go up against the Dushmen without heavy-weapon support that we don't have. A missile attack will not only destroy the facilities, but it will take enough of them out to even things up for us and will go a long way to giving us a better chance of success."

Komarov wasn't a professional soldier, but unlike many old-style Russian officials, he knew when to leave the soldiering to the experts. If Lobov agreed with Belasko, the plan had to be sound.

"I will sign off on this, then," he said. "Moscow is ready to move as soon as they hear from me."

"Good," Bolan said. "Because I'd like to leave soon. Tomorrow if at all possible. I want to have enough time so we can work our way carefully into the positions to illuminate the targets."

Again the Spetsnaz major was in agreement. "On that topic," he told Komarov, "we are going to need a second helicopter on the infiltration for my troops. His one machine cannot take us all on one lift."

"We have an Mi-8 on standby," Komarov stated. "And you can use my pilot."

"I can get all of my men on one Mi-8 lift." The major looked down at the gun emplacements Phoenix Force had marked on the map. "I just wish that we had gunship support."

"So do I," Komarov said. "I would feel much happier if I had a Hind or two to send with you."

"If we can get in position without being spotted," Bolan said, "the cruise missiles will work as well as half a dozen Hinds."

He shrugged. "But if we're caught moving in, even if we had the air support, it wouldn't help us much. The area doesn't lend itself to tac-air solutions. It's too dense and too rugged."

"Well," Komarov said, looking over at the clock on the wall, "I'll call Moscow and you two get about whatever you need to do to get ready."

USING THE RUSSIAN facilities at their airfield, the mission prep and load out went more like a real military operation. For all their many faults, the Russians knew military operations. Plus they weren't politically hampered by the Thai government considerations as the Stony Man team was. For the most part, the Thais saw the Russians as loose cannons and didn't want to do anything to provoke them. What they did on their own airfield was their business.

Jack Grimaldi flew his JetRanger to the airfield and taxied up to the open hangar. Inside, a Russian Mi-8 Hip chopper was being prepped for the mission. Three Spetsnaz troopers were clustered around the nose canopy of the Hip fitting a 12.7 mm heavy machine gun to the center panel in the lower canopy area. It could only fire forward in a limited area, but it was armament.

"This is one of the field fixes we came up with in Afghanistan," Major Lobov explained, "and I thought it might be of use. It's not as good as the gun mounts you put on your Hueys, but it's better than having nothing to shoot back with."

Grimaldi could only agree with that. The lack of guns on his bird was causing him to lose sleep, and he wished that there was an extra Hip parked somewhere he could trade his JetRanger for.

Another two men were attaching rappelling rope clips to the decking of the rear of the troop cabin. Unlike the JetRanger, the Hip didn't have side doors. The troop-carrying version of the newer Hind assault chopper had side doors, but the Mi-8 had never been designed for that role. If the Spetsnaz troopers had to rappel down to get through the jungle canopy, they would have to exit two at a time through the clamshell doors in the rear of the fuselage. It was a slower drop, but would work as long as they weren't under fire.

Other men attached auxiliary fuel tanks to the sides of the Hip's fuselage. Again, that was an advantage of the Hip's design in that it freed the cabin space for the troops.

Grimaldi didn't have anything extra to bolt on to his machine, so he just opened the inspection panels and started running through his routine maintenance.

WHEN THE Stony Man warriors sat down with the Russian commandos for a premission get-together, it didn't take Bolan long to get the Spetsnaz major to agree to blending their forces. Since the bombers delivering the missiles were Russian, the Stony Man target-marking teams would at least have to have a Russian radio operator and a translator with them. Since that was the case, it made more sense to divide the forces.

Since Bolan's team had made the recon of the main site, they would take it again this time. They knew the route in and had found a good place to keep it under observation. McCarter's team would cover the secondary site for the same reasons. When the translators for each team were picked, Dimitri Polnacek nominated himself to go with Bolan. The Spetsnaz major would translate for McCarter.

With the teams picked, they started going over the maps.

WHILE THE GROUND troops planned their attack, Grimaldi got together with the Russian Mi-8 Hip pilot for a serious map recon. Since he had been through the area, he was able to advise the Russian on how to survive in that kind of terrain when the opposition was armed with heat-seeking missiles. The fact that the missiles involved were Russian-made Grails wasn't lost on his new comrade.

"Damned Moscow Mafia," the Russian grumbled. "They sell our own weapons to anyone, even the damned Afghans."

"We have that problem, as well," Grimaldi replied.

The Russian looked up. "At least they did not sell your Stingers to them," he said. "They are worse."

"Anyway," Grimaldi said, getting off that topic as fast as he could. The massive CIA aid to the mujahideen during the war, particularly supplying them with Stinger missiles, was still a sore point with the Russians. "How much extra fuel did you say you can carry for my bird?"

Since the JetRanger would be carrying the maximum number of people on this trip, it would burn more fuel on the round trip than it could carry internally. If they wanted to get back, it would have to refuel from the Hip's auxiliary tanks.

"I can spare two hundred liters for you," the Russian pilot answered.

Grimaldi did the math and came up with a little over fifty gallons of fuel. That should be enough reserve to guarantee that they made it back.

"Now—" Grimaldi tapped the map "—make sure that you mark the layover point."

They had decided to park both choppers in the same place so they could trade off on the night security duties. The mountaintop was remote, but two pairs of eyes were always better than one. And it wasn't only the Afghans that they had to worry about. The region was crawling with displaced tribal warriors, and they weren't automatically friendly.

In living memory, foreigners had come into their homelands many times. Sometimes the strangers had come with gifts and sometimes with guns. But always they came for the poppy, and the mountain people had learned to live with the intruders. This time, though, they had seen Big Gold Liu's plan as an end to their way of life, and they had tried to oppose it. Because the tong leader didn't require their labor to process their poppies, he didn't even try to reach an accommodation with them. Instead, the Afghans had been allowed to bloody them badly as an object lesson.

If they came upon the two choppers, they would kill first without question.

## CHAPTER TWENTY-ONE

*Bangkok, Thailand*

At first light the next morning, the Stony Man warriors found the Russians already waiting at the airfield for them. After exchanging greetings and performing the final check of their weapons and machines, they boarded their choppers. The two choppers cranked up, and the cool morning air was filled with the smell of burning kerosene. After a short radio check, they lifted off into the morning mist.

The plan called for the two choppers to take off together and for Grimaldi to navigate on the run in. To keep from attracting too much attention, the ships would split up before going on to their individual insertions.

BY THE TIME the two choppers reached the forbidden zone, the morning's mist had burned off, revealing rugged islands of verdant green in a sea of even more green that was the jungle. Having plotted his course,

Grimaldi dropped down to hide in the valleys. Twenty minutes later, he clicked his radio.

"Falcon Two, this is Falcon One," he called back to the Russian pilot. The radio call signs had been chosen by the Russians not as much for their macho images as for being words easily pronounced in both languages. "I'm coming up on my India Papa and have to break off."

"This is Falcon Two," the Russian pilot answered. "Good hunting, Comrade."

Grimaldi peeled off and dropped down into the valley that would take him to the LZ for Bolan's team. The commandos were being dropped off a little farther out than the first time in hopes of finding the LZs clear of the muji patrols. The pilot also cut his airspeed to reduce the sound of his rotors and counted on the density of the jungle canopy to absorb most of the rest.

Dimitri Polnacek was riding in the copilot's seat acting as Grimaldi's observer. As they approached the designated LZ, the Russian kept a sharp eye out for movement below. "It looks clear," he said. "Nothing's moving that I can see."

"LZ in zero-three," Grimaldi announced.

"We're hooking up now," Bolan called back as the three Americans moved to the open doors.

Grimaldi flared out over the small clearing that had been picked for the LZ and once again balanced the machine between rotor lift and gravity thirty feet off the jungle floor. "Go! Go!" he called out.

Bolan and the two Phoenix Force warriors stepped out onto their ropes and made a fast rappel. When they hit the ground, they took up defensive positions around the clearing to guard the LZ for the others. Since the JetRanger could drop four men at a time, the Russians cleared the bird quickly.

Polnacek was the last man out and as soon as he touched down, Bolan radioed, "We're clear."

Counting the Russian Spetsnaz, Bolan had ten men in his patrol this time. It had been a bit crowded in the JetRanger, but now that they were on the ground, they could form up into a recon formation with proper flank security and a drag.

With the brush as thick as it was under the towering canopy, Bolan took up a long diamond with close flanks. Polnacek's second in command, a battle-scarred senior sergeant, took his commandos out to the flanking positions. Since Polnacek had been in the area before, when Bolan took point, he had the Russian follow behind him in the slack position. Hawkins took the drag position with Encizo in the center with the Spetsnaz radioman.

After a postdrop check of their equipment and the LZ, they moved out.

BOTH TEAMS had opted to bed down for the night. Bolan's patrol was up before dawn and got ready to move out. Since smell carried farther on the cool morning air, they didn't heat water for coffee or tea, but took their liquid stimulant of choice cold. It went well with a cold breakfast. A short radio call back to Bangkok let them know that the bombers were loaded and waiting on the tarmac to lift off whenever they were ready for them.

Before moving out again, they policed their RON site in the light of day to check for anything they might have left behind. Keeping this operation sterile was their best chance of survival. A single scrap left behind could warn the mujis that they were being infiltrated again.

Bolan didn't plan to take his team back down to the observation point on the plain because he had the GPS readings they had taken on the previous recon. That was a good thing because the muji patrols were thick in an area of almost a mile surrounding the camp.

Hawkins was on point when they started running into them. Fortunately, the Afghans hadn't suddenly developed jungle-warfare skills, so it was fairly easy to detect them in time to take cover while they passed. It didn't take him long to notice that the mujis were acting like typical FNGs and taking the easy way through the jungle by using the animal trails. That meant that if they went deeper into the bush, they should be able to avoid them.

Going deeper in the jungle took time, but they reached a suitable position around noon. It was a little lower on the ridge than the spot Bolan had used before. But it was dense and still high enough to keep them away from the patrols on the flat. From where they were, the jungle canopy stretched unbroken from ridgeline to ridgeline. They knew, however, that under that seemingly unbroken canopy of green, lay their primary target, a long concrete-block structure full of chemical processing equipment.

After going into a defensive formation, Bolan took a GPS reading on their new location. This reading would give him the proper azimuth to aim the laser on target. That done, they settled down to wait.

SEVERAL MILES to the northwest, David McCarter's team hadn't tried to go back to the position they had used earlier either. Like Bolan, they chose to keep farther away, but when they checked their GPS to confirm their original reading, they found that it had been corrupted.

Gary Manning shook his had. "I've got to reshoot the GPS," he said. "And, I've got to go back down close to where we were before to get the right angle."

"I'll go with you," Calvin James said.

McCarter took out the map and found a tentative location to hold the rest of his team while James and Manning went off alone.

SINCE THERE WERE just the two of them, James and Manning took extra care as they moved down the ridge. With the density of the jungle, it took longer than they had expected to reach a position that allowed them to get the sighting. Once they were in position, though, it took only a few minutes to get the sighting they needed.

"Okay," Manning said. "I got it."

"Let's get the hell out of here," James muttered.

When the two men faded back into the jungle, James took up point. They'd had no trouble going in, but now they started picking up signs of enemy movement. James shot a hand out to signal Manning as he went to ground.

Damn this place anyway; it was crawling with muji patrols. The only good thing about it was that the desert fighters were noisy. This wasn't the worst bush James had ever seen, but it was dense and it took a lot of experience to move through it silently.

He waited until the crashing and muttered Arabic curses faded and then waited another five minutes. "Okay," he finally whispered over the com link.

The two continued working their way around to the southern end of the ridgeline where the rest of the team waited.

"GROUND ONE," David McCarter's voice came in over Bolan's earphone, "this is Ground Two, over."

"Ground One, go," Bolan answered.

"We're in position, GPS confirmed and we're ready to light it up."

"Roger," Bolan replied. "I'll pass it on to the Russians and get them going. The bomber's ETA to launch point will be two hours from liftoff, so keep your heads down. Over."

"Two, roger."

Polnacek was ready on the Russian's radio and sent the code word to Komarov in Bangkok to pass on to the Russian airfield. The confirmation of the takeoff order came back just a few minutes later.

"They're in the air," the RSV agent told Bolan. "They will be at their launch point in a little under two hours."

"Good," Bolan said.

Now all they had to do was lie doggo while two hundred or so Afghan mujahideen fighters prowled the landscape looking for trouble.

*Stony Man Farm, Virginia*

IN THE STONY MAN Annex, Aaron Kurtzman had his big-screen monitors showing real-time images of the target area and the Russian bomber's approach route courtesy of the National Reconnaissance Office's deep-space satellites. When the Russians off-loaded the cruise missiles, they'd have a ringside seat and would be able to track the missiles all the way into the targets. It promised to be quite a show.

"It almost looks like they know they're on *Candid Camera*," Hal Brognola commented when he saw the tight formation the three massive Russian bombers were keeping as they cruised at thirty-eight thousand feet.

"Those old things probably know how to fly like that all by themselves." Katzenelenbogen shook his head. "They've sure been doing it long enough. No one can say that the Russians don't build tough planes."

"How long to the launch point?" Barbara Price asked.

"Their reported ETA is about two hours," the gruff Israeli said. "Once there, they'll have to get the final word from the ground teams that the targets are lit up before they can fire. But the bombers are air-to-air refuel capable, so they can afford to loiter for a couple of hours if there's some kind of glitch."

"When did you last hear from Striker?" she asked.

"Almost two hours ago," he said. "He called to say that they were going to radio silence while they made their final approaches."

Even with the Russian bombers on station, their missiles would be useless if the team couldn't get in close enough to illuminate the targets for their guidance systems. It was always the men on the ground who had the dirty end of the stick. But rarely did the ground troops get in a situation where they had to light up targets for cruise missiles. The danger they were in was unprecedented.

# CHAPTER TWENTY-TWO

*Over Central Asia*

As the three bombers approached their missile-launch point, the lead pilot ordered his bombardier to radio the ground teams in the Golden Triangle to get the initial GPS readings to program the missile guidance systems.

The two air-launched cruise missiles cradled in the belly of the aircraft were AS-15 Kents. Unlike the relatively small, compact American Tomahawk missiles with their retracting wings, these larger weapons looked like small jet fighters without pilot's canopies. They were also much faster than their U.S. counterparts and would cruise to their targets at Mach 1.6. The Bear bombers usually carried a war load of two AS-15s semirecessed in their bellies. But for an increased punch this time, an additional missile was being carried on a pylon under each wing of the planes.

To the Russian president, the threat of a flood of Asian heroin hitting the street corners of Mother Russia was all too real. Stopping that deadly traffic with a missile strike carried a political risk, but it was one that he was more than willing to take. He knew that he would get a storm of caterwauling from the international community about armed aggression against a Third World nation, and he was ready for it.

He didn't expect any trouble when he explained his concerns and knew that he would quiet them. No legitimate nation wanted to go on public record as defending heroin trafficking, not even the nations that secretly profited from that deadly trade. Even so, for this strike, the Kents had been fitted with 4500-pound HE warheads instead of their usual nuclear payloads. No matter what the provocation, popping a nuke to eliminate opium poppies wasn't going to go over very well with the world at large.

The good thing was that he'd have the United States backing his play this time. The American President had warned him, though, that while he wouldn't be able to admit that his country had been involved, he guaranteed his fullest support beyond that. The Russian government was well familiar with the schizophrenic nature of American politics. If the Yankees would only do what was in their self-interests the first time, the whole world would be a more peaceful place for everyone. But they rarely did, and now they had called on him to provide a typical Russian solution. The world really had changed since the end of the cold war.

"WE HAVE the GPS return on target one," the lead Bear's bombardier reported to his pilot. "Take up a heading of one-eight-seven and prepare to launch."

The way the AS-15 missiles worked was that they took their initial guidance from the reported GPS location of the target compared with their own position in the sky. During its flight, the bird checked in with the GPS satellites every ninety seconds to make sure that it was still on the right course. That reading alone would have been enough if the missile had been armed with a nuclear warhead. With a nuke, a hundred yards one way or the other didn't really make that much difference. With the HE warheads, though, the laser illumination from the ground teams was required to give them the literally pinpoint accuracy needed to insure destruction.

The pilot put his huge bomber into a steep banking turn to the new heading and leveled out immediately. "On a heading of one eight seven," he called up to the bombardier on the intercom.

"Bird One preflight completed," the bombardier reported. "Turbine is spooled up. Starting launch countdown."

"Launch when ready," the pilot said.

"Three…two…one…launch!"

The AS-15 under the port wing dropped off its pylon. A second later, the booster engine ignited and it accelerated away from the bomber. In a few seconds, it was flying at supersonic speeds and was quickly lost from sight.

The preflight checklist for Bird Two was completed and its turbine started. Again, the pilot ordered, "Launch when ready."

This missile also separated cleanly and accelerated into the clear blue sky.

With both of his underwing missiles gone, the pilot put his big turboprop bomber into a gentle banking turn to relinquish his position at the head of the line. The second Bear moved into launch position to launch its first two missiles. The three bombers would continue this round robin, clearing their wing pylons first before launching their belly missiles until they were empty.

"WE HAVE LAUNCH of the first two missiles," the Russian radio operator reported to Bolan. "They are targeted against our site."

Knowing the speed that the AS-15s were flying, Bolan moved forward to start illuminating the main target. The dust from the first explosion would obscure the target, but if he kept the beam on the aim point, the second Kent would lock in on it, as well.

AL HOSN WAS inspecting his antiaircraft positions on the high ground to the southwest of his main camp when he heard a thundering explosion behind him. A few seconds later, the shock wave reached him, raising dust from even that far away. He looked back at the camp and saw a billowing dust cloud shot through with black smoke rising from the blasted jungle canopy. He didn't have to check his map to know that the explosion had occurred in the main processing building.

As he stared in disbelief, he saw what looked like a streak of bright light shining through it. The light only showed where it went through the dust, and it looked like an arrow that had been shot down into the camp from the nearby ridgeline.

Al Hosn didn't know what a laser was, but he had read about the laser-guided bombs the Yankees had used against the Islamic freedom fighters in Bosnia. Since there was nothing in the camp that could produce that kind of light beam, it had to be Yankee intruders who were marking the camp for destruction.

Grabbing his radio handset, he started calling the patrols in the vicinity to immediately come to the base of the ridgeline. He was calling to the antiaircraft gun positions to take the ridge under fire when a second explosion thundered in the camp. It was followed by yet another billowing cloud of dust and smoke.

Jumping in his jeep, Al Hosn raced back to take command of his forces. The infidels had destroyed his camp, and they couldn't be allowed to escape to brag about it. He was a bare half mile away from the antiaircraft center when a third explosion took it out and yet another hit the camp.

THE MIXED FORCE of Stony Man warriors and Russians watched from their observation point. The third missile to impact the processing center had blown a great hole in the canopy, revealing the chaos under the trees.

"Does Hal want us to do a BDA?" Encizo asked as he looked down on the raw jagged scars blasted in the jungle. Fires were burning now, which would complete the destruction the missiles had started. There was no doubt that the site had been destroyed, and running a bomb-damage assessment was one of his least favorite things to do. No matter how good the bomb run was, it was a dangerous task. There were always too many of the opposition on their feet.

"He didn't mention it," Bolan replied. "I guess Aaron's going to do it by satellite."

"We got trouble, Striker," Hawkins called over the com link. He was in the northern flank of the team's position and had just spotted a large group of mujis moving into position to threaten them. "I've got a dozen or so guys trying to come up on our flank."

"They're coming after us here, too." Encizo took the field glasses down from his eyes. "I count another fifty-plus gathering below us."

Dimitri Polnacek cursed in Russian when he saw the mujis gathering below. He was too young to have fought in Afghanistan, but he had heard the stories from the veterans. It wouldn't be too long before the Dushmen started launching human-wave attacks at them.

Bolan didn't need more than a glance to see the problem and come up with a solution. "Do those bombers have any missiles left?'' Bolan turned to the RSV agent.

Polnacek's Spetsnaz radio operator spoke English and was making the call before the RSV agent had a chance to translate the question.

"There are two missiles left, Colonel," the Russian told Bolan.

"Tell them to ready both of them for launch." Bolan pulled out his GPS unit. "I'm going to use them for artillery."

"Artillery?" Polnacek frowned.

Bolan looked out across the valley. "We can't outrun them, and we're not strong enough to stand them off. But if I can get a couple of those missiles dropped in on them, it should break them up."

Polnacek's mouth fell open. Once more Belasko had surprised him. He had never heard of using cruise missiles for close-support artillery, but he saw no reason that it couldn't be done. The only question was would they still be alive by the time the missiles hit.

"T.J., Rafe," Bolan commanded, "take the rest of the team up the ridge while you still can. See if you can find an LZ on the reverse slope so Jack can get into it without exposing himself to the Triple A."

"Are you sure about this, Striker?" Encizo asked. He was well acquainted with Bolan's almost suicidal bravery, since he had seen it often enough. This, though, was pushing it even for him. "We should be able to clear out of here before they can reach us."

"I'm sure. We couldn't have completed the mission without the Russians, so we need to get them out of here. If I can get another missile in here while you're pulling out, they won't be paying much attention to you. Jack will be able to get in and make the extraction."

"I'm staying with you," Polnacek said as he unlimbered his long rifle. "You may need a little fire support until the air force gets here."

Bolan knew what a Dragunov sniper rifle could do and appreciated having the Russian covering him. For this to work, he had to keep the laser on target for the missile's final lock and dive to the target.

"The first missile is launched," the Russian radioman reported. "And the second."

"Pull back up the ridge and take cover with the rest of them," Bolan ordered him as he took out the laser target designator.

"I will stay with you," the radio operator told him. "You may need to talk to the bombers again."

If the mujis charged them, Polnacek would need some help, so Bolan nodded his agreement. With the sniper protecting him on one side and the Spetsnaz commando on the other with his AK-74, Bolan activated the laser and, checking the digital range and azimuth readout, aimed it at the center mass of the Afghan formation.

"The target is lit," Bolan told the Spetsnaz radio operator.

To his right, he heard the sharp crack of Polnacek's sniper rifle.

"That Dushman was a little too brave for his own good," the Russian explained. "That should slow them down a bit."

Bolan took his eyes from the laser's sights and saw several dozen khaki-clad fighters coming within AK range.

The radio operator started firing single aimed shots, and Polnacek's sniper rifle fired repeatedly. The Russian was as good as his heritage and rarely did he miss the muji he aimed at. The problem was that there were too many of them.

"What's the ETA of the missile?" Polnacek called out to the radioman in Russian.

The Spetsnaz commando grabbed his radio mike and spoke to the pilot over the gunfire. "They should be here soon, Comrade Captain."

That wasn't the countdown Polnacek had wanted to hear. Bringing the rifle back up to his shoulder, he zeroed in on the muji who looked to be leading the charge. A 7.62 mm slug in the center of his chest sent him backward.

Not taking his eye from the scope, he picked another target and fired.

AL HOSN WAS too old to be commanding his troops from the front, but he wasn't going to let the intruders escape from him again. He had almost sixty men with him and he had sent a second, smaller unit around to encircle the infidels so they couldn't slip away from him and hide in the jungle. This time he would have their blood for what they had done to him and his camp.

The scream of an approaching aircraft turbine made him look up to the north. When he first spotted the black speck in the sky, he thought they were being attacked by a Sukhoi ground-attack fighter. At the last second, he realized that he didn't see any ordnance hanging under the plane's wings and knew that he had made a mistake. But it was too late to warn his fighters.

The last thing he felt was the red-hot blast slamming him into oblivion. He didn't hear the second missile detonating at all.

THOUGH IT WAS traveling at supersonic speeds, the Stony Man warriors saw the Russian AS-15 missile home in on Bolan's laser beam. From their vantage point, it looked as if a high-flying jet fighter were nose-diving into the middle of the muji formation.

"Take cover!" Bolan shouted.

The Kent looked like a jet fighter, but the resulting detonation wasn't just that of the jet fuel it carried. The missile's warhead contained more than two tons of explosive, and it detonated fifteen feet off the ground. Not only did the resulting blast dig a hole in the ground and convert the rocks and dirt into killing frag, but also it shredded the missile's airframe into small chunks of secondary frag.

Most of the mujis were caught completely by surprise. Even those who snatched a glimpse of the missile in its death dive made no attempt to take cover. Those who found themselves somehow alive after the first strike were thanking God for having survived the blast and weren't expecting the second AS-15. The detonation of its warhead sent even more of them to oblivion.

When the smoke and dust cleared from the valley, there were a pair of hundred-yard-wide craters in the ground, and the brush had been scoured down to the red earth for another two hundred yards around them. This barren, smoking landscape was littered with chunks of debris, some of which still moved weakly. Other, unmoving clumps of debris leaked a brighter red into the brick-red dirt.

A few mujahideen fighters got to their feet and looked around in shock. These were battle-hardened men, but none of them had ever been through anything like this before. They had been under fire from the air, but only in the form of Hind helicopters and Sukhoi fighter bombers spitting 57 mm rockets and 23 mm cannon shells at them. Never had they experienced anything like a cruise-missile attack.

From the extent of the destruction, some of them thought that they had been attacked by a nuclear weapon and took off running in fear. Others tried to help the wounded, but most just stood and bled from the ears as they stared in disbelief.

"Okay," Bolan told the Russian radio operator and Polnacek, "it's time for us to get out of here."

No one argued with that.

AL HOSN WOKE to the sounds of both prayer and screaming. He could move his arms and legs, but he felt as if he had fallen from a great height and had landed facefirst in a gravel pit. He didn't need a mirror to know that his face was battered and bruised as badly as the rest of his body. His ears rang and his nose bled from the concussion that had knocked him out, but nothing seemed to be broken.

Choking on the dust still thick in the air, he looked around in horror. The camp he had been charged with guarding was destroyed and most of his men were dead. Not in the worst days of the first part of the Russian war before the mujahideen had been able to organize had anything like this ever happened to him. They had sent death from the sky to kill him, but he was still alive. And as long as he could still breathe, he would seek vengeance for this.

Getting to his feet, he staggered back toward the wreckage of the camp to collect a few items and to see if, God willing, one of the jeeps had survived the attack. He had an appointment to keep in Bangkok and if he couldn't drive himself there, he would walk the distance. Even if he had to crawl, he would keep that appointment.

# CHAPTER TWENTY-THREE

*Stony Man Farm, Virginia*

Hal Brognola took the conference call from Bangkok in the War Room. All the Stony Man players wanted to know firsthand how the mission had gone. Now that the dust and smoke from the strike had dissipated in the mountain air, the damage could be seen from space and it was impressive. Huge gaping holes had been torn in the jungle canopy and the debris from the concrete-block buildings was scattered widely.

The missiles had also taken care of whatever had been blocking the terrain-mapping radars on the spy satellites. Aaron Kurtzman passed around a pile of printouts of the sensor scans showing extensive destruction to the buildings hidden beneath the jungle canopy that he hadn't been able to map before. For the present, at least, the Golden Triangle wouldn't be going into modern mass production of the powdered death it was so famous for.

The satellites had also been able to get several

shots of the battlefield in front of the primary site before the muji bodies were hauled off. The IR readings showed that the body count was as high as Bolan had estimated.

When Bolan was finished with his report, David McCarter came on the line and reported a similar story of destruction at the secondary target. He, however, hadn't had to resort to using cruise missiles for fire support. But he had ordered one extra missile to take out the command post for his site's air defenses.

When McCarter was done, there was the usual round of congratulations. Bolan hated to break up the party, but as far as he was concerned, the larger mission wasn't over yet. The heroin-production facilities had been taken out, and most of the Taliban fighters who had been imported to the Triangle had been eliminated. But Big Gold Liu was still alive and his Red Door tong was still a threat.

Bolan's long experience told him that if the tong leader wasn't taken out, he would simply rebuild and continue his plan. As long as he lived, he would present a threat.

"Hal," Bolan broke in, "the pats on the back are great, but the job isn't done yet."

"I was afraid you were going to say something like that," Brognola grumbled.

"The Man sent us here to put Big Gold Liu out of business. We've hurt him badly, but he's still the top dog in this part of the world. There's nothing to keep him from rebuilding, and I don't want to have to come back here and do this job twice.''

Brognola knew that the President would be more than content to let the cruise-missile attack be considered a final political solution to the problem of the Red Door tong and its Taliban allies. But he also knew that presidential politics were characterized by chronic shortsightedness when it came to potential threats to national security. Going in to argue for a continuation wasn't going to be easy.

On the plus side, though, he had been able to convince the Man that the Algerians who planned to capitalize on the increased Golden Triangle production posed a grave risk to America. He had raised the issue that if they weren't completely eliminated, they might go back to their old pre-drug-dealing occupation, blowing things up. Since the President had been willing to go along with that recommendation, Brognola thought that he should be able to get him on board for a similar decision regarding the surviving Taliban fighters in Bangkok. They, too, were too dangerous to be allowed to run free, even in Southeast Asia.

''Let me see what I can do,'' Brognola said. ''I have Lyons working on finishing up the Algerian connection here right now. I'm afraid that Southern California's going to be on the top of the headline news on CNN again.''

Bolan chuckled. Even when Phoenix Force wasn't on mission, it was a rare day when something nasty wasn't lighting up the news from Southern California. "I want to keep McCarter's people here with me," he said, "and see if we can run some competition for them in the Atlanta newsroom."

"So far, your Bangkok street war hasn't been getting much CNN air time. Since it's not the government ordering the police to crack the heads of 'peaceful' demonstrators, it's just not news. If you can get coverage, you'll really be doing something."

"I don't know if we'll make the news," the Executioner replied. "But we'll sure as hell be sending the Taliban a positive message not to try to export their particular brand of nastiness to the Far East again."

"That will have some value," Brognola admitted. "I'll pitch it that way to the Man. The Taliban has been on the top of his daily summary frequently lately."

"We'll also be helping out the Russians a lot," Bolan reminded him. "We owe them big time on this one for the air strike, and this will show them that we're serious about backing up our friends. We need to do this so we'll have some goodwill in the bank to call upon the next time we need a hand."

"Go for it," Brognola decided. "I'll pick up the flak here."

With Brognola's approval in his pocket, Bolan and McCarter called ahead to arrange a meeting with Komarov.

*Bangkok, Thailand*

ANATOLY KOMAROV looked less harassed than Bolan had ever seen him. The usually dour Russian actually had a big smile on his face when the two Stony Man warriors were shown into his office.

"Moscow is jubilant over the success of our mission," he stated. "As you may know, our new president wants the new Russia to have as big a role in international affairs as the old regime did. He sees this as having been a good first step in establishing that. The Russian bear has shown that he still has claws."

"My President feels the same," Bolan said, "but the job isn't done yet. All we did is push back Liu's timetable, not put an end to it."

"Don't remind me," Komarov said. "That thought has been haunting me."

"I just talked to my people," Bolan told him, "and I secured permission to take Liu out permanently. I convinced them that he still has the ability to rebuild his facilities, and we'll just have to destroy them all over again in not too many months."

"You have a point." The frown returned to Komarov's face. "What do you recommend?"

"I want to take the war to Liu himself," the Executioner said. "I want us to join forces again and take him out of business permanently by wiping out him and most of his organization in one strike. As soon as he's dead, what's left of his tong will disintegrate and Bangkok will go back to being what it's always been. There will still be drugs and gangs, but there won't be an overlord shipping heroin to the Afghans to send on to Europe.''

"You don't think small, do you, Mr. Belasko?" the Russian said. "This is the second time that you have surprised me. I am curious, though, as to why your government is willing to take a dramatic step like that. It is not like your Congress to show boldness unless they have the polls and the media to back up their decision.''

"Don't judge America's determination by what Congress does or the media approves," Bolan cautioned. "The Vietnam era is a long time in the past. Remember the raid on Moamar Khaddafi? And don't forget the Gulf War. Saddam Hussein never thought that we'd move on him like that. He had one of the largest armies in the world.''

"But you didn't finish him off when you had the chance," Komarov pointed out.

"True," Bolan conceded. "That was a mistake we don't want to make again here.''

"What is your plan?''

"I think a night raid in force on his villa should put a final end to this," the Executioner said. "With both of our forces, we should have enough men to do the job.''

The Russian thought for a long moment. "I will try my luck with Moscow again.''

"Just remind them that if Liu lives, he can rebuild his facilities in the Triangle anytime he wants. And the Taliban here still haven't been defeated. That should convince them that they need finality.''

''You should have gone into politics, Mr. Belasko.''

''I can't lie well enough.''

Komarov laughed.

BIG GOLD LIU couldn't pretend that the missile attack in the Golden Triangle hadn't hurt him badly. That was the one thing that he hadn't planned on. In fact, the thought of it happening hadn't even occurred to him. In the past, that level of response had been reserved for organizations that threatened the national security of one of the major powers. He wasn't a big-time terrorist, and he wasn't manufacturing biological or chemical weapons in the jungle, so he had never expected such an attack.

All wasn't lost, though. His idea to modernize poppy processing was obviously not going to be tried again soon. To do so wouldn't only strain his resources, but would also be throwing good money after bad. It didn't mean, however, that he would stop producing and shipping heroin. Wresting control of the forbidden zone from its previous overlords had also been expensive and he wasn't going to throw that away.

He would simply go back to using the traditional, well-dispersed cottage-industry production as had always been done in the Golden Triangle. That system of turning poppy juice into the stuff of dreams had worked well for decades and would continue to do so for decades more. The downside, of course, was that the old methods wouldn't produce the amounts of product he had contracted for.

That would doubtless cause problems for him with the Taliban, who had supported him based on those estimates. But he had a comeback if they tried to hold him to their original contract. He could always point out that he had failed because the security force they had provided hadn't done its job. He knew, though, that was only a partial truth. No ground force could have protected him from the missiles.

The Chinese language didn't have a word like the Greeks did, hubris, to explain an excess of pride, but he realized that he had foolishly reached beyond his grasp. His joss was bad because he hadn't thought out this operation carefully enough. Liu didn't blame the gods for his misfortunes. The gods brought only good fortune; mistakes were made by mortal men and he had made one.

He also felt that the ramifications of this mistake might not have ended with the destruction of his facilities. He wasn't sure that the powerful forces who had decided to use missiles to destroy him would be content to let it rest there. He had roused a sleeping tiger, and that was always a danger. He could only wait to see if it had fed well enough.

But while he waited, he wouldn't be idle. He had his eyes and ears out to try to gain forewarning of any further actions the Russians and Americans might be planning to take against him. He had also made a mistake in discounting the strength of the Americans in this, and he had completely missed that they had linked up with their old foes.

Of all people, he should have remembered that enemies were only enemies for a moment. Sun Tzu had written of that many times. The winds of change blew through the dry leaves of politics, rearranging them constantly. The secret to reading those changes properly was information, and until he had more of it to work with, he decided to go into a purely defensive posture.

BY THE END of the day, Liu had ordered his operations in town closed down temporarily and had pulled all of his troops inside his perimeter. It would cost him plenty to suspend operations like that, but this wasn't the time to count the cost. He had little doubt that the Russians and probably the Americans would try to come for him, and he had to get ready.

He also had his agents increasing his largess among the Thai officials on his payroll, but it didn't look as if he was going to get much return on that money, either. Anatoly Komarov had filed an official complaint about him with the Thai government and hadn't so subtly threatened retaliation if the Thais got in his way. The Americans were more susceptible to Thai pressure, but the U.S. ambassador had gone on record saying that her government wasn't involved in this in any way. Liu sincerely doubted that, but since the ambassador was a woman, he did believe that she was in the dark.

The only way he was going to survive was to fight, and win, a war on a battlefield of his own choosing and he was preparing for it. He had gone through his operations in Taiwan and Indonesia and had ordered as many men as possible to come to Bangkok to reinforce him. They were bringing heavy weaponry with them that the well-bribed Thai customs officials would clear without even looking at. If he could hold out for three more days, he could be strong enough to fight that battle and win.

And while he waited, he thought of something he could do to throw the Russians off, or at least delay their attack.

EVEN THOUGH Al Hosn had made it safely to Bangkok, the Afghan had no intention of trying to link up with Big Gold Liu. In fact, his plans for vengeance included killing the Chinese tong leader, as well as the Russians who had killed his men even if it cost him his life. Going back to Afghanistan wasn't an option for him. He had failed in his mission, and the Taliban leaders of his government didn't reward failure. If he returned to Kabul, the best he could hope for would be a bullet in the head.

Being in Bangkok was also a risk for him, but he was a dead man anyway, so there was no risk so great that he wouldn't take it to get his vengeance. To increase his odds, though, he had abandoned his uniform in the Triangle and now wore the clothing of one of the Chinese engineers at the facility. The man was tall enough and, after being shot through the head, hadn't had any use for the clothing. He had even given up his Afghan hat in favor of a Western-style round cap with a bill in front. It bore a logo in English on the front that he couldn't read, but it covered his long hair.

There were almost six million people in the city, and while few of them looked like him, the Thais weren't an overly curious people. By hunching over to hide his height, he was taken to be a foreign worker and was able to lose himself in the crowds. The Chinese who had donated his clothing had also had a thick roll of Thai baht notes in his pocket, so the Afghan was able to eat. He was also able to use public transport to get around to further blend in.

Going to the first of the safehouses that had been set up for his fighters, he was shocked to discover that it had been attacked. The building was empty, but the bloodstains, the empty cartridge cases littering the floors and the marks of grenade explosions told him all that he needed to know. The men who had been staying there had been killed by the feared Russian Spetsnaz commandos.

The Spetsnaz fighters were the only part of the Russian Army that all Afghans had learned to fear. The Black Commandos, as they were called, usually struck like demons in the night and they were seldom defeated. Even when they were outnumbered, they fought like devils and never surrendered. The muja-hideen fighters liked to brag about the Red Army soldiers they had killed or captured, but few spoke of meeting the Spetsnaz in battle and surviving.

He was almost afraid to check the second safe-house, fearing that he would find only more blood-stains, empty cartridge cases and grenade blast marks. But it was his duty to learn the fate of those fighters, as well. Their fate was tied in with his, as was their vengeance.

THE SECOND SAFEHOUSE was in a different part of town, and Al Hosn approached it very cautiously. If the first one had been found, the likelihood that this one had also been compromised was very high. The Chinese whoremonger had no sense of military security, and he had exposed his men without providing them adequate protection.

This house was set back from the street and, from the street, it showed no signs of having been the site of a recent battle. He knew, though, that appearances could be deceptive. It was too far away for him to see a broken door lock or something as small as bullet holes in the walls.

As he approached, he heard someone whisper hoarsely in Arabic, "Commander! Over here."

He turned and saw Azzam and Seran, two of his veteran fighters, sitting against the wall of a nearby building like common beggars. Both men had also changed into local-style clothing and were wearing

Pakistani headcloths instead of their Afghan hats. They looked hungry and had obviously been on their own for some time now.

"What happened here, brothers?" Al Hosn asked. "Where are the others?"

"We are the only ones left," Azzam replied. "Black-clad commandos came in the night, and we were the only ones who escaped. We went to the other safehouse and found it destroyed, as well. We then went to the Chinese's house, but his guards would not let us come in so we returned here. We knew that you would not abandon us."

"God is truly merciful," Al Hosn said. "He saved you to help me get our revenge on Liu."

"But why are you here, Commander?" Seran asked.

"The Russian dogs attacked our camps from the air." Al Hosn's voice was hard and his face set. "Like the cowards they are, they used some kind of missile fired from far away. They flew so fast that we did not even know they were coming until they detonated. Not even during the war did they do something like that."

"God help us," Seran said. "How many of the brotherhood are left?"

"Very few, and many of them are wounded. I told them to remain up there and try to get back to the Fatherland while I came here to kill the Chinese who betrayed us."

"I will follow where you lead, Commander," Azzam said.

"And I," Seran added.

"God expects no less," Al Hosn said. "Come, we will find shelter while we plan our revenge."

# CHAPTER TWENTY-FOUR

*Stillwater, California*

The general aviation airfield at Stillwater was a small cargo hub, mostly moving fresh produce up from south of the border. Truckloads of fruit and vegetables were loaded onto cargo jets for overnight flights to northern distribution points en route to America's kitchens. Mixed in with the grocery-hauling operations were several other smaller cargo companies servicing a number of small industries in the area. With more and more products being shipped by air every day, industries had learned to expand around the nearest airfield that could meet their shipping needs.

A large number of private aircraft ranging from business jets to pure pleasure craft made up the balance of the dozens of planes on the taxiways and parking spots. Despite being in a semiremote location, it was a busy airfield, which made it a perfect place to transship contraband. With so much traffic going in and out, no one would notice one planeload more or less. Particularly when there was no routine customs or DEA inspection.

"This looks like the place," Gadgets Schwarz said as he drove their rented Hummer into the town that had grown up around the airfield.

"It's a dump." Carl Lyons's eyes slid past the minimalls, strip clubs and fast-food joints. "Find the flight-ops building and let's get this thing on the road."

"According to the sign, it's right over there."

THE ABLE TEAM'S RENTED Hummer didn't look too out of place in the parking lot in front of the flight-operations building. Other high-ticket rides were parked there, as well. Also, since the trio wasn't playing FAA inspectors looking to bust anyone's chops this time, the upscale transportation wasn't out of character for them.

For this gig, Rosario Blancanales was playing a budding entrepreneur wanting to escape L.A. and looking for a good place to expand his small manufacturing business. His main interest was the availability of cargo carriers to handle his product. Considering that the airports closer to the coast were running at full capacity, it was a natural curiosity.

Lyons accompanied him when they went inside, leaving Schwarz in the Hummer to monitor their com links. They didn't expect to run into any trouble at this stage, but their experience with the Algerians in

Washington had taught them to be prepared for anything.

BLANCANALES RETURNED from his visit with a brief-case full of information about the air-freight companies doing business at the airfield, and he was smiling. "I think we've found them," he told Schwarz. "It's an outfit calling itself Green Wings Air Freight."

The Green Wings Air Freight company wasn't the largest operation at the airfield, but it logged a lot of traffic, most of it destined to either the Miami or Washington, D.C., areas. Since neither of those metropolitan areas was known to be a big market for custom-built cedar furniture, one had to wonder why they flew so much cargo from a particular Seattle-area furniture company. Also, it appeared from the manifests that most of the cargo being delivered was relatively compact, as bundled heroin would be.

Even to the casual observer, furniture wasn't noted for being small.

"What's next?" Schwarz asked Lyons.

"Go back up into the hills and find a spot where we can look down on this place."

WITH AIR-FREIGHT schedules being the way they were, the Stillwater airfield was a 24-7 operation. The semis full of Mexican produce pulled in every half hour or so, and their cargo was quickly off-loaded into the planes. It took several truckloads to fill each plane, but as soon as the cargo hold was full, it taxied out to the end of the runway and took off. Another loaded plane took its place every fifteen or twenty minutes, and the return flights landed in between.

Finding an observation point at a roadside park in the hills over Stillwater, the Able Team trio watched the flow of goods at the airfield most of the afternoon. It was the best way to get a feeling for the rhythm of the place. While they observed, Blancanales snapped a roll of film to be dropped off at the quick-photo place on the way back to their motel. Most of the photos were of the Green Wings buildings and the activity going on around them.

"That should be about enough," Lyons told Blancanales. "Let's get back to the motel and start putting this thing together."

"One more," Blancanales said from behind the camera's viewfinder.

HAL BROGNOLA WASN'T too surprised at the report from Carl Lyons. Using an air-freight operation to move drugs wasn't a novel solution. Usually, though, drug smugglers used larger air carriers such as FedEx and UPS. Nor was he surprised at the Ironman's proposed solution to deal with the problem. Lyons always saw himself as a hammer and every problem as a nail. If Brognola hadn't known better, he would have thought that Lyons was itching for a fight to the death.

"The deal sounds okay," Brognola said. "When do you plan to launch?"

"We're going tonight," Lyons promised. "I want to wrap this thing up. We'll check back in as soon as we're done."

"Try not to make too big a mess of things down there," Brognola cautioned. "I already have the cleanup teams working overtime."

"That's going to be up to the Algerians," Lyons replied. "And so far, they haven't shown much sign of wanting to call it quits without shooting at us first. They would have had it a lot easier on themselves at the furniture place if they hadn't panicked and grabbed Pol."

That was one of the biggest reasons that Brognola had been able to get the President's approval to use the Stony Man solution in this case. The Algerians had proved to have the mind-set of terrorists, not traditional drug runners, and their automatic response was to shoot first. If the usual agencies had been given the task of taking them down, a lot of law-enforcement officers would have gotten hurt.

Brognola knew better than to try to rein in Lyons when he was working, but he had to try anyway. "Just make sure that you guys have your Justice paperwork handy," he said. "There's a state police office not too far down the road, and we don't want them responding and getting in the middle of a full-bore firefight."

"Just find a way to hold them at the gate until we're finished up," Lyons said.

"I'll try."

WITH ALL the activity going on at the busy airfield, it was easy for the Able Team trio to get into the busy cargo area. The Ironman's plan was simple—show up at Green Wings, invite the Algerians to surrender, give them five seconds or less and then kill the ones who wanted to argue about it.

Blancanales took the front entrance while Lyons and Schwarz were to go around the side to cut off the rear of the hangar.

The problem was that there were far more Algerians than they had counted on, and most of them were congregated at the open end of the hangar. From the number of cars parked there, it was some kind of conference.

Right as Lyons and Schwarz parked the Hummer around the side and stepped out, they heard a flurry of shots from the front of the building. The Algerians scattered, grabbing for their hardware as they dived for cover or raced to their cars.

"Pol?" Lyons called over the com link as he snapped a shot at a car speeding away.

"I'm okay," Blancanales responded. "Keep on them back there."

Schwarz was trying to do just that, but the Algerians who hadn't made it to a car in time were keeping him from shooting at the vehicles. For a few moments, he and Lyons blazed back until they slowly got the upper hand. This close, he didn't have a chance to use the 40 mm grenade in his M-203, but he burned through two 30-round 5.56 mm mags.

DURING A LULL in the fire, the scream of turbines and the roar of props clawing the air caught Lyons's attention. Looking over his shoulder, he saw a twin-engined Cessna with its lights off taxi to the end of the runway. Shoving both throttles up against the stop, the pilot came off the brakes and the plane started accelerating.

"Gadgets!" he yelled. "Stop that plane!"

Schwarz saw the light from the open hangar glinting off the spinning props of the Cessna as it started its run. It was so far away that he had almost no chance of getting a killing burst into the cockpit. But their Hummer was only three short yards behind him.

SLIDING BEHIND the wheel of the Hummer, he fired up the engine and slammed the gearshift into first. As he stood on the throttle, the Hummer shot forward at an angle on an interception course with the speeding plane. For a vehicle of its size, the Hummer was powerful and Schwarz had no trouble catching up with it. At the last minute, he took aim at the plane's landing gear, threw himself across the passenger seat and held on.

His aim was true and the Hummer rammed the plane's left-side landing gear, sheering off the gear leg. The wing tip dropped to skid on the tarmac and jammed the flaps in place against the windshield frame of the vehicle, trapping it under the wing.

Gadgets hugged the seat cushions as the plane pivoted around the wing tip into a screeching ground loop. With the truck caught under the wing, there was only one way this was going to end—he was going to be wearing that wing unless he could get out from under it. In desperation, he hauled up on the handbrake lever to lock the rear brakes.

Tires screeching, the Hummer broke free as the plane pulled itself away, taking the windshield with it before it skidded to a stop.

Schwarz pulled himself back up into the driver's seat, released the brake and threw the gearshift into Reverse. He was doing thirty miles per hour in Reverse when the cabin door flew open and a stream of AK fire chased him across the tarmac, the bullets sparking off the concrete.

Jerking the wheel, he pulled out of the direct line of fire behind the plane's tail and slammed to a halt. Snatching his M-16/M-203 combo from the floorboards, he stood up behind the windshield and triggered the grenade launcher. The 40 mm round flew in a flat trajectory and detonated right in front of the open door.

Had the gunmen stayed inside the plane, they would have been out of the spray of frag, but one AK gunner leaped to the ground just in time to land right in front of the grenade.

Unfortunately for Schwarz, he soaked up most of the frag and another gunman poked his head out of the door and ripped off a burst.

Snapping open the launcher, Schwarz reloaded before he shifted into first and drove off to the right side to get a better shot at the side of the plane that didn't have a door in it.

He was coming to a stop so he could shoot with both hands clear when the copilot's side window slid open and the muzzle of an AK appeared. Slamming on the brakes, Schwarz drew a bead on the cockpit area and triggered the launcher.

The 40 mm grenade slammed into the side of the canopy and detonated, blowing through the Plexiglas. The small warhead's wire-spring frag slashed through the cockpit, flaying the pilot, copilot and gunman. The copilot and the AK gunner took most of it, but the pilot was wounded, as well.

With Schwarz's Hummer on the opposite side of the plane, the remaining gunmen took the opportunity to flee the stricken aircraft. Two of them turned to send a burst of AK fire into the dark behind them, but they didn't break stride.

"You've got a bunch of them coming your way, Ironman," Schwarz radioed.

"Bring 'em on," Lyons radioed back.

CARL LYONS STOOD as if he were on the firing range, the big Colt revolver in a two-handed grip with the hammer thumbed back. As soon as the first target came into his sights, he tripped the hammer. The Python roared and the man went down.

He heard the Algerians yelling to one another and knew that the muzzle-flash of his pistol had given his position away. Still, the night was his friend. He was standing in deep shadow, and the closer they came to the hangar, the more they would be lit up. When one of the gunmen tried to break off to the right, he targeted him and fired again.

When that man went down, the others opened fire on full-auto. Most of their shots went wild, but a couple of rounds sang past Lyons's head or sparked in the concrete. Even though prudently taking cover might be called for, he had a better view of what was going on from where he was.

Suddenly, Schwarz flipped on his headlights and came roaring out of the darkness behind them. Half of the Algerians turned to face him, but the others tried to break and run. The ones who had decided to run made the wrong decision. To reach the cars in the parking lot, they would have to get past Lyons, and he wasn't moving.

During the pause, Lyons flipped open the cylinder of his Python, dumped the two remaining live rounds with the empties and stuffed in a speedloader. Snapping the cylinder closed again, he thumbed back the hammer. It was show time.

Of the three gunmen running toward him, two carried AKs, so Lyons targeted them first. He fired his first round as one of the gunmen triggered his AK.

Both bursts of fire reached out at the same time, but only Lyons's shot was true. A stray AK round ripped through his jacket, though, and it angered him. It was a new coat.

That sent him into rapid-fire mode, and he tripped off a second round at the other AK-armed gunman. A third insurance round quickly followed it, and before the target even had time to fall to the ground, he spun on the last man. The terrorist screamed and started to put up his hands, but it was too late. He should have opted to surrender fifteen minutes ago.

Lyons put a single .357 Magnum round in the middle of his chest and watched him hit the pavement.

With his area of interest now clear of targets, he snapped the Python open and quickly reloaded. Once he was ready again, he started for the hangar where he had left Blancanales.

BLANCANALES ALSO had a clear area in front of him. He'd dropped the two gunmen in the front office and one in the shipment area. The rest had rabbitted. He was clearing the shipment area, in case someone had decided to crawl into a box to hide, when he heard the sound of sirens in the distance.

"Carl," he said via his com link, "we've got company coming."

"I hear 'em. I'm on the way back."

SCHWARZ WAS still trying to round up the last two gunmen in the Hummer. After watching Lyons pick off their comrades like ducks in a shooting gallery, they had fled into the night. He heard the wail of approaching sirens and knew that Brognola hadn't been able to hold off the local law, so he had to get this wrapped up quickly.

He was running with his lights off, but had lost sight of the main man he was tracking and stopped short of the side of the runway. There was so much white light in the area that his night-vision goggles weren't cutting it, so he flipped them up on his forehead. An MD-80 hog hauler was poised at the end of the runway waiting for the flight controllers to release it, so he would have to wait for the jet to take off before he crossed the runway.

Catching a glimpse of movement to the right, he turned and saw a figure break from cover and race for the runway just as the MD-80's pilot came off the brakes and on the throttles. It was a race that could only end in a collision. The pilot spotted the gunman, but was committed and had no way to steer clear of him without crashing his plane. All he could do was keep going and hope that the collision didn't bend anything too badly.

The Algerian didn't know whether to run for it or fall flat on the ground, and the hesitation proved his undoing. He was shielding his eyes from the landing lights and at the last minute made his move. Half-blinded, though, it was the wrong move. The nose wheel clipped him, sending him rolling back into the main gear. When Schwarz could see him again, he lay on the tarmac like roadkill.

The tower had seen the gunman, as well, and had called in the local airport security to check if he had survived. Not wanting to get involved with them, Schwarz turned, flipped his goggles back down and drove back to what had been the Green Wings operation.

"We're done here," he radioed ahead. "I think one got away, but his buddy just got run over by a jet."

"Swing by the west side of the hangar and pick us up," Lyons replied.

"On the way."

With the cops on the way, the Able Team trio didn't have time to sweep the Green Wings office for intelligence information. The FBI could do that later when they investigated this latest "drug war" shootout. It would take longer for Brognola to get any information that might have been left behind, but he would get it sooner or later. Right now Able Team needed to leave.

As soon as they reached the main road through the airport, Schwarz slowed to the speed limit and flipped his lights back on. He hadn't gone more than a hundred yards before the first of the patrol cars screamed past them, emergency lights flashing red and blue. An ambulance followed with another two cars and a SWAT van behind it. "We're drawing a crowd," Schwarz said as he looked up into his rearview mirror.

"Just keep going," Lyons said. "But be ready to make a break for it if we start attracting attention."

"Break where? There's only one road back to L.A. from here."

"We'll head cross-country."

"Oh Jesus."

# CHAPTER TWENTY-FIVE

*Stony Man Farm, Virginia*

Hal Brognola was well pleased with the job Able Team had done. Once again they had single-handedly eliminated a serious threat that would have taken the federal agencies months, if not years, to do. The body count had been high and the President was doing a little tap dance trying to gloss over it in the name of a drug war, but it was a done deal. All of his problems should be that easy to conclude.

He was going over the reports from the DEA team that was investigating what Lyons had left behind in Stillwater when his intercom buzzed. "Brognola," he answered.

"It might be nothing," Aaron Kurtzman said over the speaker from the Annex, "but we just let an Algerian soccer team into the country and they came through Canada. They're not calling themselves the Sword of God, but their passport photos don't look like they spend too much of their time kicking balls around unless they're human heads.''

''What do you mean?''

''I mean that most of them are far too old to be playing with balls. And they don't have that clean-cut athletic look, if you know what I mean.''

''Who let them in?'' Brognola asked. ''I thought Algeria was still under State Department sanction.''

''It is,'' Kurtzman said. ''But this is some world congress of amateur sport, another one of the UN's brighter ideas this year. You know, one of those 'kick a ball around and we'll all love one another, put down our guns and be friends' program. They've also invited Cubans, Rwandans, North Koreans and damned near every other outlaw nation to play but the Taliban.''

''Wonderful.'' Brognola sighed. What would America do without the United Nations promoting peace, love and brotherhood at every opportunity? ''Where is this terrorist summer camp taking place?''

''That's the kicker,'' Kurtzman said. ''They're playing at different cities all over the country in a kind of goodwill tour.''

''That's even better.'' Brognola grimaced. All he needed was to have potential terrorists on a UN-sponsored traveling road show. ''Who's covering them?''

''That's where it really gets really interesting,''

Kurtzman said. "No one's guarding them. Zip. Nada. Zilch."

Brognola couldn't believe what he was hearing. "Someone has to be vetting them and providing security."

"Not this time. They all came in on diplomatic passports. According to the State Department, they're sports ambassadors."

"Son of a bitch!" Brognola exploded.

"And," Kurtzman added, "apparently at our UN ambassador's urging, the State Department told INS and customs to wave them through when they showed up at the border so as not to be disrespectful."

"I can't believe this shit," Brognola growled.

"If I can suggest a course of action…"

"Please do."

"If we can separate them from any hardware they might have packed in with their 'diplomatic' baggage, we'll have a good start on neutralizing them. Since the Ironman has whittled down their in-country contingent, it's going to be difficult for them to rearm. Particularly the explosives. You can't just go to the neighborhood We-Be-Explosives store and order a hundred pounds of RDX to go."

With this being a UN-sponsored dog and pony show, Brognola knew that he had to get the President involved immediately. But while he was making the case, having Able Team try to disarm these people made a lot of sense. If they weren't packing, their "lost" luggage could be returned to them. But if they had a few AKs and car bombs mixed in with the jockstraps and soccer balls, it would be a good argument to pull their diplomatic immunity.

"Katz is working the Bangkok finale for Striker and Phoenix," he said, "so get with Barbara and get Able Team rolling on this. I'll be right over."

"Can do."

"WHAT DO YOU MEAN that we can't engage them?" Carl Lyons asked. "What in the hell are you talking about?"

"I said that you just can't shoot first, Carl," Barbara Price replied.

"Shooting first is why I've stayed alive as long as I have," he reminded her. "Waiting around to get shot at is why I bailed out of the LAPD, remember."

"I remember," she said. "But the State Department dropped the ball big time when they let the UN issue these guys diplomatic passports. We have to pretend that they're not terrorists."

"Pigs can fly, too," he snorted. "In fact, one flew past my window just now and flipped me off."

"Carl," she said, ignoring his sarcasm, "look, I don't like this a hell of a lot, either, but we've got to play this one real tight. If you can find contraband, the President can cancel their passports and have them escorted out of the country in cuffs immediately. Hal said that even a single pistol cartridge will be all it will take.''

"Right, send them back to Canada so they can reload and come back in twenty-four hours and kill someone.''

"Once they're in custody, Hal's going to recommend that they be sent back to Algeria directly because they entered Canada on a transit visa.''

"That'll be a start,'' Lyons conceded. "Too bad we can't send them back in body bags.''

"If they give you any trouble, you can. Just wear your body armor, though.''

"Okay.'' He sighed. "Who's got the briefing on this rat screw?''

"Aaron's got their travel itinerary, and believe it or not, they're going by charter bus.''

"You would, too, if you were packing,'' Lyons pointed out. "No airport metal detectors to have to shoot your way past. One last thing, do you think Hal will mind it too much if we smoke a Greyhound?''

"I don't think so,'' she replied.

"Good.''

ROSARIO BLANCANALES had drawn the point position for Lyons's takedown plan. Rather, he and a ten-ton dump truck towing a ten-ton trailer both loaded with gravel were sharing the job. The crash helmet and shoulder harness he was wearing weren't the standard

union-truck-driver attire, but he didn't belong to the
Teamsters.

Lyons and Schwarz had decided not to wear cop
uniforms or even go in coat and ties. They were in
jeans, windbreakers over their body armor and base-
ball caps to pass themselves off as locals. They also
ditched the idea of the usual sedan and had rented a
king-cab Dodge Ram pickup. The back seat in the rig
was big enough to carry everything they'd need for
this gig.

Lyons picked up the bus when it took the exit off
the freeway and turned into town. Sliding in behind
it, he kept pace. In the passenger seat, Schwarz keyed
his throat mike. "Pol, we're on it," he transmitted.
"ETA to your location about zero-five."

"ETA in five," Blancanales sent back. "I've got
the engine running and ready to roll."

"Just don't do it too soon," Schwarz warned him.
"We don't want them to be able to dodge out around
you."

"Don't worry," Blancanales replied, sounding
rather cheerful, "I've always wanted to do something
like this and I've got it covered."

"Just don't screw it up," Lyons growled.

Blancanales waited until he could see the bus before making his move. It had taken a lot of talking
and several hundred dollars before the truck's regular
driver had explained how to do the maneuver Blancanales had in mind. Driving out into the intersection,

he delayed starting his turn until he was halfway through. With the truck's turning radius being several yards, not feet, even when he cranked the wheel for all he was worth, the truck's front bumper was almost against the curb on the far side as it came around. The trailer, however, wasn't quite clear and still tracking almost straight ahead.

Reaching down, Blancanales locked the brakes of the trailer as the same time that he stomped down on the truck's gas pedal. The massive Cummings diesel under the hood bellowed as it took up the strain and pulled the trailer onto its left wheel. The weight of the gravel made sure that it flipped over onto its side.

As soon as the trailer hit the pavement, Blancanales bottomed the clutch so as not to turn the truck over, as well. Glancing into his side mirror, he saw the bus tires smoking as the driver locked them up to keep from slamming into him. The bus slid to a stop barely two yards from him.

SINCE HE KNEW what was coming, Lyons was on the brakes even before the bus driver. But he added a twist by putting the Dodge Ram sideways in the road a bare five yards behind the bus so it couldn't back away from Blancanales's truck far enough to go out around it.

The faces in the windows were clearly hostile as Schwarz walked up to the right side of the bus, the crowbar held down at his side. Pausing at the rear luggage compartment, he jammed the flat end of the crowbar into the lock and took a strain on it.

All it took was a single pry and the lock on the rear luggage compartment popped open. He heard a shout from inside the bus and heard someone pull down a window. He didn't bother checking the luggage, but pulled a thermite grenade from inside his jacket, pulled the pin, lobbed it into the back of the compartment and slammed the door. Another grenade went into the front luggage compartment.

Lyons was flanking Schwarz ten yards out, keeping an eye on the windows. Several angry faces looked back at him, but all he was looking for was the glint of blued steel that would signal a weapon in play. It would be more accurate to say that he was praying to see a gun.

When a hand appeared with a pistol in it, he yelled a warning. "Gadgets! Duck!"

His right hand dived into his shoulder holster and came out with his Colt Python. He thumbed the hammer as he cleared leather, had it on target and fired in one smooth move. The face in the window disappeared.

The shot had barely echoed away when the bus door flew open. Lyons spun to draw down on it and saw the driver dive out headfirst. He rolled when he hit and took off running as fast as he could. With him out of the way, everyone else in the bus was fair game.

Schwarz had ducked behind the bus where there were no windows for the ''athletes'' to shoot at him from. Pulling out another incendiary grenade, he pried open the engine cover, armed the thermite bomb and laid it on top of the hot engine. Three seconds later, it popped and burst into flame. In another second, it was burning at a couple of thousand degrees and was working its way down through the engine block. Mere iron and steel were no match for the intense heat created by the burning grenade.

Now that the bus was ablaze and all need for pretense was over, he whipped open his jacket and slung his CAR-15 around in the shoot-'em position. He ducked out just in time to see another window come open and a head appear. When the Algerian saw Schwarz's weapon, he put his hands up and Schwarz beckoned him to get out.

At the front of the bus, Lyons was having to convince the passengers that they couldn't exit while armed. The first two who tried it died. By now, the fire had gotten to whatever had been packed away in the luggage. Grenades and ammunition had started cooking off, adding to the panic as the bus filled with smoke.

One of the Algerians figured out how to open the emergency window exits and they started scrambling out. By now, they had also figured out that they had to come out with their hands up and were doing so.

Only one more tried to take a Yankee with him,

but Schwarz blew him away as soon as he saw the piece.

THE MINUTE the Algerian pulled the pistol, Blancanales was on the phone to the FBI. Using his Justice Department ID, he reported a terrorist incident and requested immediate armed response. Since he had the current Justice Department code word, he didn't get the runaround he had halfway expected. For once, they were taking him seriously and called an immediate scramble. He stayed over the phone, updating their operations center as the SERT teams raced for their choppers.

THE BATTLE of the soccer team was over when the first FBI choppers carrying their SERT teams flashed overhead. Lyons and Schwarz held their Justice Department badges high in their off hands so some trigger-happy federal sniper didn't take offense to the hardware in their right hands.

They had the surviving Algerians flat on their faces, so there should be no trouble identifying the good guys from the bad. Nonetheless, with the FBI, it never hurt to make sure that they got the message loud and clear.

The first chopper off-loaded its six men in a low rappel, the kind that looks so good on TV. Able Team had been so busy they hadn't really noticed if the local media vans had arrived yet. But if the FBI was showboating, the chances were good they were doing it for the cameras.

These six black-clad commandos cleared the way for the second machine to land. Along with another six SERT men, it also carried a suit. He had a blue nylon windbreaker with "FBI" emblazoned on the back.

Blancanales introduced himself as a Justice Department special agent and flashed his tin and said, "We had a tip that this so-called soccer club might be a cover for an Algerian Sword of God action team."

"You're kidding?" The FBI guy was shocked.

"Not a bit." Blancanales kept a straight face. "It went out as an interdepartmental memo."

"Damn," the FBI man said. "I must have missed that notice. I'll have someone's butt if I find out that it wasn't forwarded to me."

No FBI agent needed to fear being called on the carpet on that account. Blancanales had made up that memo while he was talking to this guy. The way interdepartmental communications in the Justice Department went, it would take months to find out if such a memo even existed and even more months after that to get a copy.

"Anyway," Blancanales continued, "we want to turn these guys over to you and have you impound the bus. When your forensic guys go over it, they're going to find weapons, ammunition and grenade frag.''

"Yeah," the FBI man said, making a note. "We'll have to check that."

Now that the FBI was on the scene, the ambulances came in to treat the wounded and carry off the dead. Two of the Algerians had to be handcuffed while their burns were being treated, but the rest were in no mood to take on men with H&Ks in their hands. Their imams had promised them that they would be protected by the United Nations and that no Yankee cop would be able to touch them. Most of them had the attitude that God had willed them to be defeated today, but a couple of the younger men had started to doubt what their self-appointed leaders were telling them.

It was hard to believe that God was on your side when you kept losing all the time.

"DAMN," Brognola said when Barbara Price reported that Lyons had called to report mission closure on the soccer team. "That was quick. What's the body count this time?"

"One bus and four Algerians. The rest of the 'team' is in FBI custody on terrorist charges."

"How about the weapons?"

"As soon as the fire cools off a little more, the FBI plans to sift the ashes for them. But Carl said that half a dozen grenades and quite a bit of small-arms ammunition cooked off in the blaze.''

Brognola looked startled. ''What fire?''

''The one they started in the bus's luggage compartment to see if they were packing.''

Brognola slowly shook his head. ''I'll just wait for their report to get the details.''

''Maybe you should.'' She smiled. ''Oh, one last thing from Carl...''

''Yes?''

''He wants to know if they're done now.''

''I hope so.''

# CHAPTER TWENTY-SIX

*Bangkok, Thailand*

As part of their pre-Liu villa raid planning process, Bolan, David McCarter, Dimitri Polnacek and Major Alexi Lobov were making an aerial recon of their target in broad daylight using Phoenix Force's Jet-Ranger chopper. Since it was in civilian markings, they were counting on it not drawing the amount of attention that the Russian-military-marked Mi-8 would have. There was still a risk, but the available maps of the area weren't well detailed, and attacking without knowing what they were going up against was a recipe for disaster.

"He has a very good location to defend," the Spetsnaz major commented as they approached Liu's walled villa. "He has the high ground, and that wall is not going to be easy to get over if it is well defended. I can see firing steps built on the inside face."

"But it's a long perimeter," McCarter reminded him. "If we can run a diversion at a likely attack point, we should be able to suck his forces in to deal with that while we come in at another point. It would take twice the men we think he has for him to cover all of that wall adequately. I think we can make him anxious, and anxious men make mistakes. Particularly anxious amateurs. Being a tong leader doesn't train a man to be a good tactical leader.''

''You have a point,'' the major conceded.

''We also need to talk to your boss about using his chopper as fire support,'' Bolan said. ''That heavy gun in the nose could be our key to suppressing his forces long enough for us to get in at them.''

''I will see that he releases it to me,'' Lobov promised. ''You can be sure of that. When he called us down here to work for him, he promised that we would have anything we needed. He will have no choice on that.''

Bolan chuckled. The new Russian military might be subordinate to the civilian government, but the old attitudes weren't going to die out easily. The old KGB-Red Army conflicts were still remembered.

As they cruised through the heavy, smog-laden sky of Bangkok, Polnacek leaned out of the chopper's open side door and took a series of photos of the villa itself and the approach routes. They would be developed at the RSV headquarters and blown up to help them plan their strike.

They had started their survey from half a mile out and were working their way in closer to cover every square yard of the ground. They had just finished a pass over the villa itself when Grimaldi called back over the intercom.

"I think we've about used up our welcome in this neighborhood," he said. "One of those jokers down there is playing with what looks to me like a Grail missile launcher."

Bolan turned to Polnacek. "You got enough shots?"

"I'm finished."

"Okay, Jack," Bolan called up. "Break it off and head south. We'll fly out of sight before swinging around and going back to the landing field."

"Got you covered."

AL HOSN HAD hardly noticed the JetRanger fly over him on its way to Liu's villa. Choppers flew over the city all the time, and there was no way that it could be looking for him. Beyond the two fighters with him, no one else knew that he was in Bangkok. And, if he had anything to do with it, no one would know until he buried his knife in the fat Chinese's belly and gutted him.

That one was much too big to skinned alive, but he would still skin him and nail the bloody hide to the door of his largest gambling house as a warning to the Asian infidels not to betray the Taliban.

The Afghan was also on a recon, but he was doing it the old-fashioned way, infiltrating the enemy camp on foot. During the Russian war he had been known for leading night attacks on Russian camps and he knew the value of a recon. It would take him most of the day, but when he was done, he would know the villa's weak points. And, once he knew them, Liu would be his to take.

THE STONY MAN warriors were reloading magazines and going over their gear in preparation for the night assault on the villa. Going up against the overpowering odds they were facing meant carrying a double load of ammunition and as many grenades as they could carry. With the Spetsnaz bringing the RPGs for heavy firepower, they should have the tools to do the job.

"Striker," McCarter said, handing Bolan one of their cell phones, "Dimitri wants to talk to you."

Bolan took the phone and answered, "Belasko."

"There's been a change in our plans," the Russian said, his voice tight. "You should come to headquarters as soon as you can. Please bring McCarter, as well."

Bolan understood the Russian's reluctance to say more over a nonsecure land line and turned to McCarter. "Apparently something serious has come up," he said. "Komarov wants to see both of us."

"I hope the bastards aren't backing out on us," McCarter said. His experience during the years of the cold war hadn't made him a big Russian fan. Phoenix

Force had worked with them very successfully many times since the fall of the iron curtain, but he still had lingering doubts.

"I don't think so," Bolan replied. "It didn't sound that way. It sounded more like Liu making some kind of move against them."

"Rafe," Bolan said, "keep on alert and I'll get back to you as soon as we can."

"Got it covered, Striker."

THE GRIM ATMOSPHERE in the Russian ops center was back in spades. No one was smiling or joking. When Anatoly Komarov spotted Bolan, he took him aside for a private talk.

"Liu's men grabbed Marita," he said. "She was coming out of a temple and they overwhelmed her."

Bolan didn't ask what it had cost the tong gunmen to take her, but he was sure that she had at least left her mark on a few of them.

Komarov shook his head. "This is like one of your American movies where the terrorists grab the woman."

"A bad movie," Bolan said. "And if Liu's seen any of them, he has to know what's coming next."

"He thinks that he can buy peace between us by holding her captive. He thinks we are like Americans."

Komarov looked at Bolan. "Sorry."

"No offense taken," Bolan replied. Starting with

the Iran embassy incident, America's history of caving in to terrorist kidnappings was as disgraceful as it was long.

"It's obvious," he said, "that Liu isn't familiar with the usual Russian response to having one of their people kidnapped."

"He will learn immediately," Komarov vowed.

"This isn't like Beirut, though," Bolan pointed out. "Anyone that Liu cares about is safe inside his compound. A counterkidnapping isn't going to work this time."

"Killing him is still an option," Komarov pointed out.

"Freeing Marita first sounds better to me," Bolan said, "and I have an idea."

"I am willing to listen," the Russian said.

"Obviously, our attack plan will have to be modified. If we go in as we had planned, he's likely to kill her the minute the assault begins."

"A good point. What do you suggest?"

"I'll go in first and rescue her."

"Alone?" Komarov asked.

"It's best that way."

The Russian seemed to ponder that idea, so Bolan continued. "It's not a matter of national pride this time, Anatoly. I've done this kind of thing many times before, and I know what to do. I need your troops to be the assault force to cover me after I get to her. They are well-trained for that and, even with the rest of my people joining them, they're going to have their hands full during the first few moments. They won't have time to get to her before she's killed.''

''I agree,'' Komarov said, and then he smiled grimly. ''Marita will be surprised to see you.''

''If I can get in there in time.'' The tongs weren't known for having much compassion for their kidnap victims, particularly the women they grabbed. But, one way or the other, he'd get her out. ''But I can move quickly.''

''There is that,'' Komarov admitted. He, too, didn't want to think of the RSV without its top female agent. But once more the mysterious American had cut to the chase.

''One last thing,'' Bolan said. ''Before I go back to McCarter and the major to work out the details. We're going to need to borrow your helicopter because it mounts that heavy machine gun. We'll need the fire support to make sure that we can get a foothold inside.''

''Moscow is going to hang me for this anyway.'' Komarov shrugged. ''So why not? I'll have the pilot paint out the stars and the numbers on it so it won't be so obvious.''

''The Thais will know,'' Bolan warned. ''There aren't too many Mi-8s in town.''

Komarov looked at him and smiled grimly. ''What is it you Yankees say—'fuck them'?''

Bolan nodded. ''That's what we say, all right.''

MARITA WOKE to find herself shackled to a narrow bed. The smell of chloroform was still heavy on her skin. She turned her head and spit on the floor to get it out of her mouth. Her head felt bruised, as if she had taken a blow, and her face was tender, as well. Since she was still wearing her clothing, apparently they hadn't started the fun and games she knew was to come. She knew that she could withstand a little rape; it came with the job. Just as long as they didn't start cutting her or breaking her bones, she'd be okay for a while.

Looking around, she saw that she was in what had to be a basement room. There were no windows and from where she lay, she could see a stairwell leading upward. If that was the only exit, it was going to be tough for her boys to get her out of here. She knew of the coming attack, and the plans didn't include storming the villa for a hostage rescue. If they changed plans and tried to save her, good men would die.

She heard a chair scraping and turned her head to see a grinning Chinese tong gunman leering at her. Next to the mujahideen, she hated the tong gangsters more than anyone on Earth. They were all subhuman garbage, and now she'd had the misfortune to have fallen into their hands.

"Let me talk to Liu," she told the guard in Cantonese.

The guard stood and walked over to her, leering all the way. "Maybe you and me can have a little fun first," he said, sneering.

"I will bite your withered man stalk off," she hissed. "Tell your big man that I am awake."

"Russian bitch," he spit as he walked to the phone on the other side of the room.

The guard spoke in a dialect that she didn't completely understand, but she picked out that Liu was coming to see her and she steeled herself.

BIG GOLD LIU had an escort of five men when he went down into his basement room. He knew about his captive's reputation and would take no chances with her. Maybe he'd have his men break her legs to keep her where he wanted her.

The Russian she-devil had been captured almost by accident. One of his officers had been on a mission with half a dozen of his men when he spotted her coming out of a temple to cats of all things. Recognizing her from his surveillance of the RSV headquarters, he saw a chance and took it. Fortunately, he'd had a bottle of chloroform in the car and used it to good effect. As a reward, Liu had promised the man that she would be given to him for disposal when he was finished with her. The condition she would be in by then would depend mostly on her.

"And just which gangster dog are you?" Marita asked when he walked up.

"I am the man who holds your life," Liu answered. "To call me names will only shorten it. And," he added, "cause you much pain."

At Liu's direction, one of his men held a gun to her head while the other four unshackled her from the bed and carried her over to the wall. Four shackles with chains and dark stains on the wall around them told her that she wasn't the first prisoner who had been held there.

For a brief moment, she considered committing suicide by making one of her moves and forcing the guard to shoot her. But life was still strong in her, as strong as her faith in her battle comrades. The Spetsnaz had a code of never leaving one of their own behind, and while she wasn't actually one of the commandos, she was their favorite RSV agent.

Having made her decision, she allowed the guards to affix the shackles to her wrists and ankles. Once they were attached, the gunmen adjusted the chains to hold her legs apart and her arms out. When she was secure, Liu moved closer.

"I have heard about you," he said. "The locals here call you the tigress, so I will keep you well caged."

"I don't think you want to know what the Thais call you."

Without changing expression, Liu stepped up to her

and drove his fist into her solar plexus. The force of the blow left her gasping for breath. She had known that this part of it was going to start sooner or later. It might as well begin now so she would pass out that much sooner.

"You have nothing to say." Liu smiled as she fought to breathe. "That is good. Women should watch their mouths."

"As should pigs like you," she gasped.

Liu didn't let others administer punishment for him; it was bad for business. He also liked inflicting pain, and he was good at it. He had made a study of the nerves of the human body and knew how to make them respond as if he were playing an instrument.

Slipping a hand into his jacket pocket, he took out a pair of gloves that had been fitted with small needles and metal forms designed to apply pressure to nerve clusters. He slowly put them on before walking up to her. Reaching out, he put his hands on the base of her neck and went to work.

Marita screamed against her will. Her arms and shoulders felt as if they were on fire, and she slumped against the chains holding her wrists.

Liu stepped back to admire his work. This was just the opening move in what would become an artwork. He knew what this woman was, but her training and skills would be of little use to her here. She thought that she was as tough as any man, but she wouldn't have the reserves of strength that a man would. After he had sharpened her up with the careful application of pain, he would start tearing her apart and learn what the Russians were planning.

He could tell from the relaxing of the small muscles of her eyes that she had overcome the pain and moved in to give her another dose. She would control that one, as well, but there would soon come a time when all of her nerves would scream for relief. Only then would he start talking to her.

BOLAN WAITED in the shadows until he heard David McCarter's voice in his earphone. "We're in position, Striker. But wait till the lights go out and the demonstration starts."

Even on such short notice, the RSV had been able to gather a small group of their informers and pay them to hold a demonstration by the main gate of Big Gold's compound. The plan was that they would cause Liu to send reinforcements and weaken his forces on the other parts of his wall.

"Roger," Bolan sent back.

"T.J.," McCarter radioed, "anytime you're ready."

"It'll be just another minute or two," Hawkins answered from two blocks away. "Gary's setting the last of the charges right now."

Manning and Hawkins were working on one of the concrete power poles on the feeder line that led to Liu's villa. After making a last connection, Manning rappelled down to the ground. "We're a go," he told Hawkins.

Hawkins keyed his mike and said, "Fire in the hole."

Manning hit the switch on his demo transmitter. The minicharges he had placed on the transformer popped, and it shorted out, plunging a forty-block area into darkness.

"We're dark," Hawkins sent.

Losing power wasn't as big a deal in Bangkok as it would have been in a similar-sized American city. Many of the city's six million inhabitants didn't have power anyway, and those that did couldn't depend on it. To call Bangkok's electrical system overloaded would be a classic understatement. That it was also based on a 1930s French-engineered electrical system didn't help matters any. Intermittent power outages were so common that most of the population hardly even noticed them anymore. The locals either had generators as backups or lit kerosene lanterns to hold back the dark.

## CHAPTER TWENTY-SEVEN

*Bangkok, Thailand*

In the basement of his villa, Big Gold Liu hardly noticed the flickering of his lights as the power failed and his auxiliary generators cut in. The generators were well muffled, and the power room was sealed off from the rest of the house. Also, his focus was centered on his hostage, to the exclusion of everything else. She had shaken off her most recent dose of pain, so it was time to add a little physical battery to the dose. In his experience, women feared that more than anything else.

Stepping forward, he smashed his fist into the side of Marita's face, snapping her head around. She hung in the chains for a moment, her head down.

"You know what I want to hear from you," he said in English. "It will save you pain if you talk now."

"Your mother was a mongrel dog with three legs

and your father was a hairy barbarian with a bent stalk,'' she gasped in prefect Cantonese.

The tong leader bristled at the calculated insult, but he knew the game this devil woman was playing. If he killed her in anger, her pain would be over and her value as a hostage would be ended. He was moving for her again when one of his guard officers ran into the room.

"Lord," the man said, "the local dogs are holding some kind of demonstration in front of our gate."

"What do they want?"

"Who knows?" The officer shrugged. "I cannot read the barbarian chicken scratching they call a written language."

"Get reinforcements out front immediately."

"As you wish."

Liu's shutting down of his establishments had thrown a number of locals out of work. While his Red Door men held all the top and middle positions in his houses, he used locals for cleaning and the other scut work. Since the Thais were famous for labor-union unrest, maybe the demonstration was related to that. Whatever it was, he would tolerate very little of it.

BOLAN's PADDED grappling hook made no noise as it caught on one of the outward-leaning spikes on top of the twelve-foot wall. A quick tug locked the hook in place, and he quickly climbed to the top. To keep from catching his gear on the spikes, he laid a Kevlar sheet across them before wiggling over to drop down the other side.

Crouching at the base of the wall, he scanned the grounds in front of him with his night-vision goggles before moving out. The demonstration accomplished what it had been designed to do; the grounds on this side of the villa were clear. The night breeze brought him the sounds of the people chanting over the normal traffic sounds of the city. He could also hear shouted commands that had to be from Liu's men forming by the front gate.

He was breaking cover when he caught the sound of feet pounding across the grass behind him. Dropping into a crouch, he spun, his H&K MP-5 SD ready, and triggered a short burst. The subsonic, suppressed 9 mm hollowpoint slugs caught the dog full in the chest. The force of the hits slammed the leaping animal off course and it crumpled, dead, at Bolan's feet.

Even with the sound suppressor and the subsonic ammunition, the MP-5 SD subgun wasn't completely silent. Bolan stayed crouched and waited to see if a dog handler would follow the animal. But when no one showed, he figured that the dog had been loosed to patrol freely.

If there was one dog, there might be more. Slinging the MP-5 over his shoulder, he drew his Beretta 93-R and fitted its custom sound suppressor. It used the same ammo as the subgun, but it was quieter when it cycled.

His plan was to approach the main house from the rear, through the extensive Chinese gardens. He had studied the photos of the grounds and felt that the garden gave him more cover on the approach than trying to cross the broad expanse of lawn in the front. He would have to pass by one of the barracks on his way in, but he didn't think that they would have guards posted outside it. Even with the guards alerted to the demonstration, they wouldn't be expecting trouble inside their perimeter. At least not yet.

He entered the garden and took cover momentarily to scan the grounds with his night-vision goggles. Again, his path was clear. Moving through it quickly, he reached the villa and hugged the wall by the rear patio doors.

"Lion," Bolan whispered into his throat mike, "this is Belasko. I'm in position."

"Roger," Major Alexi Lobov replied. "I will call Eagle."

Lobov's Spetsnaz commandos were locked and loaded, ready to go to war. They were wearing night-vision-device-defeating camouflage uniforms in shades of black and gray. Ballistic helmets with built-in com gear and NVGs, body armor and assault harnesses completed their kit. They were armed to the teeth with their AK-74 assault rifles, frag grenades, silenced pistols and fighting knives. Double basic loads and extra grenades made sure that they could carry the fight to the finish. The knowledge that this wouldn't be a cakewalk was amplified by the combat first-aid packs they all carried on the backs of their belts.

They were going in and wouldn't come out until they were victorious. Liu had captured one of their own, and he had to be taught the price for that outrage. Everything he controlled would be totally destroyed after he was killed. They would make an example of him that no one in the region would ever forget.

"Eagle," Lobov spoke into his handset in English, "we are all in position.

"Eagle roger," a Russian voice answered. "We are inbound. ETA three minutes."

"Striker," McCarter's voice came over Bolan's earphone, "we're in place and ready to move."

"Roger," Bolan sent back.

AROUND THE CORNER of the main gate, Al Hosn knelt against the base of the wall. At the last moment, he had decided to let his last two mujahideen fighters stay back and go it alone. To do what he had come for, two more men wouldn't make any difference. He would depend on stealth and his own skills alone to make his vengeance.

He hadn't been surprised when the streetlights had gone out. He had been in Bangkok long enough to expect that to happen. Hearing the demonstrators start chanting, though, he had to investigate. When he saw the group carrying their signs and torches, he thanked God for providing him with such a perfect diversion. With Liu's guards distracted, it would be easy for him to make it over the wall.

He was ready to make his move when he heard the faint sound of a helicopter approaching in the distance. Knowing that the Russians had such a machine, he paused to see if it, too, was coming after Liu.

THE RSV PILOT was flying the Mi-8 with Jack Grimaldi behind the nose-mounted 12.7 mm heavy machine gun. He would have rather been behind the Hip's cyclic and collective, but he knew when to back off and let a better man do the flying chores. Plus, he was also a better than average aerial gunner.

The Russian chopper had been orbiting well out of sight of Liu's villa, waiting for the word to start its gun run. The first pass would be against the fortified main gate of the compound. Even the heavy 12.7 mm slugs wouldn't do much real damage against the concrete defenses Liu had in place there. But it would force the guard's heads down and give the waiting Spetsnaz RPG gunners a chance to get in close enough to use their deadly rockets.

BOLAN HAD TAKEN the call to the chopper as his signal to make his move on the villa. The blade of his Tanto fighting knife slipped in between the doorjamb and came up against the bar of the lock. Pressing upward, he was pleased to feel it move and knew that it was a simple swing latch rather than a dead bolt. Apparently, the tong leader depended on his men instead of common-sense security measures to protect him.

Night-vision goggles over his eyes, he eased the door open and slipped into a darkened room. No one was in sight, so he crossed to the nearest door. Without a plan of the villa, he would have to search to find where Liu was holding Marita. But he had an idea where she was being held. Human nature was cross-cultural and men most often tortured other humans out of the light of day.

Stepping out into the hall, he started looking for a way down into the basement.

AL HOSN HEARD the sound of the helicopter rotors grow louder, and his mind flashed back to the war on the Afghan plains. The Russian Hind gunships had sounded like that when they started their gun runs, and he took cover behind a concrete light pole. As he had expected, the blacked-out helicopter started firing as soon as it came in range. The heavy thunking of the 12.7 mm gun was also very familiar to him. The reliable long-range Russian guns had quickly become a favorite mujahideen item, and capturing one of them from the enemy was always considered a coup.

The 12.7 mm slugs were falling like steel rain with most of the fire concentrated in the elaborate facade of the main gate and the machine-gun bunkers on each side. It was an impressive show, but he knew that even the heavy slugs could do only minimal damage to concrete. Suspecting that this was another ruse, he looked out and spotted three night-camouflaged RPG teams moving up under the cover of its fire.

It was a good plan, one worthy of a mujahideen attack, and it told him that the Black Commandos were working again. Like any experienced mujahideen, he feared the Russian commandos, but he was confident that he would be able to evade them long enough to get into the villa and kill Liu.

The instant the chopper broke away from its gun run, the RPG gunners fired. The whoosh of the 85 mm rockets leaving the launchers was also a very familiar sound to the Afghan. The Russian antitank weapon was another mujahideen favorite. The three rockets streaked to their targets, and two of them slammed into the flanking machine-gun bunkers, one of them flying right into the narrow aperture.

A second, third and fourth volley of rockets followed as quickly as they could be loaded. Again the bunkers were the primary targets, but enough of the shaped charge warheads hit the facade that the air was filled with chunks of shattered concrete.

The blasted debris had barely stopped falling when Al Hosn got to his feet and sprinted into the dust cloud hanging over the main gate. He was all the way through it and on the grounds before the defenders had recovered enough to even notice him. Once inside, he took cover long enough to make sure that his way to the villa was clear.

Liu's gunmen were completely disorganized. Half of them were in full retreat while others ran to reinforce the main gate. No one noticed the Afghan when he got to his feet and ran for the villa. Al Hosn knew exactly where he needed to go. He had been a guest in the villa enough times to know where the tong leader was likely to be hiding. He had a hidden basement where he kept prisoners.

THE FIRST VOLLEY of RPGs was Major Lobov's signal for the assault. Even with the battering the main gate had taken, he had no intention of assaulting that position. Instead, his commandos would go over the walls.

With the detonating rockets as a noise cover, he signaled for his group to go over the wall fifty yards to the left of the gate. Throwing protective pads over the spikes, the major led his commandos up and over, dropping down on the other side. When the last of his Spetsnaz cleared the wall, Lobov raised his arm to signal the attack. Screaming their battle cry, the commandos charged.

McCarter had also taken the RPG fire as his signal to hit the wall. Phoenix was farther to the right on the other side of the main gate. With a one-two punch from both flanks, they thought that they'd be able to break up Liu's forces fairly quickly.

FIGURING THAT the basement entrance would be in the back of the house, Bolan ignored the big rooms in front of the villa. He was checking a door off the main room when he caught a flash of movement to his right. He spun, the silenced Beretta spit and a man screamed in pain.

Suddenly, Bolan was faced by half a dozen men who had been out of sight in the darkened main room. With the lights out and no night-vision gear, they blazed AK fire into the dark.

AL HOSN HEARD the firing inside the front of the house as he came through the servants' door in the back. He ignored it and turned the corner to the hall that led to the basement stairs. He had to get to Liu before the Russians did.

One Chinese was guarding the door to the basement, his back to Al Hosn. Drawing his dagger, the Afghan quickly closed with him, clamped his left hand over his mouth and pulled his head to the side. The dagger flashed, slicing through the guard's neck to the spine. The man's feet kicked and went still.

Laying the body out of the way, Al Hosn pulled his Makarov pistol and opened the door. He was halfway down the stairs before he could see into the basement. Liu was there with a woman hanging in chains on the back wall. Apparently, he had been torturing her.

"Liu," he called out.

When the tong leader turned, he had a pistol in his hand. "Al Hosn, my friend," he said as he let his pistol come down. "I was told that you had died in the attack."

"As you see, I am alive," the Afghan said as he took the last few steps into the basement. "It was the rest of my men who died."

"The Russians did that to us." Liu turned to the woman prisoner. "But I am punishing them. This woman is their top agent in Bangkok and I am going to kill her."

"No!" the Afghan shouted as he raised his Makarov. "I am going to kill you."

His first shot took the Chinese in the belly. Liu looked down in disbelief as the blood seeped out.

The Afghan let Liu experience fear before he fired again. This round hit him in the chest, and the tong leader collapsed to the floor.

Stepping up to the wounded man, Al Hosn stood over him, the Makarov pointed at the bridge of his nose. "God is great," he said as he pulled the trigger.

Liu's head bounced off the floor with the impact of the slug and he lay still.

MARITA SURFACED from her daze of pain at the sound of the Afghan's voice. She immediately recognized him for what he was and figured him to be the leader of Liu's Taliban fighters. She couldn't figure what he was doing here, but his first shot explained it. It was payback time for the missile attack. It also meant that her pain was ended. As soon as he was done with Liu, the muji would kill her outright. The relief that flooded through her sent her back into unconsciousness.

The third shot from Al Hosn's pistol brought Marita partially out of her daze again. "Help me," she called out weakly in Arabic.

"I will help you, Russian bitch," the Afghan snapped in the same language. "But first I have to skin a pig."

Drawing his curved dagger again, he knelt by Liu's body. A single slash cut the silk shirt from the corpse, exposing a vast expanse of flesh. Slicing through the skin from neck to navel, he worked the edge of the razor-sharp blade under the skin and started peeling it back.

BOLAN HAD eliminated the first bunch of gunmen, but more were coming. He would have to clear the house room to room to get through the villa, and he had hoped to avoid this. But since it looked as if the tong gunmen were falling back to the villa for a last stand, he had no choice. "David," he radioed to McCarter, "what's your location?"

"We're at the southeast corner of the house."

"If you can break contact," Bolan answered, "I need some help in here. The tong are retreating to the house for cover, and I need you to keep them out."

"Let me coordinate with the Russians and we'll cover the front."

# CHAPTER TWENTY-EIGHT

*Liu's Villa*

With Phoenix Force attacking across the front of the villa, the few remaining tong gunmen fled the house, leaving Bolan alone. Going into the hall in the back of the villa again, he came across a tong guard lying by a door with his throat cut. Since he hadn't bloodied his knife, someone had come into the house behind him.

Opening the door, he saw light coming from a room below and stairs leading down. There were also faint sounds from below that he couldn't identify, but he had found what he was looking for. Opening the door, he started down the stairs carefully. He was keeping the stairwell to his back with the silenced MP-5 in his left hand.

He paused where the right-hand wall of the stairwell cut off and peered around it. Big Gold Liu's body was lying on the basement floor with a bullet hole in the forehead. From the mass of blood covering his chest, it looked as if someone had been in the process of skinning him and had been interrupted.

Liu was history, but Bolan's work here wasn't concluded. He had also found Marita. She was being used as a human shield by a hawk-faced man who could only be one of Liu's mujahideen henchmen.

The Afghan was standing against the far wall, his razor-sharp curved knife held to the woman's throat. Bolan knew from experience that she was a microsecond away from having her throat slit through to the spine.

Holding his subgun at his side, Bolan carefully took the last of the stairs.

"You stop," the man said.

Bolan halted and said in simple English, "I have no fight with you. Let the woman go, I will not shoot."

"You drop gun, Yankee," Al Hosn answered. "I kill her."

Marita's head was held tight, but she turned her eyes to him. "Shoot," she croaked.

The Russian agent wasn't showing much blood, but she had apparently been worked over pretty badly. His deal with Komarov was to get her out, and he didn't want to disappoint her Spetsnaz comrades. On top of that, he had no tolerance for men who held women captive.

"Okay," Bolan said as he dropped the MP-5 from his right hand, knowing that the Afghan's eyes would follow it. Before the subgun hit the floor, Bolan's hand streaked down to his hip holster, bringing up his Desert Eagle, targeting and firing a single shot in one smooth move.

The .44 slug sang past Marita's ear on its way to the bridge of Al Hosn's nose. With his aim true, he didn't need an insurance shot. The back of the man's head had been splattered over the wall.

Crossing the floor, he knelt beside Marita long enough to check her pulse. Finding it still beating, but weakly, he picked her up carefully and hoisted her up over his left shoulder. Holding her in place with one hand, he hurried for the exit.

He took the steps of the stairs as carefully as he could so as not to jostle Marita. He had no idea of the extent of her injuries. Pausing at the top of the stairs, he freshened his grip on her and keyed his throat mike. "Phoenix, I'm coming out with the package."

"You're clear through the front door," McCarter's voice came back. "We've finished up here."

OUT ON THE VILLA grounds, the battle was all but over. The Russians were combing the grounds in pairs making sure that they left only dead tong gunmen behind.

"Over here!" Bolan called out to the first of the Spetsnaz he saw. "Marita has been wounded."

The Russians came running, pulling at the first-aid

kits on their belts as they ran. Taking her from his shoulder, they placed her on the ground and began working on her.

"Polnacek," Bolan called over the com link, "get that chopper down here. I've got an urgent dustoff."

"Who?" the Russian asked.

"Marita."

"On the way."

"Belasko, this is Lion," the Spetsnaz commander called over his borrowed com link. "We have several Thai police vehicles gathering a safe distance away. I think they are waiting to see if there is going to be any more fighting."

"Keep an eye on them and let me know if they try to get much closer. As long as they stay where they are, we should be okay."

The beat of rotors told Bolan that the Hip was incoming. "Phoenix," he called, "set up a strobe for the dustoff."

"Roger," Encizo answered. "T.J. has one."

The pulsating blue-white light of the strobe revealed Hawkins standing with his arms up, his rifle held between them and the strobe clipped to the trigger guard.

The Hip pilot recognized the international landing-zone signal and flared out right in front of him. The minute his wheels touched ground, the Spetsnaz medics rushed forward, carrying Marita. Three more commandos with bandaged wounds followed.

"Lion, this is Belasko," Bolan said. "Get as many of your men as you can on that chopper with the casualties. As soon as they're off-loaded, tell the pilot to hurry back to pick up the rest of us."

MAJOR LOBOV HAD stayed behind with the remainder of his troops for the second lift, and while he was waiting, his men were wiring the late Big Gold Liu's villa for demolition. The Russians didn't intend to leave anything behind for the leaderless Red Door tong to use to rebuild their criminal empire.

"The house is ready for destruction," Lobov's senior sergeant reported.

"Good," the major answered.

"Lion," the Russian Hip pilot radioed the Spetsnaz officer, "I am inbound. Get your men ready for extraction."

Hawkins again held the strobe for the pilot to land by. When his wheels touched down, the Spetsnaz clambered on board with the Stony Man team right behind them.

"We're a go," McCarter yelled up to the pilot as he hooked his thumb upward.

The pilot rolled his throttle past the stop, and the overloaded Hip strained to get off the ground. Once in the air, the pilot banked it to the west, barely clearing the compound walls. When they were two hundred feet in the air, the Russian major turned to his sergeant. "Take it down."

With this sector of the city being blacked out, the explosion was spectacular. The flash rocked the night and sent debris flying in all directions. The secondary incendiary charges detonated a moment later, setting the shattered wreckage ablaze.

Bangkok did have an experienced fire brigade, and as the joint commando force withdrew, they could see the lights of the emergency vehicles converging on the burning rubble. They could also see the police vehicles cautiously start to move in. The Thais were welcome to anything that was left.

IT TOOK A COUPLE of days for the Stony Man team to wrap everything up and prepare to fly out.

Right before they left, Bolan received a message from Anatoly Komarov and made one more trip into the city. The address he had been given turned out to be a large Chinese-style house in an expensive neighborhood. Like its neighbors, it was enclosed with a masonry wall. But this house had very visible surveillance equipment, and its wall was topped with outward-leaning iron spears set into mortar. He buzzed at the wrought-iron gate, and it clicked open.

The curving brick walkway was flanked with carved stone Oriental lions to guard it, and the grounds had been tastefully laid out in the traditional style. Bolan knocked on the ornately carved, red lacquered door. Red was the color of good luck in most of Asia, and houses had red doors to invite good fortune inside.

When the door opened, Bolan was surprised to see Marita herself meet him. Her hair was down her back, and she was dressed in a red, slit-thigh, high-collar Chinese silk dress embroidered with lions. Her face still showed bruises, and she moved a bit stiffly as she bowed to him. The rest of her injuries were covered by the dress.

"Mr. Belasko," she almost purred. "How nice of you to stop by. Please be welcome in my house."

Marita led him into a living room decorated in a tasteful Oriental motif. Bolan's eye picked out several antique minor masterpieces in the furnishings and sculpture. A Thai servant stood waiting for the mistress of the house, her eyes demurely downcast. Marita spoke to her, and the girl hurried out of the room.

"Please be seated," she said to Bolan.

"How're you feeling?" he asked as they waited for the refreshments he knew would be coming.

"I am very well, thanks again to you," she said. "This is twice now that I owe you my life."

"You owe me nothing," Bolan replied. "You are a comrade-in-arms and you were endangered."

The girl returned with an elaborate tea set of classic Chinese porcelain and sugared fruits on a silver tray. Marita thanked her in Thai, and the girl left.

As Marita was pouring the tea, a sleek Thai Korat

cat walked into the room as if it owned it. The Korat cats had long bodies like the Siamese, but had luxurious gray fur and full tails. The Thais considered them lucky because their thick fur was said to be the color of old silver. They also said that a Korat wouldn't stay in a house that was without luck.

The cat walked up to where Bolan was seated, stopped a foot away, sat on its haunches and stared up at him.

Marita spoke to the animal in a language he didn't recognize, and it mewled in response.

The Russian assassin laughed softly. "She does not know what to think of you, Mr. Belasko. There is something about you that interests her. I think she sees a kindred soul. She is a fierce hunter and I call her Lasher.

"Careful," Marita cautioned when Bolan reached down to the cat.

Rather than try to pet the top of the animal's head, he reached under her ear and caressed the side of her neck. Golden eyes slitted, Lasher stretched her neck to the side so he could have more room to pet her.

Marita handed Bolan his cup, and he sipped to show that he accepted her hospitality.

"I am impressed, Mr. Belasko," Marita said after sipping her own tea to complete the ritual of welcome. "I had not taken you to be a cat man."

"Call me Mike, please," he replied. "As for cats,

I've always admired anything that does its job well. For pure efficiency at hunting, nothing beats a cat.''

"She is very efficient at protecting me," Marita said. "And I've learned to trust her judgment of danger. She tells me that you are exactly as you appear to be and that you have the heart of a warrior."

Marita's green eyes flashed. "But then I already knew that, didn't I? And, now I know that even more than I did before and I want to reward your valor."

"Marita," Bolan said. "Look, I appreciate what you're offering. But as I said before, you owe me nothing."

"I know what the men I work with think of me," she said honestly. "I am seen as a prize to be won by their bravery and courage."

She locked eyes with him. "That has been my way of making it in a profession where women are not highly valued. Oh, I know that the old Soviet Union used attractive women to entrap men they wanted to compromise, but I never allowed myself to be used that way. I did not sleep with the enemy to get where I am now—I killed them."

She laughed. "It is true that I often used a flash of—how do you say it?—tit, to distract a target. Men cannot help but look when I do that. But the men I took to my bed were always the brave and they were always my comrades. The reason I never sleep with the same man twice is that I cannot afford to send a man into battle if I have grown attached to him. I am sure you understand.''

Bolan nodded.

''We have fought together as comrades, and twice now you have been there when I have needed help.

''This time—'' her hand went to her neck ''—you killed a man who was going to slit my throat. I am in eternal debt to you. And, in the way of my people, I pay my obligations.''

''Like I said, I would have done the same for any of your people.'' Bolan's eyes grew hard. ''I do admit, though, that killing the Afghan was more than a duty. I have no tolerance for men who abuse women. It goes back a long way, so there is no obligation. I will accept your thanks as a comrade and maybe someday our paths will cross again.''

He smiled. ''Until then, you can be sure that I won't forget you.''

''Nor I you.''

With a last rub of the cat's neck, the Executioner got to his feet and let himself out.

THE WOMAN WATCHED from the window as the big American walked to her gate. She was fully aware that she was the subject of erotic dreams for many of the men, as well as several of the women, of the RSV and it had always amused her. She never dreamed of her lovers. A man was either in her bed or he was not, but he was never in her dreams. She was afraid, though, that was about to change.

# DEATH LANDS

JAMES AXLER

DEATH LANDS

Salvation Road

**brings you a brand-new look in June 2002! Different look... same exciting adventures!**

# Salvation Road

Beneath the brutal sun of the nuke-ravaged southwest, the Texas desert burns red-hot and merciless, commanding agony and untold riches to those greedy and mad enough to mine the slick black crude that lies beneath the scorched earth. When a Gateway jump puts Ryan and the others deep in the hell of Texas, they have no choice but to work for a rogue baron in order to win their freedom. If they fail...they face death.

*In Deathlands, the unimaginable is a way of life.*